A Midwinter Prince
Revised edition, December 2012

Cover art by Lou Harper

FoxTales
www.harperfox.net
harperfox777@yahoo.co.uk

A MIDWINTER PRINCE

Harper Fox

FoxTales

Dedication

To Jane, as ever, my partner and guardian angel,
to Josh Lanyon, for taking the "aspiring"
out of "aspiring author"
and to Jan McKay, whose love for this story
makes me particularly proud to have written it.

Chapter One

Laurence Fitzroy, nineteen years old, heir to a baronetcy and who knew how many acres of Suffolk countryside, stopped on the steps of the Lyceum, oblivious to the exiting crowd he was forcing to part around him. He fastened his pale silk scarf over the open neck of his shirt, wondering vaguely what had happened to the bow tie he'd impatiently ripped off during the performance. Laurie liked opera well enough, but first-night shows where his father's only motivation for being there was the need to be seen in the best box in the house… He drew a deep breath of the lung-catching air, feeling himself wake up, become alive once more to the lights, the blistering cold, the living river of human souls parting to accommodate him. He was bored, restless, lonely.

Taxis were pulling up by the pavement, two abreast, almost blocking the thoroughfare. No sign of the limo. Charlie must have had one cigarette too many with Mrs. Gibson down in the kitchen before setting off. Laurie sighed. That wouldn't please the old man one bit. He glanced up the Strand as if he might turn and walk in that direction instead, into the night.

Sir William Fitzroy stood on the pavement in the crowd, Laurie's mother clasped to his side like a decorative, blank-faced doll. As Laurie watched, his great red face swung around and darkened still further with angry blood upon spotting his son hanging about on the opera house steps, looking as usual completely disoriented. He raised one meaty hand and made an unmistakable gesture. *Here, boy. Now.*

Laurie was not in the habit of rebellion, and now would be a stupid time to start. As for walking off into the night, wealthy or not, in real terms he had on him the price of a bus fare and one night in a B and B. Then, without further cash injections from the huge, grim-faced man waiting on the far side of the road, he was...well, he was that shape in the blankets over there, that fragile-looking piece of human flotsam huddled in the doorway to Lindley's. Except, knowing him, he'd have let someone else steal his blankets. Laurie sighed and began to make his way across the road. His mother, frail little sparkling figure in the circle of Sir William's arm, was looking for him anxiously too. What the hell was the hurry? There was still no sign of the sleek Daimler in which Sir William liked to be seen going home from events like this. Lesser mortals, Laurie couldn't help but notice, had piled into their taxis and even their buses and underground train stations and made their escape by now.

The boy huddled in the blankets outside Lindley's was asleep, his head tipped back against the concrete pillar of the doorway. He had close-cropped black hair and skin Laurie thought would be olive in daylight, though now he was painted by the lights of passing cars, the shifting spectrum of the window display. His face, passive and grave, had a sculpted foreign beauty Laurie had never seen before.

He was terribly still. Laurie noted how his own body heat had leached away in just the time it had taken him to cross the road, how he was pulling at his thin tuxedo jacket and starting to shiver. How long would he survive without shelter on the streets of London tonight?

He didn't know if it was curiosity or fear that drew him closer. This boy was his own age, not dissimilar to him in looks and build. What were the real differences? What force dictated that Laurie would go home in a limo tonight and sleep between warm sheets, while this image in the transforming mirror remained here, abandoned in the bitter night to live or...

God, was he breathing? Slowly, barely aware of what he was doing, Laurie struggled through the last currents of the crowd, entered the doorway, and crouched beside him.

He was not more philanthropic or caring than the ordinary run of teenage boys. Up till now, his horizon had been so crowded with his own joys and pains that he'd spent little time looking past them. And this was far from the first down-and-out he had seen on the pavements outside theatres and opera halls while all around him denizens of another world—his world—glittered and burst and disappeared like bubbles from a glass of champagne. Those others had not touched him. Laurie had not yet been sufficiently human himself to accept properly that they were too. Something in the line of this boy's smooth, exposed throat, the abandonment of one hand, which had fallen palm up out of the blankets and lay within inches of passing women's spiked heels... "Hello," Laurie said, uncertainly. "Are you all right?"

Brown eyes flicked wide. The open hand snapped shut like a clam, plunged inside the parka for a knife it either did not find or chose not to deploy, and emerged a second later, thrust out toward Laurie in a gesture of desperate warding off. "Please. I don't have anything."

"I...I know. I'm not going to hurt you." Laurie sat back on his heels. He was trying to place the accent—not Hungarian, though not far off. Something Eastern European, rich and softly modulated. "I was just afraid you were dead."

The boy gazed up at him. Then to Laurie's surprise, the fear drained from his fine features, and they lit up with a wide, compelling grin. "Perhaps I am. I have never seen a city sky so full of stars. Perhaps you're the angel of death."

"That should bother you more than it seems to," Laurie said, helplessly smiling back. But the boy's attention was no longer on him. He was looking up over Laurie's shoulder, up beyond the rooftops of the Strand. Instinctively Laurie glanced that way too.

The sounds of the midnight street faded around him. No, he had never seen a sky like this, either. Even on his family's estate down in Suffolk, light pollution from nearby houses and farms had spun a web across the night. And in London—well, it never happened. You were lucky to catch a moonrise. Yet suddenly the tops of the buildings were bearing between them a river of light, a thousand-hued pinprick blaze that stole the breath from his lungs. "Beautiful," he said, then recalled himself to reality. "That means it's going to be bloody cold, doesn't it?"

The boy returned his gaze to him. It was serene now, looking for some reason at Laurie as if he was the one in need of help, the one lost in the night. Laurie felt it like a kindly brush to his skin. The boy said quietly, "'Oh, God, make small the old star-eaten blanket of the sky…'"

Laurie ran the words through his mind. He did know them, though he couldn't be sure where from. "'That I may fold it round me and in comfort lie.' Where did you learn that?"

Reaching into the pack wedged behind him in the doorway, the boy produced a dog-eared paperback book. *Twentieth Century Poetry*, Laurie read in the passing headlights, remembering now with embarrassment that he'd learned the lines for himself while stuck for an hour in a broken-down Tube train. Part of London Underground's campaign to bring literature to the masses, a few well-loved verses on the trains' walls between the ads for flights and cosmetic surgery, seemingly the only way to get it through his thick head.

"Look," he said awkwardly after a moment. "I can't make the sky into a blanket for you, but…" He reached into his pocket, pulled out the twenty-pound note his mother had given him for drinks and ice creams tonight, as if he had been ten years old. "Will that get you into a shelter tonight? I think you'll freeze to death if you stay out here."

The boy studied him, shadowed eyes fathomless. "What's your name?"

"Laurie."

"Some advice for you. Don't start seeing us, Laurie. Once you do, you won't be able to stop, and it will take you years to teach yourself to pretend again that you don't."

Laurie opened his mouth to reply. Before he could, a large hand descended from out of the night and grabbed him by the collar of his expensive tux. He scrambled upright, trying to make the effort look like his own, not wholly the result of his father's grip on his scruff. On his way, he managed to drop the twenty into his new acquaintance's lap. He did not see if the boy took it, was too involved in the effort of tearing away from Sir William's iron clutch, turning his shove into a voluntary walk toward the limo now waiting by the pavement. It was the only way of dealing with the old man: to do what he told you and make it look like your own work. Laurie shot a glance back toward the boy, smiling in unquenched mischief. "Yours?"

"Sasha," the boy returned quickly, like a secret thrown between them, so soft the word was almost lost in the whisper of traffic.

Laurie shook off his father's grip just in time to avoid being tossed into the backseat like a sack of flour. His father slammed in after him, so forcefully the pressure change made Laurie's ears pop.

The argument began straightaway and was very predictable. Slouched in the limo's backseat—noticing in some way for the first time how delicious and unlikely its warmth was, how embracing its leather upholstery, how complete its protection against the night—Laurie folded his arms and let it happen. No argument at all, really—just a trick of endurance, while his father thundered out all the rage inside him, against a world that contained idle chauffeurs, scrounging tinker tramps, and children of his who felt the need to rub shoulders with them, handing them cash earned by decent British citizens to go and buy drugs with. Laurie seldom tried to reply. If he did, all he gained was the terror of watching his mother's beautiful, poised, aristocratic little mask begin to crumble into tears. Besides, there was almost an interest to be had in listening to Sir William, to learn, apart from anything else, how many epithets he could find to apply to the subspecies of humanity who inconvenienced him by huddling in the doorways of his city at night. *Beggar, scrounger, tinker, gyppo*. "Mangy little pikey," Laurie heard, staring out into the darkness beyond the glass, watching his own pale reflection. He'd never even heard that last one. He'd have to look it up.

"Here! Are you damn well listening to me?"

Laurie blinked. He'd started to fade out. "Yes, sir," he said automatically. He looked at his mother, sitting across from him beside her irate husband. She, too, was taking an intense interest in the streets outside. For once, irritation stirred in Laurie. She had chosen the old sod, hadn't she? Whereas her children were merely stuck. The old man had drawn breath for another salvo. Laurie, to his own surprise, sat up a little, leaned forward, and met his eyes. "Wait a bit. Do you honestly think that anybody would *choose* to be out there tonight? That anyone would be freezing to the pavement if it wasn't their last bloody option?"

A bad idea, of course. Now Laurie had to sit through a familiar rant on the subject of thankless little bastards who never lifted a finger to earn a penny of their own but had the cheek to sit in Sir William's car, in the clothes Sir William had put on their back, and give him their lip. It wasn't a logical argument, but it was an effective one. The worst of it was that Laurie was in partial agreement.

His mother, for once, shifted in her seat and turned her deep sapphire gaze on Laurie. Laurie could read compassion there, sorrow, and a bitter amusement. She used to defend him a lot, he remembered, perhaps while he was still young enough to be defensible. "William," she said in her pretty French accent, laying a hand on her husband's arm, "leave him be." Her face lit up with a half-sardonic, half-appeasing smile Laurie seldom saw nowadays. "It's only the moral absolutism of youth. Not worth your time. It will wear off soon enough."

Sir William glanced from one to the other of them. For a moment, he looked almost bewildered. Laurie wondered if it was hard for him, to see nothing of his own face and everything of hers whenever he laid eyes on his son. He gave a kind of snarl. "Don't get into his corner, my lady Marielle. Not unless you're willing to fight there."

Her eyes went blank. After a moment, she returned her attention to the night outside. Sir William, without looking, banged his fist against the glass divider behind him. Laurie saw Charlie reach obediently to open the intercom. "Get your bloody foot down, Wilson. I need a drink."

* * *

Back at the enormous six-floored Mayfair house, where the family rattled around like peas in a barrel and the staff outnumbered their employers, Laurie did his best to creep to bed. But he and his eight-year-old sister shared the same far-flung corridor on the top floor, and she knew every creak of the boards.

"Laurie!"

He froze, then let the shoes he was carrying drop to the floor with a thump since the jig was up. Reluctantly he pushed open her bedroom door. She was bolt upright in the bed, a shawl arranged primly around her shoulders like a little old woman expecting grand company. "God," he said tiredly, "are you undead? Do you never sleep? It's nearly one in the morning."

"I know. You're much later than you promised."

Laurie looked at her. Like him, she was a carbon copy of her mother, and he wondered at the weird genetic selectivity that seemed to have winnowed out the old man's contribution to the way his offspring looked, moved, functioned. She was quite composed, but there were shadows in her eyes, and when he stopped to listen, he understood why. Muffled yelling rose up from the floor below, sometimes bass, occasionally a brief, high-pitched response. It turned the air in the child's room static with unease. Carefully Laurie shut the door behind him. He sat on the bed. "There was traffic," he said. "I'm sorry. Did you have a good day?"

"No. Eleanor Browne's boring party was bad enough. Then you get taken to the opera and I'm left here with Mrs. Gibson. And opera's wasted on you, Laurie. You know it is."

"Yes, I do," Laurie agreed. "You'd be much better at it." He paused, long enough to hear continued sounds of conflict from below, a hiss and a vibration that had made his heart contract with fear at Clara's age. "Do you want to know what happened? I think I took some of it in."

He shoved a pillow down his shirt and morphed into the luckless heroine, bouncing back and forth across the room with hands clutched to his makeshift bosom, belting out an aria whose Italian libretto consisted of improvised English with an extra vowel tacked on to every noun. The villain of the piece arrived, pulling him offstage from behind Clara's wardrobe by his own hair, whence he emerged basso profundo and hunchbacked, prowling around the squealing child's bed with dire, mostly culinary threats concerning his intentions for poor Helga. At the climactic moment, Helga emerged once again, feminine attributes enhanced this time with a second pillow, which provided useful cushioning when she plunged to her death over the cliff between the two beds. By this time Clara was doubled up and threatening to wet the bed with a sincerity Laurie knew was real, so he laid off, resurrected himself, gave her back her pillows, and kissed her good night. The sounds from downstairs had ceased. With a kindly firmness he had learned in the years since he'd become more of a father to her than an elder brother, he directed Clara to lie down and sleep, switched her light off, and padded down the corridor to his own room.

* * *

The trouble with Sir William's outbursts was that they always contained enough of a grain of truth that his son could not dismiss them outright. The poison grain would find its soil in Laurie's mind and put out shoots, always holding Laurie back from outright rebellion against him. In the morning's bleakest early hours, Laurie sat up in the bed that had been his since he'd outgrown his nursery cot, in the big, shabby room he had always occupied. He laced his arms around his knees. He thought about the grand bedrooms on the floor below, any of which were his for the asking. But, putting aside his need to keep distance from parental rows, Laurie knew he did not feel enough like the young heir to the place to take on even that much of the trappings of the role.

In which case, what was he doing here at all? If he shared his parents' ideals for his future, it would have been fine—acceptable, anyway—for him to get sent down from Oxford in disgrace after failing his midterm exams, to agree to the month of tutoring and cramming his father had paid for, to creep back under the parental roof and work for the second chance he suspected Sir William had more or less bought for him.

But the truth was that he scarcely cared. He couldn't imagine making the effort it would take to focus his wandering, dream-filled brain on the maths and politics that his father, more fancifully still, was convinced would carve out a respectable career for him. He couldn't even manage trig, and the political world seemed a swamp to him, a miasma, a chamber of horrors where unimaginable superpowers played out apocalyptic games beyond the reach of any normal human influence. He knew he had no real intention to try, and on those terms, it was wrong of him to stay. He should stand up to his father and tell him the deal was off. That he would make his own way, as hundreds of thousands of young men so much less privileged than he managed to do.

Christ, as even a homeless kid on the Strand was doing, after his fashion.

Laurie envisaged the scene in which he had this conversation with his father and ran a hand into his hair, shivering. If the old man had been an unrelenting brute to him, it would have been easy. His powers would have evaporated along with Laurie's childhood, leaving him free. But, until his only son had developed a mind of his own, Sir William had been a decent dad. Domineering, intolerant of infantile vagaries—always ready though with rough fun, a leg up onto the horse he'd bought, way too big for his ten-year-old, but Laurie had known better by then than to show fear and had mastered the animal on a do-or-die basis that the old man plainly still hoped for and expected from him now. It was only since Laurie had begun to question the gold-plated world in which he lived that their ways had diverged violently. At every confrontation, something inside Laurie would tangle up in memories of love and authority, and his strength would dissolve. The old man was much worse now, his temper heating up in proportion with his disappointments, but even the worst, most vituperative rants Laurie could not quite bring himself to dismiss. What if he *had* simply put money into a lost soul's hands tonight for him to go and hurt himself some more?

Well, if he had, Laurie hoped his toxin of choice was keeping Sasha warm. Laurie got out of bed, suddenly sure that sleep would evade him tonight. He grabbed a quilt off the bed and went to huddle on the attic's broad window ledge, where he could look out over the ice-glimmered rooftops. His own sole experience of hard drugs was that they could indeed pull down the night into a starry blanket that would wrap around him and drive off cold and pain forever—which was why, after that, he had touched nothing stronger than the occasional snitched handful of his mother's ample sedative prescriptions. Which was bad enough, he supposed, but did the trick on the warfare nights, when the roar of his parents' disputes crept through every floorboard and there was no one to drown them out with amateur theatricals for him. Drawing up his knees, inhaling the quilt's faint scent of cedar chests and dust, Laurie hoped Sasha was warm—or believed himself so—and free.

* * *

Sasha. Black hair, brown eyes—a face which was, in its own way, as aristocratic as the one Laurie saw in the mirror. He wasn't sure why he couldn't shake the image from his mind. The tutor who'd been charged with knocking him into shape for resitting his exams was not due for another two days, and Laurie had time on his hands.

At least it was London time, which meant he had resources. There was a scatter of small playhouses in the area, around whose backstage areas and greenrooms he had made himself familiar over past school holidays—never doing more than helping shift scenery and run errands, but buying himself contented hours in the one environment where he felt really at home. He'd been asked a couple of times to undertake extra and bit work but had never dared accept. He held a deep conviction that some kind of alarm would go off in his father's study the second his foot touched the boards. A great admirer of drama was Sir William, but not as a career for his boy. Laurie might as well have announced at once that he was going to become a prostitute or join the Chippendales. He made his way down the Strand toward the Twilight without allowing himself to look into doorways.

It was another world anyway at bright December noon. Laurie found himself wondering if he had imagined his encounter of the night before. The entrance to Lindley's was washed, gleaming, thronged with Christmas shoppers. No traces of the night and the shadow people who belonged to it. For a few minutes, walking briskly down the Strand, warm in his sheepskin jacket, Laurie tried on the idea that this was the real and only world, the day side, where everyone he saw looked rosy and well-heeled. It was a nice thought. Experimentally he fitted himself into it, straightened his shoulders, and looked around. He was a wealthy young man of good family. In his wallet was a credit card of unspecified limit. He had nothing to worry about, really. If he closed his eyes, shut down those inconvenient parts of himself his mother assured him were mere youthful sentiment anyway, ready to burn off in the arid light of adulthood…

No way that he could find Sasha again in that bright world, even had he wanted to. Laurie pushed open the backstage door of the Twilight, the warm gust of air that greeted him a reminder of contrasts from the night before. He slipped into the shadows, quietly greeting the stagehands who remembered him.

Not quietly enough. Two racks of costumes down at the end of a corridor gave a warning shudder and broke apart, expelling a plump shape in pink cashmere. Dora, the

Twilight's talented and faithful dresser, paused for a moment as if scenting the air, then got a fix on him and came cannoning down the corridor to intercept. "Laurie! Darling!" She hadn't learned the art of air kissing, and he stood, resigned, while she planted a lip-glossed smacker on each of his cheeks. "God, I swear. You get more knicker-dampeningly gorgeous every time I see you. Are you of legal age yet? Please say yes."

Laurie looked at her—her nice smile, her luminous eyes. Soft, fragrant hair, a body as generous and easygoing as her nature. She had made a massive, unsubtle pass at Laurie every year since he was fifteen. It was almost a festive tradition. He smiled at her. "Hi, Dora. More or less, I think. But…"

"I know, I know. Don't tell me." She raised her hands in mock surrender. "You're gay. It's always the same. They come through here year after year, these gorgeous boys, and then the second they're legal—boom—they're after cock. Don't you worry, darling." She deposited a third noisy kiss, this time on his brow. "Dora's used to it. I tell you what. Before someone comes and nabs you for set painting, you come down here and help me steam press a few cloaks. I don't know what they think I'm made of here, but I can scarcely lift the bloody things."

Dazed, Laurie followed her. She set him a load of industrial ironing and wandered around him chattering, requiring little by way of reply. Laurie liked her a lot. She was kind, and her offers of a no-strings roll on the trapdoor mattress were quite sincere. But when he tried to imagine going through with it, all he could envisage was Sasha and a pair of dark-lashed brown eyes.

The one thing he dared look at even less than his love of the theatre and reasons for remaining at home was his sexuality. He had sealed it up, set it determinedly aside. In public school, you either leaped for the safe moral high ground of loudly stated straightness, to include lurid tales of weekend conquests with Roedean girls and cutouts of topless tabloid models stuck to the inside of your locker. Or you drowned among the rest of them—boys who hadn't learned to conceal the fact that a natural consequence of being trapped for years in a single-sex school was to fall in love, however temporarily, with other boys. Life for this second group, this underclass, Laurie had soon seen, was barely worth living. You moved from being an older boy's fag to being his or someone else's faggot, and these two terms might as well have been seared on your brow. You went from polishing shoes to being buggered in the locker room. Every single boys' school cliché was true and had not altered from the eighteenth century to the twenty-first. Laurie was not sure how he had walked the line between these two extremes. The pressure to be one thing or the other was incredible, and he hadn't even been bright enough to clamber into an ivory tower and raise a flag of frigid intellectualism. He'd had a couple of girlfriends, carefully selected scions of other good families, and enjoyed their company with ill-defined longings for touch. If ever he dreamed of greener grass and the other side of the fence, he took fervent precautions to hide the fact from himself and anyone else. If Sir William had a thing about foreigners and Jews, you should see how he could make himself pleasant on the subject of homosexuals.

Probably Laurie should come down off his stepladder and take hold of Dora's warm hand. He had been rescued from the steam press by the set builder's assistant, who had put him to work on a giant fantasy background for the Twilight's Christmas satire of Narnia. Laurie looked at his paint-stained hands and tried to imagine them closing on soft, white female flesh. Why not? She was sweet, and she'd given plenty of his fellow backstage lads a useful sexual initiation. He could hardly take her home, but Sir William would be delighted to hear of his prowess. *You young dog, Laurence.*

Laurie chuckled, shaking the stepladder dangerously beneath him. In the magical shadows of the stage below, Dora flitted back and forth, never failing to give him a glittering smile or a wave. Nevertheless, as the afternoon began to close in to December dusk, he climbed down, washed the paint from his hands with eye-stinging turpentine, and set off—not in the direction of home.

Chapter Two

Sasha had been right: once you started seeing, you couldn't stop. He jogged down the lane that bordered Charing Cross station, feeling as if either he or it had been newly made. It was a magnet for down-and-outs, scooping up those who came here from the eastern counties, just as those from the north arrived and sold themselves around King's Cross and sometimes got no further. For every coffee vendor and stall of trinket souvenirs, there were at least ten lost-looking souls curled up on the steps and the pavements between them. God, was it just that he was hungry that his senses seemed so keen? The contrasting shades of the fruit on the greengrocer's stall reached up and hit him. Everything on the stalls, he saw for the first time, was placed just out of reach of any thin, grasping hands, and was watched over narrowly by the vendors. The scents of fresh-ground beans shivered in the back of his throat. And he could not stop noticing the dispossessed.

Laurie found it hard to understand. These routes across the city were not new to him, were his jungle paths. Mayfair and the Strand, across the Hungerford Bridge to the only part of South London considered appropriate for young men of his class to visit—the South Bank development with its film houses and Royal Festival Hall. It wasn't that he had not noticed that the steps up to the bridge and the space underneath it were scattered with huddled human shapes in blankets; how could he have failed to? Sometimes it was a case of stepping over oblivious outstretched legs, or the patient companion dogs who, in this heartland of English values, extracted more attention and handfuls of change from passersby than their owners. Had he simply dance stepped or dreamed his way past, distracted by his companions, head full of whatever film or play he had just seen?

And yet each one of these was as real, as individual, as Sasha. As Laurie himself. And they were legion. If Laurie threw down a twenty—or even a few pence—here, what would he do for the next and the next?

Pausing in the entrance to the Charing Cross Tube station, Laurie felt his mouth go dry, his head spin as if he had suddenly been placed on the edge of a yawning precipice. This was the pit of human need, the world on which his own lay like a glittering crust. It was bottomless. Laurie could pour a family fortune into it, cause Sir William to die of apoplexy when he found out, and make no difference at all. To think of his father was to conjure his voice in his head, reminding Laurie that not all the flotsam here were without choice, lost, deserving of sympathy. That the majority were drunkards, junkies, scroungers. Laurie shook his head. He didn't want to hear this litany now. There was a dreadful comfort in it, a cop-out from all responsibility. Layabouts and crooks could be ignored.

He hardly knew what he was doing, continuing his path through the station and out into the light on the other side, streaked here with shadows from the riverside trees stripped of leaves. A few down-and-outs were clustered here too, on the plaza the city council was so diligently trying to make bright and multicultural. Almost at random, Laurie cautiously approached an old man propped against the foot of Nelson Mandela's statue. Pigeons waddled around him. As Laurie crouched, they went up in a dusty, clattering rush. Laurie repressed a flinch. His heart was beating violently anyway. "Excuse me," he said, suddenly painfully aware of his own soft but definitely upper-class accent. "Do you know of a boy sleeping rough near here—Eastern European, I think, about my age—called Sasha?"

It was such a long shot. Laurie was ashamed, almost before the question was finished. How stupid of him, to assume that this man would know of the existence of one homeless boy, just because they shared the same social substratum—about as stupid as the occasional Americans Laurie had met who asked him if he knew such and such a person because he too lived in the UK.

The old man squinted up at him. "Not gonna offer me a bed for the night at the cost of my dirty old soul, then?"

Laurie blinked. Then he understood. He had seen, without taking it in, the usual type of young man who stopped to talk to down-and-outs. Neatly suited, ties tied tight, often clutching a well-worn Bible. As far as he had thought of them at all, Laurie had wondered if they were not simply another kind of predator.

He said cautiously, a little unnerved by the bitter, amused gleam in the old man's eyes, "No. Seems a bit of a steep price. I hope they throw in supper." He pulled out a few pound coins from his pocket. To his surprise, as he straightened up, the old man jerked a thumb in the direction of the next bridge upriver.

Repeating the question to the hard-eyed young thug who intercepted him under the arches was more difficult.

"Who wants to know?"

Laurie kept his spine straight, resisted the temptation to look down. He wasn't afraid, exactly. Anyone who had incurred the wrath of Sir William Fitzroy was not easily daunted by the prospect of physical confrontation. But now, as well as his accent, he was acutely conscious of his whole presentation—his clothes, the difference between his own slender but healthy build and the rawboned emaciation of this gatekeeper. Beyond him, in the shadow of the arches, Laurie could see small bonfires, a shantytown of boxes, black plastic bags, ragged tarpaulin sheets rigged into tents. He supposed this boy took his turn on guard duty, stalling visitors long enough to let the others conceal what they had to or make themselves scarce. Laurie didn't think he was likely to be taken for an undercover cop or the world's least convincing social worker, but he was going to have to say something to account for himself. "I'm a friend of his," he said awkwardly, then added, with surprise at his own cunning, "I owe him a bit of money."

His interlocutor snorted. "Oh, right, Prince Harry. Did he win it off you at a polo match? Give it to me. I'll see he gets it safe."

There was something in this sardonic offer that made Laurie's heart give a bump. *He is here, then. What are the odds*? Keeping his own tone clear of answering dryness, he said, "I'd rather give it to him myself, if that's okay. Is he around?"

"I'm afraid my lord Sasha is transacting a piece of business at present," the young thug informed him, dropping his Glaswegian accent for a creditable imitation of Laurie's own. He glanced off to his left, where the arches plunged down into fire-painted shadows, and Laurie did too—in time to see what looked like a well-to-do city trader emerge from behind one of the piers and scuttle away.

A moment later, Sasha appeared, pale and unsteady, wiping his mouth. He saw Laurie and stopped dead.

"What's the matter?" Laurie's companion demanded, plainly amused by his blank-faced astonishment. "Did he give you one on credit? How good of you to come and settle up."

Laurie was suddenly tired of him. His own temper rose only rarely, but when it did, it burned far more fiercely than his father's—a clean, cold flame. He rounded on the other boy. "What bloody business is it of yours? I'm here to talk to him, not you. Now back off!"

Interesting, Laurie. He surprised himself again, glancing around him to where one dangerous-looking lad had multiplied to half a dozen, with as many again coalescing from the shadows as he watched. He'd make good pickings, he supposed, between his watch and his coat and the contents of his wallet. Still the fear refused to spark in him, even now when it would have been in his best interests to break and run.

A warm hand closed on his wrist. It tugged him lightly back and to one side. Before Laurie could move or react, Sasha had stepped in front of him, a glimmer of steel flashing back firelight in his fist. "Forget about it, Len," Sasha growled, his voice the same exotic music Laurie had heard the night before, turned ominous and chilly now with anger. "All of you. Leave him alone."

Whatever status Sasha held in this demimonde and whatever he chose to do to make ends meet, he was well enough respected for the little crowd to part as he steered Laurie through, back toward daylight. Only a few catcalls and falsetto cries of "Oh, Prince Harry!" came after them. He'd put an arm protectively around Laurie's back, the gesture at once shaming him and touching him indefinably.

"Thanks for that. But I can take care of myself, you know."

Sasha nodded, continuing to guide him out, casting the occasional backward glance. He was nervy even by the standard of the street people Laurie had observed up till now, his wary gaze scanning the riverside promenade constantly. "I'm sure. Fencing? Boxing?"

Laurie flushed. He had learned judo too, but knew he required a courtly bow over the mat before engaging in combat.

"Forgive me, but Len won't say en garde to you. Laurie, what the hell are you doing here?"

I dreamed of you all last night and thought of you most of today. You're like a new source of gravity, drawing me in. I think I fancy you. Laurie's mind shied off from these truths, and he said, almost casually, "I wanted to see you were okay after yesterday. It was perishing cold last night."

"Yes, enough to freeze the balls off brass monkeys," Sasha agreed, the expression in his velvety, faraway accent making Laurie smile. "But I don't understand how you found me. I…"

He stopped and carefully let Laurie go. Laurie turned to face him, aware of a cold place around his shoulders where Sasha's arm had been. "What is it?"

"I've…seen UK border agents come down here in all shapes and sizes. Police too. Sometimes they're women. One came once dressed as a nun to round up a runaway Catholic. But I've never seen one quite like you."

Laurie snorted. He spread his hands. "Are you kidding?" he asked. "Did you ever see a border agent's dad come along and haul him off by the scruff?"

Sasha smiled. To Laurie it was like an undiscovered type of sunlight; he took a helpless step toward it.

"All right. I'm sorry. Street people get suspicious. I thought perhaps you were their latest secret weapon."

They continued along the riverside promenade. Sasha had not replaced his arm around Laurie's shoulders. They made a conspicuous enough pair as it was—the skinny down-and-out and his elegant, glossy-haired companion, two sides of the same coin if you knew how to look. Laurie said, not much caring for the answer—he could have walked like this at Sasha's side forever, as if in a dream, on and on downriver until the Thames spread wide into the sea—"Where are we going, then?"

"I'm going to take you to lunch," Sasha told him serenely. When Laurie's eyebrows went up, he reached into one of the parka's deep inner pockets and produced a twenty-pound note. "I couldn't use this. The police check the shelters, and I'm not supposed to be here."

They stopped outside an elegant little café on the Embankment. Heading automatically for the door, Laurie noticed Sasha had remained behind him, rooted to the spot.

Laurie saw fear in his eyes. "What's the matter? Don't you want to go in?"

"Love to. If you want the embarrassment of having them ask me to leave, or calling the police to make sure I do."

"Sasha, for God's sake. You can go anywhere you want when you're—"

"When I'm with you?"

Laurie looked away. "I…didn't mean that."

"No. I know you didn't. Street people aren't welcome anywhere but the street, that's all, and nine times out of ten, not there. Here." Smiling, letting him off the hook, Sasha held out the twenty. "Go and get us something. I'll wait for you on the fountain steps in the gardens."

Laurie emerged a few minutes later with long beef-and-mustard sandwiches and two extra-large coffees clutched to his chest. It occurred to him belatedly, sitting down at Sasha's side the whispering shadow of the fountain, that he should have asked him what he wanted, but Sasha only shook his head when he expressed the concern.

He took the sandwich carefully from Laurie's hands, shot him a quick, half-apologetic glance. "Wait a moment, please."

Laurie watched, half in amusement, half in sympathy, while he demolished his meal. Wherever he came from, he hadn't left his manners behind him there. The process was not messy, but it was thorough, and Laurie guessed it was an urgent priority, certainly over small talk. Once he had finished, Laurie offered Sasha the remaining half of his own sandwich, which he accepted with a shamefaced grin.

"I was worried you might be vegetarian or"—Laurie cast about for his limited knowledge of dietary restrictions—"or Muslim or…"

"Nn-nn." Heaving a deep breath, Sasha patted his mouth with the paper napkin. "As it happens, neither. But if

I had been…well, I wouldn't be anymore. Not down here. Thank you. Now we can talk."

Laurie's throat promptly went dry. The brown eyes on his were without expectation, but so steady and calm that they unsettled him. "How stupid," he said, faintly. "Now you put it like that, I don't know where to start."

Sasha reached for the coffee, wrapping both hands around it. They were strong-looking hands, though wasted and chapped with cold, expressive even in their grasp on the polystyrene cup. "Well, you can start by telling me how you found me. Nothing personal, but it's not good news for me that you did. It would help if I knew."

"Don't worry. It was mostly luck. I turned right instead of left outside of the Tube station, and I asked an old guy on the plaza, that's all."

"By the statue?" Laurie nodded. "Gyorgy told you where I was?"

"Not exactly. He just did this." Laurie reproduced the old man's vague directing gesture. "Don't be angry with him."

"I'm not. I'm just surprised. He's one of us." Sasha smiled at Laurie over the rim of the coffee cup. "He must have liked your face. All right. I'm glad he did. I'm glad your luck brought you here. But you have to promise me you'll never do it again."

Laurie tensed. He fought not to betray a sharp sting of disappointment. Stupidly, he had not considered that his arrival might bring more evil than good to Sasha. That this might be a last time, not a beginning. "I'm sorry. I didn't mean to make trouble for you."

"No, stupid. Trouble for *you.* The likes of Len will eat you alive. It's no place for *gaje.*"

"Gaje?" Laurie echoed. "Is that what I am?"

"Just one of you, so *gajo*. Oh, everyone's got their own name for them—the people who live on the topside. Gaje's a Roma word—in Romania, anyway. You'd call us gypsies."

Laurie couldn't help it; a thrill went through him. Childish of him, he knew, but the word conjured for him stories his mother had read to him of a people whose lives were so free, so different to his own narrow existence that he could scarcely believe in them. Frightening figures too, or they became so after his father had chased a group of them off their grounds in Suffolk. Horse thieves, child snatchers, ghosts who silently unlatched windows and doors to rob the cradle. He felt a blush rise, as if Sasha could read these paranoid gaje thoughts. "Gypsies…" He thought for a moment, then remembered an article he'd read in the *Guardian*—because it certainly wasn't the kind of political awareness he'd ever been taught at Eton—and said, "But the right word's *Romany*, isn't it?"

Sasha turned to him. The chatter of the people on the esplanade, the paths that wound through the winter-bare park, seemed to fade out to Laurie, replaced by the thump of his own heart. He watched, motionless, while Sasha put out a hand and, just for an instant, touched his face. His palm was warm from the coffee cup, soft as suede. He said, "You're…very sweet, aren't you?"

Laurie frowned. He wanted to protest that he was not. He might not live on the streets or earn his keep giving blowjobs under bridges—might not carry a knife, but he wasn't naive. Not a child.

But Sasha lowered his hand, smiling gently. "*Romany's* a good word," he went on, only when he said it, the emphasis fell on the second syllable, not the first, and the *y* transitioned into a soft, foreign *i* sound that made Laurie shiver. "That's what I am. Now…what about you, my visiting prince? What are you doing down here among the Romani?"

"I…" Laurie paused. The compulsion, the repeated inner tug that had drawn him here, would sound poor in plain words. But he didn't want to dress it up, much less lie to Sasha, so he said, shrugging, "I just wanted to see you again. I couldn't forget your face."

Too much, surely. He braced, waiting for Sasha to betray disgust or get up and walk away. But although Sasha's expression became serious, all Laurie could detect there was a kind of concentrated, deep-seated pleasure. "Thank you," he said. "And…you came a long way off your beaten track to find me, didn't you? A long way from the beautiful car and—your father, was it, who dragged you off? Does he do that often?"

"Oh, only when I'm talking to people wrapped in blankets on the Strand."

"And do you do that often?"

"No. You're my first. I…never even looked twice before."

"Don't be ashamed. Why would you? It's two different worlds, Laurie, and I think you live up on a mountaintop, even in yours. Last night I was afraid I *had* disgraced some kind of royalty."

"Oh, not even a minor aristocrat, until he dies. He's only a baronet because his great-grandfather made enough money to buy himself a coat of arms and half a county." Laurie pulled himself up. He wasn't about to lessen the gap between this new friend and himself by trying to do away with his family or their wealth—by trying to make himself ordinary. "It's my ma who's the real blue blood. I think her lot owned the Languedoc while his were still working out which end of a woolly mammoth was which."

Sasha broke into brief laughter. "French?"

"Oh, very. And you? Romanian?"

"Yes, by birth. Although my own mother…" Sasha trailed off, his attention refocusing on a point beyond Laurie's shoulder. "Well. She was English, but nevertheless…I am an illegal immigrant, and when that policeman making his way down the promenade sees me here with you, he'll assume I'm soliciting you for money or you're soliciting me for sex. And he won't like either, so..."

Sasha began to get to his feet. Halfway there, he stopped and looked down at Laurie in astonishment. "Laurie, what...what's the matter?"

Laurie drew a breath and resurfaced. He could feel, in the muscles of his face and brow, the expression that had been there a second before. He'd never seen it himself—had never been looking in a mirror at the right time—but had gathered from friends and from seeing his mother very occasionally do the same thing, that his response to disgust or outrage was not a grimace but a stern and absolute blank. A mask of aristocratic thunder. He never meant it or at least never meant that dawning aspect of his nature to show—the latent imperiousness he had from his mother's blood and his father's conduct. *There isn't a policeman in this city who would dare question me*, that haughty bastard would say, *let alone make such a vile implication.*

"Sorry," he said to Sasha, who had gone pale beneath his patina of city dirt and looked ready to run for it. "All right. Let's go."

"Not you. Just me." He grabbed up the sandwich papers and his pack and broke out suddenly. "Look, you saw me under the bridge back there! You know what I do."

Laurie did. All that bewildered him, when he thought about it, was his own faint shiver of excitement at the thought. He should simply have been horrified, shouldn't he, that a boy his own age should be forced to such a living, and to all intents and purposes he was. But underneath his dismay, like a vein of hot lava... "Yes!" he said. "I mean...it doesn't matter to me. You don't have to be afraid of the police, is all. Not while you're with me."

Sasha gazed down at him. The pain in his dark eyes dissolved to a bright amusement. "Oh, my God. You *are* Prince Harry."

"No. He's a nice enough bloke, but they'd never let him roam around down here. My father, though…" He trailed off. The esplanade policeman, still far enough off for Sasha to make good his escape, was indeed turning his stately steps toward them. *My father's high up on the Metropolitan Police commissioners' board.* Oh, yes. And what would he do to help Sasha or anyone else not white, rich, Protestant, and provably British since the time of the Norman invasion? He'd help him by arranging for his deportation on the next boat out. "Never mind. Okay, go. But I'll see you again."

"No, you won't. It's better, Laurie. Trust me."

"I'll see you again. Will you let me give you some cash? To"—he paused, grinning—"to buy your friend Len a pint, show there's no hard feelings?"

"No." Sasha was smiling back, his expression oddly gentle. "I don't want it. Not from you."

"At least keep the change from the twenty. Otherwise…" Laurie paused, then once more surprised himself with his own guile. "Otherwise, how can you say you bought me lunch?"

I'll see you again. Laurie sent the thought after Sasha's retreating back. He didn't have long in which to do so. Between one glance and the next, Sasha was gone, melting into the crowd and the dazzling winter sun. His disappearance set a dry knot of pain in Laurie's throat. He'd read somewhere that twenty thousand people went missing each year in Britain alone, just dropped off the radar and were never seen again. He had wondered at the statistic, wondered how it could happen. Well, he had just seen it. It happened like that.

The policeman was still making his steady track through the park toward him. Laurie turned to look at him. This time he let the cold, forbidding mask come down deliberately, got to his feet on the fountain steps, and stood, hands on his hips, against the rainbowed backdrop of

Neptune and his mermaids. The policeman paused for a second, then as if on purpose, swung around and pursued his beat along the Embankment.

* * *

Laurie's tutor arrived the next day, and from then on he scarcely had an hour to call his own. Sanderson, a thin, bespectacled young man who had obviously been told by Sir William to educate his son or die trying, threw himself with nervous energy into the task. He set up shop on the top floor. It made sense; there was an old schoolroom up there, complete with massive dark oak desks and blackboard, and maybe Sanderson shared his student's instinct to put as much space as he could between himself and Sir William. But it gave Laurie the chills to be back on the scene of so many grim childhood hours. Homework, extra tuition during holidays, when the happy shouts of other kids would rise up to taunt him from the square. At least, he thought, settling into a chair and giving Sanderson his best look of respectful attention, he now more or less fitted the furniture. Could see over the desk's top. He patted his algebra textbook, to all appearances businesslike and ready.

The sole alleviation to Laurie's misery during the grim battles that ensued was Clara's presence. She turned up for every class with a view, as she put it, of *bettering herself*, though she spent her time discreetly reading *Charmed* novels behind the cover of one of Laurie's mathematics texts. Laurie wanted to tell her the deception would go down better if she put McKay's *Algorithms* the right way up, but he didn't want to tease her. He appreciated her loyalty too much for that, though he could have wished she was not seeing her elder brother daily revealed as such a dunce. He crawled off to his attic afterward, too numbed out for a while to do anything more than sit on the windowsill watching the traffic come and go in the slice of the real, living world he could see between two imprisoning Regency facades. He even experienced a brief envy for the pigeons, who might be dying of cold out there but at least could fly, feed, and cheerfully shag one another as they chose.

Except he was *not* stupid, was he? Laurie had once known some of the things Sanderson was trying to teach him, or he would not have scraped through his A levels and into Oxford, no matter how many strings Sir William had had to pull to help effect this. Although the shadowy unknown scope of his father's influence sometimes made Laurie shudder, he did remember slowly picking up enough of the methods and equations he needed to get by and amassing, albeit without much comprehension, enough dry facts and data to make himself sound intelligent on the subject of politics, at least until he met someone who actually was.

That was the problem. Enrolled as an undergrad at Oxford, Laurie was constantly surrounded by people for whom these matters were daily meat and drink, their lives' work, not a schoolboy game for sliding your way through exams. Laurie could recite chapter and verse on every English government that had held sway since the system was invented, giving the information as lines to an imaginary character in a history play; he could sing, for Clara's entertainment, the value of pi to a hundred decimal places. But these tricks would cut no ice with Oxford dons. His cover, over the course of his first university year, was slowly and systematically being blown apart. He felt as if the walls were closing, his mind clouding over. A kind of low-level panic ran always in the background of his days.

Had he ever been really good at anything? *Yes*. His faltering self-esteem tried to defend him. He'd loved English lit at school, mostly for its drama component but devouring poetry and novels too. That had been all right with his father. Reading was a gentlemanly hobby; a knowledge of literature was a gentlemanly acquisition. When it came to drama, however, Laurie had excelled, learning lines overnight that should have taken weeks, transforming effortlessly into anyone from Hamlet to Hermione, his unself-conscious gender-swapping a boon to those entrusted with the task of teaching drama in an all-male school—frustrating those teachers in equal measure with his absolute refusal to take part in any play that might receive a public airing, especially on parents' evenings. Knowing Sir William's prejudices, they had not tried to force the boy, and on those nights he had been their most talented nonperformer, tirelessly prompting from his secure hidden place in the wings.

Except at Christmas, when he came blazing forth as Cinderella's stepmother, the Widow Twanky, or a disturbingly handsome Ugly Sister. Pantomime was British, traditional, and his son a jolly good sport for taking part in the fun. If it ever occurred to Sir William that the pantomime dame was Britain's last remaining trace of revered, societally condoned transvestitism, he gave no sign.

Laurie hadn't tried to join any of the dozens of drama societies looking for members at Oxford. He had felt as if he would be exposed as a fraud there, as he was afraid he was every day in the lecture halls and his tutors' studies. He let himself think less and less about the theatre. It had been okay for a schoolboy to mess around there, but now he was working toward a career—which, however little he had had to do with its choosing, must someday lead him out of his father's house and into a life of his own. Mustn't it…?

So he tried. He set aside his disinclination and did his very best to learn from poor young Sanderson, who, if nervous, was sincere and not unkind. By the end of each day, tutor and student were invariably in such a state of frustration with themselves and one another that the sound of the clock ringing four in the hall downstairs came like a clarion of freedom.

Chapter Three

Four o'clock, any moment now. Laurie stared at the clock on the study-room wall, willing its second hand to make that last climb, until his eyes stung. Sanderson, absorbed in a text on abstract mathematics with the same chuckling thoroughness another man might have brought to a juicy porn magazine, seemed unaware of the time. Laurie blinked; he'd misjudged the clock, and had another minute to go. He restrained a gigantic, whole-body twitch, wondering why his mistake had rendered the last minute scarcely bearable. He drew a deep, silent breath, set himself to count the dust motes floating in a wedge of sunlight between his desk and the tutor's. It was last light, bloodred and tarnished, hardly visible against the room's overhead neon. Another breath, unconsciously registering the scent of beeswax from the endlessly polished old floorboards…

The clock issued its first gentle chime. Sanderson didn't appear to notice until Laurie's irrepressible restive movement knocked his geometry set to the floor in a rattle of plastic and metal. "Oh, four o'clock already?" Sanderson said, a note of regret in his voice that couldn't possibly have been authentic from anyone but him. "Well, off you go, Laurence, old fellow. I'll stay here and finish this chapter, if you don't mind."

"God, no." Laurie gathered up the fallen instruments, stabbing himself in the palm with the compass point without a flinch, dumping them randomly back into their box. "Knock yourself out, Sandy. I'll see you tomorrow."

Admittedly, as bitterly as he resented them, the exercises Sanderson set for him were his only chance of redeeming today's stupidity and rescuing him from tomorrow's. But first, freedom. His mind restored to him for a few hours before he had to sit down and tackle the exercises. A few hours in which he could retire to his top-floor room and think about Sasha. Today he wouldn't even have his sister on his hands, and much as he welcomed her faithful presence in the study room, he was glad. Clara had a bruising social schedule in the weeks running up to Christmas, as one after the other of her friends threw parties of increasing and competitive magnificence. Laurie, jogging quietly down thickly carpeted stairs to make himself a sandwich, reflected with amusement that she'd be exhausted after this one. The nine-year-old Lady Sophie of Ravenscliffe had no doubt pulled out all the stops, and Sir William, unashamed to schmooze those greater than himself, even at a little girls' tea party, had volunteered, with rare paternal condescension, to escort her. He would be hip-deep in port with Lord Ravenscliffe for hours. Laurie's mother was out too, so for once Laurie had the house to himself barring staff, who bothered him as seldom as he tried to bother them.

God, he could lie down on his bed and think of Sasha. The prospect of this was such a relief that Laurie's breath caught in his throat, and he paused on the landing, clamping both hands tight to the carved banister while the rush of excitement passed through him. His own need astonished him. What were the chances of them ever meeting again? Sasha had said it. They did not live in the same world, and Laurie's efforts to travel between the two had put Sasha in danger, made his already marginal existence more perilous and difficult still. Sasha himself had bidden him not to try again.

But even if Laurie had been forbidden to seek him out, his mind could create for him a thousand scenarios where no such restrictions applied. He could run into Sasha by chance in Regent's Park and walk with him silently into a grove of trees whose branches closed around them in tender concealment. He could march into the shantytown under the bridge with a pistol, hold Len at gunpoint, and demand that Sasha be released from this life of degradation—even though he knew Len had nothing to do with it. He could command Sasha leave behind the scuttling shamefaced businessmen who came slumming it down here for their treats, and come with Laurie to a place unspecified but safe and beautiful, where Sasha would stand before him, smiling, dark eyes glowing, and silently undress. Once, to Laurie's utter shame, in the fantasy *he* was the businessman, propped against the pillar, lost in bliss while Sasha sucked him off. Laurie didn't even know what that would feel like—from another boy or from a girl. His entire sexual experience in his nineteen years of life amounted to a tumble with a debutante, randy and willing, if too drunk to know who he was next time she saw him. But his imagination was good. Oh, a couple of hours to himself and he could find his way almost anywhere and conjure Sasha there to join him.

A ripple of laughter rose up from the ground floor. Laurie jumped as if caught in the act he'd been planning. Clara and Sir William must have come home early. Stifling a sigh, he continued on his route downstairs. He might as well let his presence be known. She'd seek him out anyway, and, if he couldn't have his mind-created grove, his armed rescue mission and seamy encounter beneath the bridge, her droll, jaded account of the party would be good for him, better probably than his own company. Eight going on thirty-eight, his Clara.

The door to the living room was open. Landing silently in stockinged feet from his customary vault of the banisters, Laurie froze. His father was sitting in one of the big armchairs, Clara on his lap. Laurie racked his brains for the last time the old man had touched her. He tended not to. His rages—and, young as she was, Clara was not immune to them—seldom culminated in violence. As for carrying, hugging, and all the benign contact of parenthood, the girl had her mother for that, as well as Laurie and a small team of domestic staff.

She looked happy enough now, if a bit startled. Sir William was gently jouncing her, and whatever he was saying to her was making her laugh. He was bright red in the face, perspiring slightly. Something in the position of his hand on her skinny little back made Laurie go as cold as death. He broke paralysis and continued across the hallway, far enough to open the door to the library. It gave its characteristic squeak. Clara spun around and jumped off the old man's knee, her face lighting up. "Laurie!"

He put out a hand to her. No, she wasn't going on thirty-eight. She had her few sweet adult ways, but she was as clear as daylight, barely out of babyhood, bright and untouched. Laurie calmly drew her to his side. He said to his father, "Good evening, sir," and remained there in the doorway to the library, motionless, staring at him. Sir William got to his feet. For a moment he seemed to struggle for his usual bluster, and Laurie wished he would. Wished he would demand what his son was doing, hanging about like a mooncalf in the hallway. Wished he would look like anything other than a man caught with bloody red hands. "She's got to do some of her Christmas holiday homework," Laurie said. He added, conscious of his ghost of a smile, "So do I. We'll see you later."

Laurie took her into the study and sat with her while she worked through her exercises. They were just English grammar, and even Laurie could help her with those, though he conscientiously tried to show her only her own route to the answers, not the answers themselves. She was completely undisturbed, chattering away to him about the party between her efforts to distinguish a noun from a past participle. Laurie listened as best he could, both hands knotted on the desk. In his mind, two scenes were playing themselves out. In the first, a boy who looked just like him but whose soul was untainted came trotting down the stairs of the big old house and saw his father playing with his little sister, smiled at them both, and passed on. In the second, a different version of the boy, marred but unswervingly brave, took Clara and went straight to the police, to social services, because no matter how many commissioners' boards Sir William Fitzroy headed up, no matter if he had half the Met in his pocket, there was justice in the world, unassailable justice and protection.

But Laurie was neither of these, and his world was what it was. When Clara had finished her homework, he suggested to her a sandwich supper with Mrs. Gibson, and Clara, never one to pass up an escape from the usual dreary family dinner, beamed at him in acquiescence. He took her down to the kitchen, and once she was settled chattering to Charlie at the old pine table where he too had hidden out from so much grim formality over the years, he drew the old housekeeper aside. "Gibson, I don't want Clara left alone." He shivered. That wouldn't bloody do it. The child wasn't *alone* with her father. "Do you know when Lady Fitzroy's due home?"

Gibson wiped her hands on her apron and surveyed the young man she had striven to look after since he was old enough to walk. "Not until morning, I believe, sir. She's staying with her sister over in Kensington. Why, Master Laurie, you look like a snake's bitten you. What on earth's the matter?"

"Nothing. That is…I think he might be drinking again. My father."

"Oh." Gibson looked down. There had been a bad few years when Sir William had added alcohol to his natural deficiencies of character—but had reined himself in rather than lose his foothold among his peers on his various boards and commissions. "Oh, dear. Are you sure?"

Laurie swallowed. He wasn't sure of anything. "No. But…I can't take any chances. I tell you what. Is Hannah at home for Christmas?" Hannah, the youngest daughter of local family friends, had been Clara's preferred babysitter since early childhood and still welcomed the chance to earn a few easy, enjoyable quid with her little charge when Laurie wasn't around.

"Yes, sir, as far as I know."

"Send Charlie to fetch her, would you? It would be good if she could stay over for a couple of days."

"Yes, of course. But...aren't you going to be home, Master Laurie?"

"Yes. I will, most of the time. I want somebody who can stay with her overnight, though, sleep in her room, and if I do have to go out...I just want her to have a companion. Do you understand?" Gibson, who plainly wished she did not, nodded sadly. "Tell Hannah she's been having nightmares. I'll square it with my mother and Sir William. And I'll pay."

* * *

Laurie waited until Hannah had arrived, bright-eyed and flushed with the cold, and was installed with the delighted Clara in the games room, laughing and shrieking over *High School Musical 3* or whatever similar god-awful DVD the child seemed able to watch with undiminished joy as often as she got the chance. He sat with them through the trailers, then as soon as the male lead's moony face appeared, retreated to the library, waving a *thanks, but no thanks* at their efforts to make him stay. He moved Clara's books from the table, packed them neatly into her satchel, and got out his own. Dutifully he worked through Sanderson's elaborate stratagem for making him understand and apply the pi concept, as opposed to reciting its value in the manner of a doomed Wagnerian hero or Valkyrie.

He left the library door open but saw no more of his father. Probably he had gone out to dinner and his club if his wife was not coming home. Laurie tried to concentrate on his work and the happy noise seeping out from the games room. At the proper hour for an eight-year-old's bedtime, the well-trained Hannah emerged with Clara in tow, and he bade them both a casual good night. Once they were gone, he tried not to let every creak in the floors above, every unidentifiable sound, become the bogeyman. Tried not to lapse into infantile fears. His father had seldom laid a hand on him—and never in that way—but his looming, angry bulk, especially when stinking of scotch, had been enough to place the fear of God in Laurie's heart, a fear he was still too young and trapped to place in context and dismiss.

And there was another shadow self in Laurie's head, one even less worthy than the equivocator who had gone down to the kitchens and tried to arrange some kind of inadequate shield for his sister. That one, when the house was quiet, folded up his books, went upstairs, and, creeping into his mother's bedroom, found by touch in the street-lit darkness the drawer where she kept her pills. Temazepam, in Laurie's experience, produced a strongly amnesiac effect. Three or four of them would not only ensure he slept, but might also wipe his mind clear of what he'd seen this afternoon. Hannah's presence in the house might puzzle him, but he'd find a way around it.

He was halfway up the vast carved staircase before he knew he had moved. God, the temptation was strong! Laurie, who normally did his best not to think of how often he had fallen back on this escape route, now made himself count the times. Over school holidays, maybe once or twice a month, when the rows had been bad or his fear of his own nightmares strong enough to keep him from sleeping at all. Had she never noticed her supplies were going down? Possibly not—she seemed to have several prescriptions from different doctors.

Pills for his mother, booze for his dad. Laurie knew, again from the *Guardian*, that children of substance-abusing households were much more likely than average to become addicts themselves. That was nice, he thought. If he didn't, it was a bit of a victory, kicking the trend, and if he did—well, it was on the cards, wasn't it? Not entirely his fault.

He sat down on the steps and buried his head in his hands. It would be a rich comfort to him, no doubt, fucked-up and lurching in and out of rehab in his twenties, to be able to think he wasn't to blame. Loneliness went through him like a knife. He seldom let himself consider this: his isolation, in this house, in his glittering social matrix, surrounded by friends who wouldn't give a toss if he disappeared tomorrow as completely as the other nineteen thousand nine hundred and ninety-nine…

The pain, now that he let it rise up, was almost unbearable. Flinching from it, he tried to think of something else, any associated train of thought he could ride out on. What else had he read in the *Guardian* lately? Yes, a review of the statistics on the numbers of migrant workers entering the UK since membership of the European Union had been extended two years ago. That was it; that was the thought that had been tugging at his mind since he had learned where Sasha was from. Romania had been admitted. What did it mean? Laurie did try to retain facts like these as part of his student-of-politics persona, but he knew he'd been flicking through the paper for cinema times and the Steve Bell cartoon. It meant, he thought, that Romanians could enter the country without a visa. They were free to travel here, work here.

Perhaps there was no need for Sasha to be in hiding at all. He was Roma, a gypsy, part of a societal underclass who perhaps did not have access to such information, who instinctively stayed beneath radar. Maybe he didn't know. Laurie got up. This thought was inspiring to him, driving off the shadows of his day. Sasha had tried to make him promise not to seek him out again, but this would be in a good cause. After Sanderson's classes tomorrow, he would go down to the Embankment.

For now, though, he would go to bed. Without pills and without guilt. He had done as much as lay within his power. Laurie felt his mind clearing, and remembered the night sky he had seen above the Strand, that unlikely perfection of starlight. The house no longer felt threatening around him, and he made his way calmly to the front door for a breath of fresh air before turning in, to see if tonight was the same.

Opening the door into the black-and-white tiled porch, he gasped. The massive old house cost a fortune to heat, but Sir William had several fortunes sensibly invested, and his mother, delicate hothouse plant that she was, liked the place kept at subtropical temperatures. Stepping from hall to porch was like diving into cold water. Ice flowers painted the delicate stained glass on the inside. Shivering, feeling his lungs catch with the change, Laurie went to touch them. They did not melt but slightly adhered the skin of his fingertips to their wild fractal ferns and blossoms, burning him as he pulled back.

He unlocked the front door and stood on the top step in the golden glow from the fanlight and the carriage lanterns that adorned both marble pillars. Yes, the skies were clear again, eerily lucid, each star like a separate human cry. He could scarcely breathe. This night would sweep like a scythe through London's lost souls.

They were legion. Laurie couldn't help them. His father's voice said, *Damn good thing. Cull the buggers like foxes*. "Fuck you," Laurie whispered fiercely, turning back indoors. You just did what you could, didn't you? And he could rescue one.

He made his way downstairs and tapped cautiously on the door to the chauffeur's rooms. It was after eleven, and he knew Charlie liked to turn in early on nights when he wasn't needed. But Charlie opened up straightaway, his dressing gown over his day clothes. "You all right, son?"

"Yes. Are you waiting to hear from my father? Do you reckon he'll want the car again tonight?"

Charlie shrugged. He had been Lady Fitzroy's driver since before her marriage, and Laurie was aware that he had no illusions about her or her husband. Probably Gibson had already spoken to him. "If he does, he can call a taxi, for my money. Do you need me to take you somewhere?"

Laurie considered. It was tempting—he was a decent driver, but the Daimler was like a whale in the narrow London streets. He didn't have the right, though, to ask Charlie to collude in what he was doing or acquiesce to it, even by his silence. "No," he said. "I've just got cabin fever from all this cramming. I fancy a run."

Charlie nodded sympathetically. He was a practical soul. No doubt he thought the young heir ought to be out chasing girls and getting into trouble like a normal embryonic baronet, not taxing his unremarkable brains over textbooks. "Off you go. She's got a full tank. Have her back by morning, that's all, and don't bloody speed."

* * *

Driving through the winter night. It felt to Laurie more like sailing, in this vast car whose suspension absorbed every bump in the road. He touched buttons and heard invisible whispering fingers wipe away steam on the windows' insides before it could form. Unreal. Floating past brilliant shop displays, the wealth of the world laid out in them, absurd bathrooms of Carrara marble, bedrooms, dining suites, beneath whose unreal outward-looking windows huddled unreal human souls—stripped of reality, of human status, by poverty. Laurie, having chosen one of them to save, was now beginning to understand his hypocrisy in ignoring the rest. He told himself that he would never accept the injustice. But nor would he let it make him bring the Daimler to a halt until he found the object of his search. He swallowed down the contradictions with an effort. He had to find Sasha; that was all.

His place in the doorway to Lindley's was vacant. A dull ache of anxiety went through Laurie. Had he drawn too much attention to Sasha the other night, only succeeded in driving him from his patch to somewhere even less hospitable? Continuing down the Strand, looking out for police cars and trying not to go conspicuously slow, he scanned the pavement. A taxi braked sharply in front of him, and he missed its rear end by three inches, drawing his attention fiercely back to the road. He could not afford an altercation, the lengthy exchange of insurance details. He had a sense of sands running through a glass, time running out. Why? It was nerves only, the feel of the strange car, ice forming under the wheels. Sasha must have survived winter nights before. Probably he had found shelter—sold his soul to Christian Outreach in exchange for a bed, and maybe not such a bad bargain as Laurie had thought, not on a night like this.

The Strand broadened out to the multilaned chaos of Trafalgar Square, and he concentrated on negotiating around it, keeping to the inside until he could escape and go back the way he had come. A fine hail was beginning to fleck the windscreen, bouncing and stinging, floating veils of light across the square. Nelson's Column drifted in and out of view. Just a little farther, indicating left and moving with the mix of assertion and courtesy he'd learned from Charlie, lane after lane and back out onto the Strand in the opposite direction, past coffee shops and all-night grocery stores.

There. Not Sasha but Gyorgy, barely distinguishable from the group of black plastic bags where he had taken refuge. Laurie was sure of it; every detail of that sunny afternoon on the Embankment was crisp in his memory. Every word. "*He's one of us*." Right. Gripping the wheel, Laurie prayed the solidarity extended to the pavement, to places to get through the night. Snapping the Daimler's hazards on, ignoring the chorus of bus and taxi horns that immediately began in his wake, he pulled to a halt, got out wearing his mother's mask of blue-blooded thunder—what Hannah had once less politely referred to as his fuck-off face—and indicated to them, with one brusque gesture, that they should just damn well go past him. Resisting the urge to vault the Daimler's front end, he walked around instead, blinking in the rainy headlights, and cautiously approached the old man.

"Gyorgy?"

He was sleepy. It took him a moment to look up. Half-blinded by dazzle, it took Laurie almost ten seconds to work out that he was cradling Sasha in his lap.

"Christ," he whispered and dropped to his knees among the bags. Sasha was barely more than a loose arrangement of bones and old clothes in the old man's arms, drained of the bright energy which, in the riverside sunlight, had made him look almost strong. "What's wrong with him?"

Gyorgy raised an eyebrow. He did not seem much surprised to see Laurie here. "Cold," he said simply. "Too much cold for the young ones tonight." He made an effort to close the dirty blanket over Sasha's chest. "More blood in them to freeze than in old men like me. You see?"

"Yes. I see." Laurie barely could, for sudden tears. "Is he…?"

The old man made no attempt to reply to the half-formed question but lifted his burden a little, as if proffering him in Laurie's direction so that he could find out for himself. Laurie reached out shaking fingers to touch the pulse at Sasha's neck.

Yes. Alive. Skin like a fridge-cooled peach. Laurie took a deep breath. “Listen,” he said. “I want to take him away, off the street. I swear to you, I won’t hurt him.”

Gyorgy’s dark brow rucked. “Not mine to give or keep,” he said. “But he won’t sell his soul, gajo.”

“I know. I don’t want it. I just don’t want him to die here. Help me?”

Together they got him to his feet. He came around a little at the movement and regarded Laurie with unseeing eyes. Laurie saw with a pang that frost had caught in his lashes. Quickly Laurie ducked beneath the arm Gyorgy was holding and drew it over his shoulders. “There. I’ve got you. Don’t be scared.” Taking most of Sasha’s weight, he turned to the old man. “Thank you. What can I do for you? Where can you go?”

“With you, wouldn’t hurt,” came the rasping reply, and for one wild moment Laurie considered it. Why the fuck not? The Daimler would take six, the house in Mayfair probably fifty if it was used to capacity. Maybe he should just harvest up as many as he could, drop them at Sir William’s feet, and let him deal with it.

But Gyorgy was backing away, grinning, waving a hand. “Tenner keeps me in St. Martin’s overnight, boy. They let you stay as long as you can buy their coffee.”

Laurie handed him twenty, not so much generosity as the fact that he had nothing smaller—seldom did—that anything smaller felt like loose change to him, scarcely useful as currency. He opened the Daimler’s passenger door, pushed it wide with one foot, and eased Sasha in. The leather-scented warmth breathing out into the night was suddenly intoxicating to him, even after such short exposure to the bitter dark. Sasha took a startled breath and opened his eyes wide, stiffened from head to foot in a kind of convulsion of terror, and tried to launch himself straight back out onto the street, as if the night, however deadly, must be preferable to falling into a stranger’s hands. God alone knew what he thought was happening to him—abduction, arrest…

"It's just me," Laurie said helplessly.

The confused gaze found him and focused. "Laurie!"

"Yes. Just hang on. I'm going to get help for you."

But where from? Laurie thought a normal person might know, one who went to ordinary hospitals from time to time instead of discreet private healthcare clinics in leafy suburbs. He glanced around for signs that might jog his memory. Charing Cross was nearby, but the station and the hospital were in two different parts of the city, weren't they? A choking panic rose in him. He had only thought as far as getting Sasha into the car—that fantasy of transfiguring cold into warmth for him, giving him refuge, like Laurie was some alchemical magician or god. He hadn't thought what he would do with a dying boy in the passenger seat beside him. He put out a hand. He remembered how Sasha's had closed on his wrist beneath the bridge. *Fuck, Sasha didn't have to think twice, did he*? He knew what to do to protect people. He wasn't useless, not like Laurie, who didn't even know quite what he was looking for, the right place to feel for the pulse.

But Sasha stirred and suddenly clasped his hand hard in return. "Laurie," he repeated, as if it was the only name that could mean anything to him. He twisted around in the seat—almost too weak to fight the belt that Laurie had automatically fastened for him, just as he always did for Clara—and stared at him, wide-eyed. "It *is* you. I was on the pavement, and…I saw lights. I saw my mother, and then…I saw you."

"You'll be all right," Laurie told him past a raw, dry pain in his throat. "You've got hypothermia. I'm going to get you to a doctor."

"Oh, God. No hospitals."

The grip had tightened. Laurie was grateful for the Daimler's automatic gears; he couldn't have brought himself to break free if both their lives had depended on it. "Look, I don't think…I don't think you have to hide, Sasha. It's what I came out here to tell you. You don't need a visa to come to the UK anymore. Did you know that?"

Sasha stared at him. His pale face began one of its slow, compelling transformations, from stoic stillness to the broad, loving grin Laurie couldn't work out what he'd done to deserve. "Of *course*, stupid. But you do need a passport. Papers of some kind."

"Oh."

"Or I wouldn't have come over the Channel in the back of a container truck full of frozen yogurts. It was"—he trailed off and shuddered, eyes becoming distant even while he took in Laurie's face with that loving hunger—"it was colder than I am now. There were twelve of us. Five of them died. I ran for it while they were checking the corpses at Dover."

"Oh, God."

"I tried to tell you. I'm not legal. I'm no good. Let me out, Laurie. Go home."

"We're both going home." Laurie heard, with surprise, the snap of decision and authority in his voice. What made him think he could do this, or even that it was right? It was as if Sasha's grip on his hand could squeeze out of him all uncertainty, all mistrust in himself. "If you won't go to a hospital, you have to let me take care of you."

"Your father…" Sasha paused, caught in a fit of coughing as the Daimler's warm air fought the chill in his lungs. "Your father will take me by the hood of my coat and hang me from the nearest lamppost."

"Oh, screw my father," Laurie said with a brave insouciance, smilingly undermining himself a second later with, "Anyway, he's out. I won't let him anywhere near you." He hesitated, knowing what it was to be without choice, even in the best gilded cage. "Okay. Look, I'm sorry. Just say the word and I'll stop. I'll take you back to Gyorgy, or anywhere you want to go."

A purring silence fell inside the opulent car. No word came. After a moment, Sasha relinquished Laurie's hand, placing it carefully back on the wheel. Still no word. At the next junction, Laurie took the turn for Mayfair.

Chapter Four

The great house had several portals, each appropriate to the class of person who might be expected to come and go through them. Gibson and Charlie, as long-term family staff, had their own quarters and their own route to the street. Day staff—Lady Fitzroy's floating population of au pairs, companions, personal shoppers, and music tutors—used a lowlier doorway from the garden at the side. Best of all for Laurie—always had been, on occasions when he needed to escape the cage without the grand parade through hallway and down steps—was a seldom-used door around the back, once the method previous Baronet Fitzroys had used to conceal the comings and goings of coal men, maids, and other such personnel as did not fit well with the mansion's magnificent facade. An old stone stairwell led all the way down to it from the garret where Laurie and Clara now kept their roost. Back then, an underpaid Victorian workforce could do their work and retire to their sleeping quarters without being seen by the family at all.

Reflecting on the ironic beauty of this, Laurie parked the Daimler in the alleyway that led to it. Only the first stretch of the alley was visible to surrounding houses. Once he'd negotiated the corner, he was invisible, safe in a refuge he knew he was outgrowing but could not work out how to abandon.

Tonight at least it served a purpose for somebody else. He went around to the passenger door and half lifted Sasha out into his arms.

* * *

His room was filled with firelit shadows. Similarities suddenly hit him between this sparsely furnished garret and the place beneath the bridge—uncertain light making odd shapes flicker on the walls, a sense of hiding away.

Enormous differences too. The most significant: the bright gas fire designed to look like an open one, convincing enough but for its inexhaustibility. Effortless heat at the touch of a switch. Feeling as if he were seeing it for the first time himself, Laurie guided Sasha to kneel by it. "There. Not too close. I think you're meant to warm up slowly. Here, let me take your coat." Their hands met as he reached for the damp parka, warm skin brushing on cold, and Sasha looked up at him, expression hard to interpret. Gratitude, certainly. Some kind of frightened promise.

Laurie gave up trying to read him in favor of practical concerns. "Right," he said. "You stay there. I'm going to get you some food."

He ran downstairs. A cracking good short-order chef, Laurie was. Between his parents, for whom each meal turned into a long, turgid ritual, and a kitchen full of staff determined to wait on him hand and foot, he had learned the art of the lightning raid. He knew where Mrs. Gibson kept the frozen-ready meals she and Charlie would serve up for themselves after a late-night Fitzroy party, knew which cooked fastest and tasted best out of the microwave. That was the extent of his culinary talents, but it would do for tonight. He made a mug of instant coffee, put it on a tray, then added a pitcher of fresh orange juice. Hot food and vitamins, those were what he should provide. He picked out the best-looking apples and grapes from the fruit dish. Would that do? He had no idea, but it would be academic if Sasha starved to death upstairs in the meantime. Balancing the tray with unconscious grace on the flat of one hand, he let himself back out onto the servants' stairs.

In Laurie's room, Sasha was waiting for him. He had taken off every stitch of his clothing and was lying on the hearthrug in a posture even Laurie's total inexperience told him was meant to be seductive. "Christ!" Laurie said and dropped the tray, then caught it before it had fallen an inch, with the reflexes that made him such a valuable backstage props handler. China and glass clattered but remained upright. "What are you doing?"

"It's what you want, isn't it? Nothing's for nothing."

Laurie came to the fireside and carefully set the tray down. Then he strode over to his bed and grabbed the warm dressing gown he'd discarded there that morning. This was convenient, in a way, he told himself through the racing thud of his own heart. All his visitor's clothes were soaked and filthy; he'd been looking for some way to part Sasha from them. He took the dressing gown, crouched behind Sasha, and said, "Here. Arm. Arm," just as he did for Clara on those school mornings when unwillingness to go made her forget the basics of putting on her coat. "Yes. Some things *are* for nothing. This is. God, Sasha. How could you think that?"

"Why would I think anything else?"

Sasha's voice was unsteady, cracked with shivers. Laurie shook his head. "Because…we met. Twice. Did I look like I was trying to"—he didn't even know the right word—"price you up?"

"No. But just so you know, this is the price."

"What?"

"This room. Heat. Food. I've done it for a lot less." He shuddered, and on impulse Laurie wrapped his arms around him from behind. "I'd give you change if I could."

"Well, it's just a house. And a grocery-store lasagna. And…I prefer girls, so you're all right." Laurie squeezed him, let him go, and went to pour juice for him. "I tell you what, though—while you've got your clothes off anyway…"

* * *

Laurie sat by the fire, knees drawn up to his chest, arms encircling them. In the next room, he could hear gentle splashing sounds that he hoped meant Sasha was enjoying the hot bath Laurie had run for him. He surveyed with amusement the tray, which, if it had been a chicken, would now be a neat pile of clean-picked bones. They hadn't talked while Sasha had quietly taken the lasagna down to the plate pattern and the fruit to its core.

Laurie welcomed the silence. He was trying hard to assimilate the idea of poor Sasha's price. That Sasha would think he'd been rescued, warmed, fed, just so that Laurie could…

God. The idea was repellent to him, and yet he could not shake the vision of that naked, firelit frame laid out and waiting on the rug. He'd been on his side, hadn't he, with his back to the fire, so the painful hollows of his ribs and hips were not apparent and you could only see his shape—wide shoulders, the elegant curve of his torso down to slender hips. I prefer girls, Laurie repeated silently, this time almost making himself laugh. He hadn't really had enough of either to know, but based on the evidence so far, what he preferred at this stage of his life was Sasha.

Who had arrived in England among the corpses of his friends and lived rough ever since, selling sex to strangers until he could no longer accept or believe in human kindness. Laurie leaned to turn up the fire. No matter what he felt, he mustn't show it, or…

The bathroom door creaked gently open. Sasha appeared, safely wrapped in Laurie's dressing gown, subtly transfigured. Laurie had had no idea how he would look when clean, fed, and thoroughly warm. His black hair was damped down in short feathers: raven's-wing hair. For the first time, his skin was softly flushed, rose under olive. When his eyes met Laurie's, they seemed to have a light of their own, independent of the firelight, making the flames suddenly tawdry and dim.

"Thank you," Sasha said, with an intensity to match their blaze.

Laurie smiled. "Good bath?"

"Religious experience."

"Ah." Aware that he was staring, Laurie turned his attention back to the gas flames and did not watch while Sasha came to kneel beside him on the rug. He could smell him now—nothing but the tang of Laurie's own citrus soap and shampoo, somehow intoxicating when underlain by this particular skin. Awkwardly reaching for distraction, he said, "You speak really good English, for an immigrant." Then, afraid he had been rude, added, "Better than me, I mean. And…even that doesn't sound right."

"It's not," Sasha told him, settling comfortably on the hearthside. He was so close that Laurie couldn't help but meet his gaze. "Do you know why?"

"Oh, God… I did for about five minutes in fourth-year grammar. Something about subjects and predicates and intransitive Christ-knows-whats. It's all gone now."

"No, it hasn't. You wouldn't say 'better than me do,' would you?"

"No, I wouldn't. Oh. I see." Laurie did, for the first time. It was crystal clear. He fought the sensation that a big cartoon lightbulb had just popped on over his head. "Why did nobody explain it to me like that before?"

"Blinding kids with science helps a teacher keep his mystical authority over them. 'Better than me' is fine in everyday speech. Everyone knows what you mean, and 'better than I' sounds pompous. But you can just add the *do*, to work out which one is correct. I think I told you my mother was English. She…ran away to join the gypsies, I suppose you would say."

Laurie stared at him. *I can see how she came to do that*, was in his mouth, on his tongue. A slow wave of warmth passed through him. *She looked into a pair of eyes like yours, and the rest of the world faded to nothing.*

Remembering himself—his resolution, his obligations—he tried to make a sensible reply. "Oh. Is she—"

But Sasha leaned toward him. For a moment his hand clasped and unclasped in the wool of Laurie's sweater as if he could not decide whether to seize him or push him away. Laurie, astonished, sat still, and a moment later felt the swift, warm-velvet press of Sasha's mouth against his own. It was tentative, exploratory. As Sasha backed off, Laurie saw him clouded with anxiety, trying to work out the effects of what he had done, his smile contradicting but not hiding the fear in his eyes. Sasha said faintly, "I'm sorry."

"Don't," Laurie said, his own voice a strange, dry rasp to him. "I mean...don't be sorry. It's okay. But I told you, you don't have to—"

"Oh, I know."

"You don't have to do anything at all," Laurie finished awkwardly, reaching helplessly forward to kiss him back.

Time passed. Seconds. Minutes. Laurie didn't know. All he could feel were Sasha's hands on his shoulders, Sasha's tongue in his mouth, probing so gently it brought tears like meltwater to Laurie's eyes. As if he had been the one freezing half to death on the pavement; as if *he* had been dying of cold. He shuddered and sobbed, took hold of the edges of Sasha's dressing gown and pushed them back, blindly feeling for the shapely collarbones beneath. Sasha moaned, a rippling vibration in Laurie's mouth, and they broke apart for an instant, only long enough to exchange a startled glance, before pushing urgently mouth to mouth once more. Laurie felt his eyes close. Burning down his spine was a signal he had seldom experienced and never at this intensity: the knowledge that he was about to become erect, not at the controlled, controlling touch of his own hand, but in response to another living creature—a creature like himself, another boy. He cried out, half in fright, and felt Sasha's hands come to rest warmly on either side of his face, steadying him, a silent reassurance.

His bedroom door clicked. Laurie froze. He opened his eyes and met Sasha's, surely as wide and scared as his own. "Oh, God," he whispered, feeling the prayer shape itself against lips still pressed to his.

But he would not allow the fear. Laurie would not let anything happen to Sasha. If this was the time—right now, apocalyptically, when he had to stand up to his father, so be it; the old sod could kill him and toss him out the window if he wanted. Twisting around, Laurie got to his knees and then his feet, shielding Sasha behind him just as he himself had been protected against all odds beneath the bridge. He heard his own voice ring out, levelly, unfazed. "Who's that?"

"Me. I'm sorry, Laurie."

"Clara." Laurie swallowed convulsively. "You know, I swore to your mother I wouldn't swear in front of you, but fucking *hell*, Clara!"

She pushed the door tentatively wide. "I know. I won't tell. I was having bad dreams, or I wouldn't have…" She trailed off. "Laurie. Do you know there's someone in your dressing gown?"

Laurie sighed, dying adrenaline shivering off him like glitter. "I'm aware of it. Yes." He took an unsteady step back, seeing Sasha unfold from the rug and rise to stand beside him. "He's Sasha. He's…" Laurie thought quickly. If he asked her to keep quiet, she would do her best. But she was so clear, so straightforward, that the truth would fall from her over the breakfast table straight into her father's lap. Ask her to keep a romantic secret, however, and she'd probably take it with her to the grave. "He's a gypsy prince." He heard Sasha's faint choking sound but forged on, deadpan. "And he's in exile, so you mustn't tell anyone he's here."

Clara gazed at them both, her eyes enormous. "A prince? I won't say anything. I swear it on my life."

"Just a promise will do. Well, Clara, this is Prince Sasha of Romania. Sasha, my sister, Lady Clara Fitzroy of Mayfair."

"Enchanted," Sasha replied with impressive solemnity and stepped forward to give her a courtly bow. "I'm sorry to hear you have bad dreams."

Laurie watched with a painful tightness in his throat while she tried visibly to rise to the occasion. "Oh, they're nothing," she said. "A childish phase, apparently. Forgive my intrusion." Bobbing him a neat convent-school curtsy, she began to back out.

"Wait, Clara." She was pale, Laurie thought. He'd assumed she was too young to feel the constant low-level sense of oppression in the house. Assumed she'd been happy enough with her father. God knew what she took in, what she knew. "Hannah's with you, isn't she?"

"Yes. Snoring."

"You can wake her up, you know, if you have nightmares."

"I know. But she doesn't…"

"Doesn't what?"

"She doesn't know Reduced Shakespeare," Clara whispered, going paler still, eyes filling with tears. Laurie forgot with instant totality any shreds of irritation, strode to her, and swept her up.

She said to Sasha over his shoulder, as if making apology for somebody else, "Oh, dear. I'm not normally such a nuisance."

"Not a nuisance at all," Laurie said, sitting down with her on the bed. "Which one in particular doesn't she know?"

"*King Lear*, I think."

"Good. A cheerful one." This was easier than opera, Laurie thought. He'd been to see the whole Reduced Shakespeare Company series twice last year, not that it had taken much time—they'd done tragedies one night, comedies the next, and grouped together histories and mysteries on the third. He'd reduced them still further for Clara's benefit on his return home, and they'd become a frequent choice for repeat performance. Settling her on a pillow, Laurie darted an apologetic glance at Sasha, but he'd gone back to sit by the hearth once more and was watching him with smiling curiosity. Laurie took up a position roughly central in the room and bowed to his small audience. "There once was a mardy old king…"

The performance took less than ten minutes in limerick form. It required all of Laurie's ingenuity to leap from wicked Edmund to doomed and dim-witted Cordelia, and he almost sprained an ankle in the mad scene on the heath, but the effort was well worth it. The shadows left his sister's face—and, to his astonishment, when he glanced across the room, he saw that Prince Sasha of Romania was curled up by the fire, tears of silent laughter streaming. Giving the ending his usual twist, Laurie had the old king and his daughter tango offstage together, alive and well and discussing their plans for revenge.

He emerged, sweating and trembling with exhaustion, to noisy applause. "Ssh, both of you, for God's sakes. Lady Clara, will that do for you?" She was too far gone to reply, but he took her weak nod for assent and gathered her up. "I'll be back in a minute, Sasha."

She was almost asleep by the time he shouldered open the door of her room. He took her quietly over to the bed and laid her down beside Hannah, who was sleeping the sleep of the innocent but smiled vaguely and threw an arm around Clara when she felt her weight. He straightened up, ran both hands through his hair and stood in the streetlight for a moment trying to convince himself of her safety.

In his own room, Sasha was waiting. He stood up as Laurie reentered. "You're a good, kind brother," he said, holding out a hand. "And an amazing bloody actor."

Laurie walked into his arms.

The bed was narrow. Their limbs tangled, awkward, Laurie's now colder than Sasha's. They sank down wordlessly, no time even to pull back the duvet and blanket. No time to divest Laurie of more than his sweater, though he almost died of fright and excitement when Sasha seized that and pulled it over his head. Sasha lay looking up at him, then ran both hands across his naked chest with a dry sound of longing and hauled him down to lie beside him. In the dark they found again the interrupted kiss, picked it up with bruising urgency. This time Laurie felt Sasha's mouth open to admit him, and flickered his tongue uncertainly inside and back. "Oh, God. Sasha."

"Yes. It's all right."

"Is it? Am I doing it right?"

Sasha gave a soft, half-choked chuckle. "Yes. Doing it fine. Come on; come here."

Moaning, Laurie obeyed him. It was as easy as obeying gravity, easy as falling. He pushed his hips forward and felt Sasha shove back hard against him, then subside before pulling him up to lie on top. Together they undid his dressing gown's belt and opened the garment wide. Then Laurie held breathlessly still while Sasha deftly undid his jeans—hesitated for a moment, as if he had shown too much expertise, dark eyes troubled, seeking Laurie's in the amber streetlight. Laurie said, in his turn, "It's all right," added incoherently, "Please," and shuddered in relief when Sasha understood him and shoved jeans and boxers down around his hips.

Their bodies met, hard and hungry. Laurie cried out at the feel of Sasha's cock against his own, a hot, dry slide. He wondered fleetingly if he ought to be doing something more sophisticated than this, more than thrusting for contact as if his life depended on it, but Sasha didn't seem to mind—had opened his thighs as if to welcome and direct his efforts. His hands on Laurie's backside were firm, his face rapt, lips parted on quickened and quickening breath.

"Oh, Laurie," he whispered hoarsely, beginning ragged thrusts up to meet him. "Come on."

Laurie gasped. He'd thought he was fully erect, but the whispered command sent a surge through him. His movements took rhythm, barely voluntary, some ancient music that had been there all the time only now becoming audible to him. He briefly longed for his cock to be enclosed—he knew what gay men did, though it seemed barely feasible—and Sasha, as if reading him, reached a hand down between their bodies. "Lift up a sec," he murmured, hot against Laurie's ear.

The brushing caress of his mouth, his sudden clasp on Laurie's cock, almost brought Laurie over on the spot, but he hung on; the touch was full of intent, pushing his shaft down so that at his next thrust, it was caught and clenched hard between Sasha's thighs. He heard his own astonished cry with shame. That was it; that was the grip he had needed.

Instinct told him it was vital to keep Sasha with him, not to let the soaring pleasure take him yet. If he came first, he might leave Sasha thinking he had only served him, like a…*like a client*. The words whispered coldly through Laurie's mind, and he pushed them away.

No! Like lovers, like lovers.

He shifted, and smiled down at Sasha. Waited until Sasha's next movement had brought Laurie's cock to lie between their bellies. Now when he thrust, they would both feel it, both have the heat, the pressure, and the refuge of one another's flesh. Sasha's face changed—lost its mask, the faint trace of readiness to hide pain or sorrow, flushed up and contorted like that of any other healthy young man about to shoot to climax—and Laurie let go and pounded at him. Sasha closed a crushing grip around the tops of both his arms and hung on, writhing up, loosing a short, desperate cry at every thrust. Wet heat burst on Laurie's belly, in the tight place where they were locked together.

He braced, the beginnings of the seizure almost too much, almost making him afraid. He didn't recall coming with the girl. But this…*this* he would remember until he died.

"*Christ*," he rasped out, shuddering, aware of the rush of his semen between Sasha's thighs as the tip of the iceberg. The rest of him—from prickling scalp to curling, scrabbling toes—was caught up in the firestorm, incandescent, lost.

* * *

He thought he must still be glowing faintly in the dark. He lay, beached and wrung out, at Sasha's side, listening to their breathing slowly lose its ragged edge, unable to think or to move. Yes, he must be luminescent, shining. Sasha too. If he opened his eyes, blinked the tears from them, he would see Sasha, bright as an angel in an old tale, in the bed beside him.

"I…I should go now."

Laurie snapped back to his senses. He looked and saw poor Sasha was not shining at all—that his lights had gone out, and he was up on one elbow, ready to get out of the bed and leave, as if…

"No!" Laurie whispered, reaching for him. "For God's sake, please don't tell me you thought that was…"

"Business?" Sasha finished for him, smiling weakly. "You think my punters try to stop me leaving? The last one kicked me out of his car. It's almost a pity, because"—he paused, voice catching—"I wouldn't have minded enjoying my work for once."

"Oh, Sasha." There were tears in Sasha's eyes. Somehow the sight of them shocked Laurie to the core. "Hang on a minute." He scrambled out of the bed and gestured to Sasha that he should stand too, just long enough for Laurie to turn back the duvet and the wool blanket that covered it. "There. Get back in." When Sasha hesitated, he gave him a little encouraging shove, stripped out of his jeans, and followed him, burrowing down with him into the warmth. Their limbs laced together, Sasha, after a moment's stiff awkwardness, grasping at him fiercely. "Stay with me," Laurie whispered into his hair. "Just for tonight. Stay."

* * *

Morning found them locked together still. Laurie breached the surface of his dreams with a deep inhalation; they had been hot and sweet, and his cock was hard, crushed to Sasha's thigh. "Oh," he rasped, as Sasha woke too and turned smiling to look at him. "Sorry."

"Mm," Sasha commented, rolling to face him. He'd divested himself of the dressing gown during the night.

For a long minute, the joy of being skin-to-skin with him overwhelmed Laurie, and he could only cling to him, blindly pressing kisses to his throat.

But Sasha ran shuddering hands down his arms, down his sides, and suddenly Laurie wanted more. Much more, as if in his few hours of sleep he'd grown up, vaulted barricades out of shy, awkward boyhood… An instinct rose in him, opened darkly like a rose. He turned his back to Sasha's gentle pushing, rolled to face the wall.

"Laurie, no. Not that."

Sasha had gone still. His grip on Laurie's shoulder, on the hand he'd flung back to him, was bruising, damp with distress.

"Why?" Laurie softly demanded, already half-aware the question was stupid.

"You must know. I'm not sure I'm clean. There's a doctor who comes around the homeless people sometimes, tests for things, but I…I haven't wanted to find out. Do you understand?"

"Yes." Laurie did, with painful clarity. He wriggled back over and pulled Sasha into his arms. "Listen to me. You can't live like this. Maybe you don't have to, even if you're illegal. Why did you leave Romania?"

Sasha moaned. He tried to escape Laurie's grip, then subsided into it, letting go a ragged breath. "It doesn't matter. Doesn't make any difference."

"Tell me anyway."

"My father was a political activist. Not much of one; he just wrote poetry. Made the mistake of trying to get it published abroad so that people would know what Ceauşescu was doing in Romania, to people like him—gypsies, intellectuals, anyone who disagreed with the regime."

He paused, and Laurie lay watching him, arousal and compassion competing for space in his mind. With an effort he dismissed both in order to think about history, or the little he knew of it. Nikolai Ceauşescu—that had been the mideighties, hadn't it? When the Romanian people had risen up and overthrown their Communist dictator in a bloody coup. "What happened to him? You're only my age, aren't you? You couldn't have been born."

"No. He was sent to the Piteşti prison in 1984. He was Roma, but he'd had his own house north of Bucharest, where there was a big gypsy community. He and my mother gave lessons in their living room, the only education most kids there got. They were doing all right, but when he was released after the revolution, he was…different. Broken. He didn't really care for anything anymore—or he couldn't. The state had stripped what assets he had, and…he and my mother went to live in the *mahala* in Sofia, the Roma ghetto. Conditions there were terrible. Still are. I think becoming pregnant with me was the last straw for my mother. She waited until I was born, and then she left me with him and came home."

"To England?" Laurie asked it softly, leaning on one elbow, running a hand over Sasha's hair. His eyes were wide and distant, and he had told his story as if it belonged to someone else. "Did you try to trace her? I don't know how the law works, but if you've got someone here, a close relative who could vouch for you…"

"I thought of it. I haven't had the chance. I only got here a couple of months ago." He smiled faintly and shivered, tugging at the duvet. Reflexively Laurie moved closer, covering him. "Somebody told me the winters were warmer here, you know."

"You need shelter. I…I'd help you find your mother, you know. There're ways, using the Internet. What about your father? Is he still alive?"

"No. He died a long time ago. Look, Laurie—"

"Then you've been surviving by yourself in the—what did you call it, the mahala? The ghetto? You might be a refugee. You could apply—"

"Laurie. Why are *you* living like a refugee, here in your own home?"

Laurie caught his breath. He felt as if he'd missed a gear on his mother's little Mini Cooper and stalled her out. He stared down at Sasha, who was back in the moment with him now, intense, eyes fixed unblinkingly on his. "We weren't talking about… What do you mean?"

"This great big house. Why are you hiding in one of its attics?"

"I'm not. It's just my room."

"Okay. How old are *you*?"

"Nineteen. Why…"

"Because you're terrified of your father, and you've got everything you need to walk away and make a life of your own. Education, money… Why don't you?"

Laurie shifted uncomfortably. He wasn't sure how he had ended up in the spotlight, and he felt oddly trapped there, as if Sasha's questions were more valid than his own.

He didn't know why and fought a brief rush of irritation. What could Sasha possibly understand, about the task of self-extraction from the honeypot, the web of family wealth?

"I don't really have either," he said. "He gives me...pocket money, for God's sake. And I'm home for the winter to study because I stuffed up my first-year exams. He's paying for my tutor." Put so plainly as that, his reasons sounded so inadequate that Laurie felt a deep flush of shame rising up in him—then remembered, almost with relief, that he had other motives. They were none of Sasha's business, but the quiet, dark gaze on his was not judgmental, only waiting. "He's a bastard," Laurie said quietly after a moment. "I'm afraid he'll hurt Clara, and my mother too. I try to be around as much as I can."

"But when term starts, you'll go back to college and leave them. The only real way to help them would be to find your own life, your own place, and give them somewhere to go. Wouldn't it?"

Laurie swallowed. "Jesus, Sasha. You don't know what you're asking. I'm not...I'm not like you. I can't do anything."

"What are you studying?"

"Maths and politics. With the old man's connections, I might get a seat in the Houses of Parliament or go into law, but..." He trailed off. To his bewilderment, Sasha was beaming at him. Laurie could feel repressed laughter trembling in the muscles of Sasha's chest and stomach. "What?"

"I thought you must be at... What's the big drama school called here? RADA?"

"The Royal Academy of Dramatic Art," Laurie confirmed dryly. It was where, when he was eighteen, he had hoped, prayed and even dared to assume he would be. But that was before his subject choice for A levels had had to be made and he had run up against Sir William, who had turned out to have assumptions of his own.

"No wonder you don't think you can do anything. Laurie, if I had half your gift, I'd be doing street plays, finding any way I could of crawling onto a stage every chance I got." He lifted a hand and rubbed the backs of his fingers up and down Laurie's cheek.

Something in the gesture made Laurie want to burst into tears.

"Forgive my saying this. We've just met. But you don't seem to me to be…much of a maths-and-politics person."

"I'm not." Laurie wanted to shout it, to smack his fists against the wall to make his point, but he had learned to tread too warily through the mine-loaded no-man's-land that stretched between his father's ambitions and his own. His voice remained flat and quiet. "But it's not as simple as that."

"No, I'm sure it's not. I'm sure…each of our lives, our circumstances, looks far simpler from the outside. Listen to me, Laurie. I can't believe I've met you. I'm still not sure that you're real; I keep thinking I died of hypothermia with poor Gyorgy last night."

"No. He's okay. He said he could go somewhere."

"Because you gave him enough to get him off the street. That's what I mean. You're so bloody sweet, and last night—coming here, doing what we did—it was perfect. You made me want to live for the first time in as long as I can remember."

"Then live." Laurie choked. His throat had filled with coppery salt. "Let me help. You *might* die the next night you're out there. I couldn't bear that. Come back here—I'll find a way."

"Shh. You know that wouldn't work. Look, I can't trace my mother's people. There's reasons for that. But I know there are Roma gypsy camps here too, on the outskirts of London. Would you look online for me, see if you can find out where?" He smiled, shrugged. "They don't welcome the likes of me in Internet cafés."

They would, if I dressed you in my clothes. If I took you out and bought your own for you, sent you to my hairdresser. If I kept you. Maybe the old man is right—there's nothing that money can't buy.

Biting back a moan, Laurie drove off the darkly shining thoughts. "Of course I will. I'll do it now."

He pushed the duvet back, but Sasha's grip closed tenderly tight on his arm. "Not right now. What time is it?"

"About six."

"And still pitch-dark. It doesn't feel like morning yet to me."

Laurie wasn't sure how he had ended up on his knees beside the bed, except that there had been a dispute, a brief silent tussle, which he had unexpectedly won. He was stronger, he supposed—better fed, anyway. Once Sasha had had a few more hot meals down him, he would be a force to be reckoned with. Nothing Laurie would have liked better than to have let him get where he had been trying to go, plunging down the bed, planting hot kisses on Laurie's chest and belly en route, but he remembered the look on Sasha's face as he had emerged from his transaction under the bridge—the weary, dead sickness—and he did not want Sasha even going through the same motions.

Laurie would go through them for him, though it was a first and he had very little idea where to start. He'd seized Sasha by the armpits, pulled him back up. Yes, that was how he'd come to be down here: the moment Sasha had understood his intentions, he'd bolted upright and tried to escape the bed. Laurie had stopped him, but only by main force, a dirty tackle that had tipped Laurie out onto the carpet. He'd scrambled to his knees, got between Sasha's thighs, and stilled him with a passionate embrace of his waist. "No. Let me."

"No. It's dangerous, Laurie. I'm not sure I should even do it to you."

Laurie wasn't too sure, either. Like most of the boys in his year, he had spent his single school-hour of sex education staring in desperate embarrassment at the scuffs on the classroom floor.

He said, in a valiant show of confidence, "It's okay. I'll pull back when you—" And that was no good, was it? If he couldn't even say the word, he probably shouldn't be doing it or trying to get someone else to. "When you come," he finally blurted out, blushing hotly, looking hopelessly up at Sasha, who somehow seemed to find his nonplussed ineptitude rather endearing than otherwise. Who was smiling down at him even while he tried to detach Laurie's grip. And when Laurie sat back, there was no doubt who had won this round. Sasha's cock lifted straight and clear. Laurie whispered, shivering at its explicit shape and detail, so close, so very close, "I've never done this before."

"You chose a great place to start, didn't you? A homeless rent boy."

"Sasha, don't. Tell me what to do."

"Nn-nn. I should be stopping you, not…" He released an unsteady breath, and Laurie saw his shaft lengthen, its tracery of blue veins pulsate a little more clearly. "Not giving you instructions. Oh, God. I want you, though. Just…"

His hand brushed across Laurie's nape. Not a pressure—a silent assent, a signal that he should begin, uninstructed. Guided by whatever instincts he had, Laurie closed his eyes. He loved the sight of Sasha, but it was too much, overwhelming, to look at him and do this—to lean forward, parting his lips, the blind movement bringing him straight into contact. He heard his own shattered moan with embarrassment and opened up, letting the head slide in over his tongue, hooking one arm tight around Sasha's thigh.

God, what now? His mouth was full; he couldn't take him any deeper without choking. Then Sasha made a faint sound of need. Peripherally Laurie saw that he took one hand from its caress of Laurie's shoulder and used it to brace on the mattress. His touch on Laurie's neck became damply urgent, his thigh muscles stiffening.

Oh, Sasha was struggling not to thrust up into him, not to drag him down. Laurie understood and, with a sense of revelation, drew back and plunged down again, creating the movement Sasha was forbidding himself. Sasha gasped and writhed helplessly to meet him, making Laurie choke as his cock hit the back of his throat, but he snatched a breath and recovered. Breaking down Sasha's good manners was a powerful aphrodisiac to him; his own cock was hardening again. Tears stinging his eyes, he kept up the back-and-forth movement, bolder and stronger as he lost his fears of the act, until Sasha jolted as if electrocuted and gasped out, "Oh, no. Let me go now!"

Almost too late. And Laurie would have disobeyed him if he could, even knowing the risks. Wanted, more than anything, to feel in his throat the explosion that had happened on the skin of his stomach before—but Sasha's desperate grip closed on his shoulders, shoving him frantically back. "Laurie!"

Christ, he was starting to come—alone and untouched, taut shaft spilling. Laurie saw the lonely anguish on his face and on instinct put a hand to him, clasping him tight. "It's okay," he told him roughly, from a sore throat. He might not know much about much, but he had at least this much experience—all his own lonely nights; he knew this touch. Unfolding from the floor, he carefully tumbled them both back into the bed, never letting go his grip on Sasha's cock. And now Sasha could thrust as hard as he wanted. Lying over him, pumping him fast, Laurie cried out at the feel of him losing control, his wild last movements, rhythm breaking down to rigid stillness as he came.

"Laurie, come here."

Laurie barely heard it. His blood was roaring in his ears, and Sasha's voice was a ragged whisper. "What?"

"Come here, *ves'tacha*. Before you explode."

Soft laughter touching the voice. Emerging slowly from the universe where the only thing that mattered was getting Sasha off, Laurie became aware of his own condition, which he had to admit was a hopeless one, and painful too, now that the mists were parting. Sasha struggled up onto one elbow, pushing Laurie down. He put one arm beneath Laurie's head and cradled him, smiling, planting worn-out kisses on his brow, on the corners of his mouth.

"Ves'tacha," he repeated, and Laurie guessed this time he was not being called an outsider or foreigner.

Sasha reached down, seized his straining, disregarded cock, and stroked Laurie to orgasm in a dozen slow, firm movements, holding him tight when the wave hit, stifling Laurie's cries in his embrace.

* * *

Laurie sat huddled on the bed, the blanket—damp in places, but he couldn't bring himself to care, or find its scent other than lovely, viscerally reassuring, like a caress in the dark—wrapped around his shoulders. There wasn't much to distinguish now between him and Sasha, was there? Both clean and fed, stripped of the clothing that denoted their status and rank. What would be the difference to the world if Sasha stayed here and Laurie went out to some street corner and curled up as he was now, a young male body in a blanket, just like the thousands of others that starred the London streets? Maybe on balance the planet would benefit, if Sasha were installed as the son of this great house with all its privileges. He would surely use them better. His brightness, resourcefulness, ability to survive…

The pain in Laurie's chest, the edge of panic resting like a blade on his heart, stemmed from his inability to extract from Sasha a promise that they would meet again. Something had darkened between them since they had woken for the second time. God knew they had sailed close to the wind; it had been rising eight before the gathering December light outside the attic window had called them from their entwined, satiated sleep, the household coming to life around them. They had lain still, breathless, while Clara and Hannah chattered their way down the corridor outside; then Sasha had slithered out of bed like a startled cat, and none of Laurie's assurances that they would be okay, that nobody else would come up here, had slowed him down as he padded to the bathroom, then returned and began to put on his clothes.

The sight of that stirred Laurie from his thoughts. He'd had vague plans for purloining the filthy garments and taking them down to the laundry, but the night had got away from him. "Sasha, hang on."

Sasha glanced up, dark eyes clouded and apprehensive. Beginning to look hunted…

Shame touched Laurie. How many times had he asked him to stay, pressed him to agree to their next meeting? "At least take some of my things," he said. "We're about the same size."

Sasha paused, doing up such buttons as remained on his jeans. He stood for a moment, naked from the waist up, silhouetted in the morning light. Then he came and crouched before Laurie. He stretched his hands out and placed them in Laurie's lap, palms up, the gesture one of pleading. "Listen," he said very quietly. "I go back onto the streets in one of your cashmere sweaters, your Savile Row coats, by ten o'clock tonight I'm mugged and stripped naked. I come back here, spend nights here, every morning

I…go back to the underworld. I'd got used to it, Laurie. Begun to stop minding. And just one night with you here… Well, this morning I already mind a bit again. Do you understand?"

Laurie did. Instead of telling Sasha so, he broke away from him and scrambled out of the bed. "Not all my clothes are from sodding Savile Row," he said harshly. He pulled open first a wardrobe, then the drawers of the pine dresser that stood beside it. Homely items, these—lumber-room furniture, in a house otherwise fitted up with priceless antiques and bespoke modern masterpieces.

"*Why are you living like a refugee, here in your own home*?"

Impatiently he tugged from drawers and hangers some of his older things, jeans and sweaters he used for backstage work, a thick fleece jacket. They were worn but clean and good and could feasibly have been bought from a charity shop. "Here," he said, holding them out to Sasha. "If you put your parka on top, you should be okay. I'm never going to see you again, am I?"

Sasha dropped the dirty sweatshirt he had been about to pull on. He let it fall and walked up to Laurie, bare feet silent on bare boards. Laurie briefly wondered why he was only noticing now for the first time that he didn't even have a carpet in here except for the threadbare fireside rug where Sasha had held him and kissed him. Then he could only stare at Sasha in hopeless longing. How bloody lovely he would be if he ever lived long enough to lose his starvation thinness. He moved like a panther now. He'd surged in Laurie's arms like the sea.

"I don't know," Sasha said, reaching up for him. "Don't make me make any promises now, ves'tacha. I wish I could explain."

* * *

Laurie straightened up from his desk. All the spartan features of this room were of his own choosing, a reaction against Sir William's wealth, although until now he hadn't allowed himself to see it. He was a refugee, a far more hopeless one than Sasha. But his studies required a good computer, and this his father had installed for him, together with a top-end printer and fast broadband.

Sasha was waiting by the door. It was broad daylight now, the whole world awake. It gave Laurie bleak comfort to know his own clothes, dry and warm, were next to that beautiful skin. He knew—they both did, Sasha's anxious look confirming it—that they were out of time. Laurie handed him a printout. "There's an encampment near Birchwood Heath. There were some news articles about it. It's all the way out on the Metropolitan line to East Hill, and then you'll have to take a bus, so please, take this money, just to get you out there, okay? Please don't argue."

"Okay," Sasha whispered. "Thank you."

"And this envelope. Take it, Sash. It's just a note for you. Don't even read it until you're well away from here."

They slipped silently down the corridor. At the door that opened onto the concrete stairwell, Sasha turned. He planted a hand flat to Laurie's chest, reached up, and briefly kissed him. "Does the door open to the outside?"

"Yes. I…"

"Shh. Don't come down with me. Please, Laurie. I couldn't bear it."

Laurie stood for almost five minutes in the doorway after he was gone. A thin December sunrise was making its way into the stairwell through its cobwebbed skylight. When Laurie let his gaze rest on the dim space below, let himself listen past the distant daily noises of the waking city, he could recreate his last glimpse of Sasha—a concentration of shadows slipping into shadows, a fish into unknowable seas. He put out a hand—closing his eyes, reaching into the air, as if he could clasp some last trace of him. Then a door banged on the floor below: Sir William exiting the bathroom, probably, in his usual lovely morning mood—and he shivered back into the moment, turning away.

Chapter Five

Laurie's winter resumed. He felt now as if he were trapped behind a glass wall and supposed he always had been. Not until now had he wanted something beyond it badly enough to make it real. He sat every weekday from ten till four with Sanderson, learning nothing, acting out the part of a boy who had learned something well enough to convince the poor tutor that they were making headway. On nights when his mother and father were both at home, he sat down to the family dinner and acted out the part of a good son who still had something to say to his parents and could make entertaining small talk for his bored little sister. Sir William, Laurie noted with weary satisfaction, seldom met his eyes on these occasions and otherwise avoided him. Steered well clear of the child too, which was Laurie's only real concern now. Once Hannah arrived after dinner as she did every night, he picked up his books and, acting out the part of someone who gave a fuck, politely excused himself and retreated to his garret to study.

He even did so, usually, for a couple of hours. It often took Laurie a while to come back to himself if he'd been lost in a role. Not the fooling around he did for Clara, that schizophrenic clowning, but the serious parts he'd undertaken for performance. A natural method actor, his drama teacher had called him, bemused by a sixteen-year-old who could, without a costume change, stand in his T-shirt and jeans and suddenly convince him that he was in the presence of Macbeth. Laurie, the Good Student, often convinced himself just as thoroughly and would spread out his books and sit quietly at his desk watching strings of numbers and facts that meant nothing to him dance across the pages until he felt sick.

On the third night after Sasha's departure, he allowed himself to remember he had not incinerated all the dirty clothes that Sasha had left behind. Sitting up from an unequal tussle with the Corn Laws, Laurie smiled at the blank wall in front of him. There had been an awkward moment. He'd managed to get down to the basement unseen, the clothing bundled up with the bed linen, which could probably have used incinerating too, after the night it had had, but needed at least a discreet wash, and not by Mrs. Gibson. The boiler had been blazing away; no trouble to drop the soiled garments in—except one scarf, a soft blue scrap that had been wrapped around Sasha's throat, its ends tucked down to shield his chest. It was good, by contrast with the other things. Perhaps he could use it again, perhaps…

Perhaps he'll come back for it, had run through Laurie's mind, causing his fists to clench in the fabric, his eyes to fill with angry, painful tears. Sasha had opened the door to the stairwell, let himself out, closed it behind him, and been gone. Had made himself, in one instant, a nothing to Laurie, only empty air where the second before he had been vividly, vitally present. Laurie had tried to reconcile Sasha's absence with the lingering scent of him, with the traces of semen dried onto his belly, his pubic hair, his fingers. He had stood in the boiler room, struggling with this anomaly, the blue scarf clutched in one hand, for a second too long, while Gibson had appeared in the laundry next door, linen basket majestically balanced on her hip. She had been put out, at first, that her boy wished to wash his own sheets; she didn't mind, not at all, that he'd spilled coffee all over them. Then all of a sudden, she'd cottoned on—or thought she had—bestowed upon Laurie such a look of gentle comprehension that he had prayed to die on the spot, and left him to get on with it.

He had neither burned the scarf nor washed it. He'd taken it back upstairs with him, tucked it into the bottom drawer of his pine chest, and left it there. Swallowing dryly, Laurie stood up from his desk. He went to the chest, ran his hands over its fine old wood, polished smooth with use. Then he pulled open the drawer.

He lay down on the bed, all made up with clean linen now. He couldn't go through that again—reached under the mattress and scrabbled around until he found a box of tissues.

Shame was tearing at him. He didn't know why. Despite all the conditioning that might have made him think so, he had never found his own touch dirty or degrading; pleasure was pleasure, and he'd taken a deep, quiet joy in it, in the escapes and visions he could achieve.

Ah, no, not shame. Instead sorrow. Yes, sorrow and a crushing sense of hopelessness, that he was about to try to recreate what he had done with Sasha, whose scent was rich in the scarf. Inhaling it deeply, burying his face in the wool where it lay on the pillow, Laurie heard his own choked sob and fell fiercely silent. What had they done? The first time, when they'd hit the mattress in a tangle of limbs? Laurie had landed on top, yes, and Sasha had opened his thighs for him, then closed them and held him tight. Gasping, Laurie grabbed for a handful of the tissues, tore open his jeans, and shoved them into place. He had not meant this. Had meant to build the memory slowly, give himself a half hour's comfort in his arid, glassed-in world, even if it was sad and degrading beyond measure to try to do on his own what the two of them had made—that fire, that communion. He tried for an instant of control and failed, shooting violently into his own clasp. He broke into tears and dragged pillow and scarf down over his head. "Oh, God! Sasha, Sasha!"

* * *

On Thursday morning at ten fifteen, a light, cautious rap came on the study-room door. Clara looked up from her latest edition of *Star Girl*, and Sanderson hung fire in the middle of a trig equation. He looked at Laurie, who, even as his pupil, was also the son of Baronet Fitzroy and a natural master to a man like Sanderson, who found it reassuring to be mastered. Laurie, who could not speak—who was bland, calm, and cool on the outside, and racked on his interior by an impossible hope—gave him a nod of permission. Sanderson called out, "Come in."

My education's no good to me, but you could use it. I'm leaving a key to the back stairwell under the garage door. As you come in, there's a room to the left that nobody uses. I'll put a box in there with some clothes in it. My Savile Row stuff, I'm afraid. You'll have to look the part if you're going to share my tuition. You can change in there and come up. The study room's the last on the corridor. Laurie had stopped there for a moment, then added, *Just think about it. Whatever you decide, keep the key. I don't ever want you stuck outside on a cold night again.*

The note Laurie had sealed up in an envelope for Sasha had yielded a result.

Sasha looked good, and it wasn't just the clothes, though they suited him well. He entered the room with a quiet poise that fitted Laurie's background story for him perfectly—useful and impressive too, since Laurie hadn't had the chance to tell him what it was. He was clean, and although still thin, there was a difference. Had he found shelter? Closing the door, he nodded to Sanderson. Turned a brilliant smile upon his friend. "Laurie."

Clara dropped her baby-teen comic. "Prince Sasha!"

Oh, God. Not quite the approach Laurie had had in mind. Well, he would have to run with it now. Clara pattered over to Sasha, who took her outstretched hands and shook them gravely. Laurie stood up from the big library table where his work was spread out, and said to the tutor, "This is the friend I said might be joining us, Sandy. The Romanian ambassador's son."

"Oh!" Sanderson's watery eyes had gone wide. "Of course, Laurence. I didn't..." He lowered his voice and took a few steps toward Laurie. "I didn't know the young gentleman was...royalty. What's the correct form of address, sir?"

"Just Sasha." Laurie shot a glance over Sanderson's shoulder to meet Sasha's eyes. "He's very informal." Keeping his gaze steady on Sasha's, which was kindling with astonishment and laughter, he continued, with all the casual lordliness he could muster, "I'd be just as pleased, Sanderson, if you wouldn't mention this to anyone. Prince Sasha failed his midterms too, and his father isn't as generous as mine. The ambassador knows Sir William, so..." He drew himself up, allowed his tone to acquire the edge of disdain appropriate to so vulgar a subject as money. "I'll see that you're remunerated for the additional work."

"Oh, no, Laurence." Sanderson rubbed his hands. Laurie could envisage him back at home that night telling his collegiate housemates that he was confidentially tutoring a Romanian prince. "It'll be my pleasure, I'm sure."

Sasha came quietly to sit down. He took the chair next to Laurie's, a discreet distance away, still close enough to touch. "You found the encampment," Laurie said softly, passing Sasha a pen and unused notebook. Sanderson, in his nervous excitement at this new arrival, had swept his whiteboard clean and was now busily covering it with a set of fresh equations. "Are you okay?"

"Yes. Better than. I've slept in a bed for three nights." He gave Laurie a luminous glance across the textbook he was opening for them both to look at. "Well, four. Thank you."

"Don't mention it." Please, Laurie silently begged him. Don't mention any of that, or I'll crack and disgrace both of us right here, tutor and little sister notwithstanding. I can hardly breathe as it is. "It's this chapter. I hope you can make something of it, because I haven't got a clue."

"My education stopped when I was thirteen, so I doubt it. Also, you didn't happen to warn me that I'm a prince."

Laurie grinned. "Blame Clara. I thought you were just an ambassador's son. Don't worry; either way, you look the part."

"All right!" Sanderson had swung around to face them, pale face alight with the joy of abstractions. Laurie and Sasha sprang apart and into attitudes of polite attention. "This morning, gentlemen, we are going to solve the mystery of trig, I think. I must say I feel very optimistic. Laurence, would you like to begin?"

Wincing, Laurie began where he always did—at what he'd been told was the correct place, breaking the equation Sanderson was pointing at down into its component parts. He could usually get so far as that, but the trouble was, once he'd done so, he couldn't see where to go next. Why it mattered. Nevertheless, he gave his good-natured best shot. Sandy had his living to make, and he lived in terror of Sir William too.

Struggling with values, cosines, and tangents, Laurie was vaguely aware that Sasha had slid the textbook out from under his elbow and was running a thoughtful fingertip down the pages—not over the text and explanations but the diagrams. A quick, assessing triangular dance… Laurie flashed back to the feel of that fingertip brushing the hair back from his brow, and lost the thread entirely. "Sorry, Sandy," he groaned. "Clara's gonna get this before I do."

"Nonsense, Laurence. You'll be fine. Let's just start with the next one, or…" Sanderson paused, clearly concerned by the etiquette of asking a prince to do a sum for him. "Or perhaps your friend—er, Sasha—would you…?"

Sasha looked up. "Not that one," he said quietly. "I'd need to see it as a diagram, I think. But..." He scooped up a protractor from the desk, got to his feet, and went to one of the two tall windows that looked out over the Mayfair rooftops. It was a bleak December morning, but to Laurie, who had stood up and followed him as if entranced, the grim old slates seemed bathed in light. Sasha leaned both hands on the sill. "Okay. I can see the Hilton tower from here. Laurie, if you go and stand at the other window, which I reckon is about three yards away..." He waited till Laurie had obeyed, then smiled at him and said, "You and I are the baseline of a triangle, A to B. I'm just going to take a rough measure of the angle from my point to the tower, and..." He tossed the protractor to Laurie, who caught it adroitly. "You do the same from yours. Hilton tower is C. So we know the length of one side of the triangle, and now we've got two of its angles, and if you do the tangent equation..."

Laurie went back to the desk. He grabbed a pencil and notepad and quickly sketched out the line of the roof, the wall, the distant tower. Couldn't resist, even now, adding an ornamental chimney hood and pigeon strutting on the sill.

Sasha grinned as these additions vividly appeared. "All right, but put the numbers in too," he gently admonished.

Laurie did so. He checked it with a calculator and turned to Sanderson, bright with comprehension. "Yes," he said. "It fits."

Sanderson, frozen by the whiteboard, stared at them. Laurie could not work out if his expression was more impressed or chagrined. It must have come as a relief to him, surely, that his least apt pupil had finally understood the point of trigonometry—that his pupil's infant sister had just got the grasp of it too, to judge from her awestruck little face—but he must be discomfited too. As if aware of this, Sasha gave a small, deferential shrug and went to sit down again. "I still need to learn how to state it mathematically, Mr. Sanderson. If you don't mind."

Sanderson did not. He laid down his whiteboard marker and sat with his students at the big table. For the rest of that afternoon, he worked through the rest of the exercises in the chapter from the diagrams, as if Sasha's methods had come as a revelation to him too.

The class went more quickly than any Laurie had ever known before, fast as the hours he spent backstage at the Twilight. He was astonished to hear his watch beep four o'clock, and to see his tutor, looking more relaxed than ever before, gathering up his books. "Well, gentlemen!" Sanderson said. "I do feel we've made progress." He hesitated, looking at Sasha, then finished, pale cheeks flushing up at his own daring, "I trust you'll be joining us tomorrow, sir."

Laurie followed Sasha out. The study-room door clicked shut under his dampened fingers as he pulled it to. Clara and Sanderson were still in there, comparing notes on what she thought Sandy should wear for his dinner party that night. Sasha was at the far end of the corridor, a graceful, tensely poised shape in the dim light. As Laurie watched, he pulled open the door to the concrete stairwell and slipped through.

It was not the movement he had made four days ago in the same place. Not *please don't follow me*. His eyes had met Laurie's for a fraction of a second before he disappeared, dark lashes lowered, a soft brilliance glimmering through. Heart lurching, Laurie sped after him.

They rounded the last flight of steps into the utility room at full pelt, Laurie hard on Sasha's heels. Choking with laughter, Sasha grabbed him, whirled him around, and pushed him up against the wall, banging the door shut behind them with one foot. "Help me out of my princely disguise, then."

Laurie drew a ragged breath and took hold of the close-fitting black cashmere—his own, but which became Sasha so well. He pulled it up over Sasha's shoulders, ran both hands over his finely articulated collarbones, the shoulder blades that shifted like wings to seek his touch. "Oh, God. I thought you were never coming back."

"I know." Sasha abruptly sobered. "I'm sorry. I got scared. But I missed you so much, and…"

Laurie lurched forward, silencing him with a kiss. He felt, with disbelieving, vertiginous pleasure, Sasha's knee push up to part his thighs, and pressed himself, gasping, against the invasion. Running his palms down Sasha's chest, he brushed both nipples—accident only, but when Sasha twitched and cried out, Laurie repeated the caress, fascinated at how the tissue tightened and came up against his palms. "Is that good?"

"Yes. Everything you do…" Sasha shut up, and Laurie, who had dared duck down to suck one taut little mound into his mouth, held him while Sasha slammed a hand to the wall and muffled a shout against Laurie's shoulder. "But we can't do it here, you idiot."

"No?" Laurie came up for air for a second, then went to attend to the other nipple. His cock was hard and tight inside his jeans, aching where it pressed against Sasha's firm thigh. He could feel Sasha too, trapped and ready. A rush of need swept through him. "I think I've got to. God, come here!"

Wrapping both hands around Sasha's backside, he ground them together, Sasha now kissing him frantically, throwing out a hand to grab at the washing machine for balance. The imperfect feel of baffled contact, sealed off behind layers of fabric, was at once terrible and beautiful. They had to push hard, hard, and the touch was packed with so much promise of how it would be when briefs and boxers, jeans and Savile Row trousers finally got themselves unzipped and out of the way.

"Laurie, stop."

It was urgent. Laurie went still at the pitch of one thrust, though it was like jamming the brakes on at eighty miles an hour. His heart almost clawed its way out of his chest with the effort, but he would rather die, he knew, than impose on Sasha one touch he didn't desire. "What? What is it? What's wrong?"

"I can hear someone."

"Fuck." Laurie let him go and spun to face the door, listening. For a moment all he could hear was his own blood rushing, and then…yes, footsteps scraping on the concrete stairs. At the very best-case scenario, Clara, though she found the old staircase spooky and usually avoided it. Even then, some adjustments were required. Handing Sasha his sweater back, Laurie ran both hands through his hair and willed his erection to subside.

No. Oh, God. A male tread, slow and heavy. Glancing around, he saw Sasha bone white—more terrified even than Laurie himself, and in a worse way, as if whatever was beyond the door might not be human. *It's all right*, Laurie mouthed to him, seizing his wrist and drawing him into the shelter of the old larder cupboard, no place to hide but perhaps enough cover to shield them from a cursory glance into the room. They clung together, barely breathing. Then Laurie heard the back door open and Charlie call out cheerfully up the stairs, "Back in half an hour, Mabel. Just gonna pick the old goat up from his club."

The door slammed. A moment later, the garage door creaked, and the Daimler's distinct purr began. Laurie subsided against the wall, limp with relief. "It was Charlie."

Sasha stared at him, eyes so dilated with shock Laurie could not distinguish sable iris from fathomless jet-black pupil. "Who's Charlie?"

"My driver."

"Your… Okay. Who's Mabel?"

"The housekeeper."

"You really are like something out of a book, you know. And...the old goat?"

"My father, I suppose. I had no idea they called him that."

A snort of laughter escaped Sasha. Laurie, who'd been seriously frightened, made a desperate grab for sobriety, but the sound infected him in a flash, and they fell to their knees together, tangling in the cramped space. "Oh, God!" he choked. "We can't do this. We can't do this, Sash. We're gonna get caught. We can get away with the classes maybe, but not the fooling around afterward."

He trailed off, wondering what sort of a spectacle he presented, flushed and sprawled in his corner, erection dying an uncomfortable death in his jeans. But however he looked, Sasha didn't seem to find it off-putting. Instead he smiled at him as if he were the loveliest sight in the world and said, on a note of rough longing, "I think I'd rather have the fooling around."

"Oh, me too," Laurie whispered, embarrassed by the longing in his voice. Sasha would always look bloody elegant, wouldn't he? Dying on the pavement in Gyorgy's arms, he had formed a sort of pietà in Laurie's memory, and even now, half in and half out of the borrowed sweater, irresistible. "But that's not gonna get you a job, is it?"

"Depends what kind you... Wait, though," Sasha said, smiling broadly. "I have one. I meant to tell you. A real one, washing cars at a while-you-wait. I had an address, because of you, so they could hire me."

"A...car wash?" Laurie stared at him. He knew the kind of places. They mushroomed up overnight and disappeared just as fast, usually when immigration shut them down. "Sasha, no. They'll exploit you. What are you doing—ten-hour shifts for fifteen pounds a day?"

"Twenty, actually. It's not so bad—I can pay some rent on a bed in a van and spend the rest on food and coming here. What more do I need?" He reached out to cup

Laurie's face in his hands and kissed him fervently. "I'm doing fine. I'm doing better than you, my beautiful captive prince."

Closing his eyes, Laurie submitted to the warm mouth exploring his own—leaving it to brush over his eyelids, his brow, as if trying to erase the marks of his imprisonment—until the touch became unbearable, threatened to crack him to tears or roll them both down onto the utility room floor and to hell with the consequences. Laurie pushed him reluctantly back. "God, Sasha. Stop. I'm not gonna risk you."

"All right. But promise me, Laurie, you'll think about getting out of here somehow. Run away with the gypsies, if it comes to that. Anything's better than a cage." He took Laurie's hands. "I saw how you looked when you thought it was your father coming down those stairs." Letting Laurie go, he turned away.

Laurie watched him getting dressed, slipping out of the beautiful, tailored things and into his street clothes. "Will you come again tomorrow? For the class?"

Zipping up the parka, Sasha nodded. "Yes. For the class. Thank you, Laurie."

"Thank *you*. I've spent nearly five years failing trig. Be careful at your car wash, will you? They raid those places. And…" He dug in his jeans pocket, pulled out his wallet. Sasha's face immediately shadowed, but he forged on, "It must be costing you nearly twenty bloody quid to get here and back. At least buy yourself a fare card for the Tube."

* * *

The next day Sasha was there, and the next, and so they began a strange kind of routine. Sasha would make his dash across the city between his split shifts at the car wash, leave his clothes—often damp and soap-stained, but at least he had more than one set of them now—in the utility room, and turn up on the top floor, insouciant and smiling, every inch the foreign prince. Laurie varied the things he left for him, and if Sanderson ever noticed they shared clothes, he never saw fit to mention it. He seemed only too glad to have someone in the class who kept his pupil happy and alert, especially when Clara's social engagements kept her away. Sanderson also seemed genuinely intrigued by his new charge's ability to transform abstracts into concrete situations that Laurie, who had been floundering, would then grasp easily. Within a week, they were somewhere near the point in the syllabus they should have been two weeks ago, and catching up rapidly. Laurie could read the relief in Sanderson's face and the set of his shoulders. If Sasha had gone about his magic arrogantly, it would have humiliated Sandy, but the boy had a gift of presenting his ideas so quietly and obliquely that he often left Sanderson to think he'd come up with them himself. Laurie concluded that diplomacy must run in the blood.

For Laurie, these days were sharp-edged joy. He opened his eyes each morning knowing Sasha would come—the dangers of his world permitting. That he would be able to sit with Sasha, elbow to elbow, watching his face become intent and pleased as one after another of Sanderson's mysteries opened out before him—and that this would be all the contact they would have. That he would walk Sasha down the corridor after the class but leave him, with rigid discipline, to run down the steps on his own. He could move like a ghost, Laurie knew. For all his own grace, Laurie had never had to learn the skills of prey. If he went with Sasha, he would at least double their noise.

And make their partings even harder.

Sometimes Sasha stole a kiss—or bestowed one—on the threshold of their separate worlds and gave him a look that told Laurie plainly that he would gladly trade their classroom afternoons for one refugee night. Laurie would ease him back, eyes closing in hunger and pain. Although he had no very clear idea of how this tuition would help Sasha out of his car wash and into some better life, he was grimly determined that Sasha should have the chance. The tension rose between them. Laurie wondered sometimes that Sandy did not feel it, the crackle in the air, although the two of them sat like demure English gentlemen throughout, only the occasional brush of hand to hand flashing off silent sparks.

The days flowed on, one to the next, shortening as the year got old, until one freezing, brilliant afternoon, Sanderson announced he had to leave early and would be setting a batch of exercises to be completed in his absence. Laurie glanced up, caught Sasha's eye, and quickly looked down at the page once more. Sasha was looking well these days. He rippled with energy, and at times his gaze would shine with a pure gypsy glimmer—mischief and promise, strange dark fires. Laurie's self-control was disintegrating. The obvious outlet was no longer enough, and he seldom bothered touching himself, alone in his room after those silent partings; he could remember too clearly the real thing.

Nevertheless when Sanderson had gone, Laurie turned his attention to the task. They both did—Sasha in companionable silence at his side, occasionally stopping his own work to explain to Laurie what *x* would do to *y/z* if these various quantities were weights, measures, cranes, cars, spaceships, instead of inscrutable little glyphs on a textbook page. Once he was done, he slipped away from Laurie as if aware of his power to distract him, and went to sit quietly on the window ledge, looking out into the sun.

Laurie slogged on for a while. Sasha made things easier, but Laurie'd had a long morning before he arrived, and his head was pounding dully. Eventually bogging down, he sighed and rubbed his hands across his face. When he looked up, he saw Sasha had turned and was watching him, poised catlike on the ledge, his arms wrapped around one knee. Laurie pushed aside his book and faced him, smiling, waiting with interest to hear his conclusions.

"Tired," Sasha said. "Bored, frustrated. And pale, even for a gajo. Would you be missed if you vanished for the afternoon?"

Laurie gave it thought—or tried to. His heart had suddenly bumped up into the base of his throat. He said carefully, after a while, "By Clara, maybe. Otherwise, I don't think I'd be *missed* as such if I vanished into thin fucking air and never came back."

Sasha nodded, weighing this statement for all its bitter worth. "All right," he said. "Come with me."

Chapter Six

He had bought a fare card, and Laurie had one too, for the rare occasions when he had to use public transport. The tickets took them all the way out on the northwest wing of the Tube network, from the central zone onto the overground stretch past Finchley Road. Seated beside Sasha on the rattling, bumping train, Laurie smiled as the tunnel abruptly disappeared, shooting them out into the light. He'd never been this far out on the Metropolitan before, and the sight of unknown streets, long terraces, and allotments flashing past—bare trackside trees, factories, the occasional glimpse of water—set inside him a bright sense of freedom. His headache evaporated, leaving him spaced-out, exhilarated, the press of Sasha's shoulder to his own completing the high. Sasha, too, after making his usual scan of the carriage and platforms, was looking out the window, but Laurie could feel at least as much of his attention smilingly fixed on himself, probably in amusement at his town-boy reactions to new scenes.

Laurie felt an irresistible urge to touch him, to find his hand in the hidden space between their bodies. When he did, Sasha turned to him, silently questioning, eyes full of assent. He drew their joined hands out so both were lying on his lap, and Laurie, after flinching in shock, gave thought to the public displays of intimacy he'd seen on buses, tubes, and London's streets over the years. Not just boys with girls, either. Late at night, the clubs emptying, young men too embraced each other. He'd averted his eyes, telling himself it wasn't right, in the open like that—wondering at the same time if the grapes were only sour because *he* didn't have anyone to kiss half to death on a street corner. He looked at his hand, bony and pale in Sasha's. His father, as far as he knew, did not own the Tube network. The carriage was almost empty at this hour. Only a couple of old ladies sat with their backs to them down at the other end. Extracting his hand, Laurie took hold of the seat bar behind them. He hauled himself up onto one knee against the jolting of the carriage, leaned over Sasha, and kissed him, feeling his head spin at the heat of him, the longed-for returning press of his mouth. Sasha's hands came up in welcome, steadying him, clasping in his jacket. Laurie could also feel laughter shaking him and, after a moment, drew back, smiling too. "What?"

"You. Very bold."

"Yes, I…suppose so. Do you mind?"

For answer, Sasha pulled him back down by his lapels.

* * *

The bus from East Hill to Birchwood took half an hour. Laurie watched—Sasha kindly having conceded him the window seat, promising he'd seen the route often enough—while the last far-flung suburbs of his city began to thin out into fields and trees. The driver put them down at an unmarked stop halfway along a stretch of tree-lined road, and Sasha caught Laurie's hand, pointing to a stile over a fence into a sunlit lane. "It's this way. Not far."

Laurie didn't care. He would have walked with Sasha forever like this. They were in the wings of London still—a road purred in the distance, and Heathrow-bound planes glimmered in the sky—but other than that, the world felt empty and serene. The lane, half grassing over in some places, reverting to track, stretched out before and behind them. Dark hollies and gleaming birches where a few gold-coin leaves still clung gradually transformed into beech cover, tall graceful shapes receding into churchlike distance, bronze carpet beginning to crunch underfoot. Laurie said softly, because it felt like a place between worlds, "Will they mind me coming here? Your friends?"

"Not if I vouch for you. That's the arrangement. We all take complete responsibility for anyone we bring in from outside. So"—Sasha reached out and drew Laurie to him, encircling arm a comfort as well as excitement to him now—"so you'll have to try not to disgrace me, okay?"

* * *

The Birchwood Heath camp was both everything and nothing Laurie might have expected such a place to be. The cluster of caravans and trucks was buried deep in the trees, invisible until you came within a few yards of it, the first signs of its presence a drifting scent of wood smoke in the air. Dark-eyed faces appeared at windows as they approached, and a burly, brindled dog shot to the end of its chain, barking frantically. Sasha went forward to it fearlessly and knelt down, intercepting its rush. "Quiet, Zaga. This is a friend. Come here a second, Laurie."

Apprehensively Laurie obeyed him. He wasn't sure now what he would not do at Sasha's command, even though the bulldog's rolling eyes and continued growls were far from inviting. "Here. That's it. Let her sniff you. So she'll know you next time and not make such a fuss."

"*Hoi*, Sasha, *mora*! Who the hell's that?"

Laurie looked up. A chill touched him. He didn't think the introductions were going to be so simple from now on. The clearing around which the caravans were grouped was suddenly full of silent men and women, watching, fronted by a huge, shaven-headed blond who would have looked more at home at a right-wing British National Party rally than here. "Sash," Laurie whispered. "I don't want to make trouble. Is this a good idea?"

"It will be." Sasha got to his feet, leaving Laurie to deal with the dog, who to her credit now seemed more interested in slobbering on him than pursuing her attack.

"What's the matter, Gunari? Didn't I agree to your contract? Aren't I allowed to have friends?"

The crew-cut Gunari surveyed Laurie, who instinctively stood up too. He wasn't afraid, and he didn't like to see Sasha's impulse to protect him.

"Friends like this?" Gunari growled. "I'm not sure. Where'd you pick him up—the back lane outside Harrods?"

"Fuck you, Gunari," Sasha returned good-naturedly enough. A ripple of laughter had run through the crowd, making Laurie fervently wish he'd taken time to put on an older coat before letting Sasha whisk him off here. "He's the one I told Mama Luna about, the one who helped me, so back down, okay? Where is she?"

"Where she always is," a hoarse female voice responded. It was little more than a rasp but carried clearly through the cold air, and the group in front of Sasha parted slightly, revealing an old woman sitting by the fire. If the modern silver vans and TV aerials had jolted Laurie's expectations, the sight of her conformed exactly to his gajo vision of the Romani world, the stories he had read in childhood of painted horse-drawn carts and black-eyed fortune-tellers crouched in the firelight. He could not judge her age; her bright, analytical stare contradicted her tiny, hunched-up frame. She was wrapped from head to foot in scarves and shawls whose brilliant shades seemed to change as Laurie looked at her.

She made a gesture at Gunari so tiny that Laurie barely saw it, but the big man fell back as if she'd poked him in the chest. "More courtesy to visitors, my boy, when they come peacefully. Sasha, bring your friend over here. The rest of you..." Another movement of her skinny hand, and the small crowd scattered like chickens. "Yes. Mind your business."

Sasha led Laurie to the fireside. "Gunari is Mama Luna's son, Laurie," he said, pitched just loud enough so that Gunari, who was still lingering, would hear. "It's useful he looks like a big thick neo-Nazi. Puts people off the scent."

Gunari glowered, but the old woman didn't seem to mind her unlikely offspring being called names. She rocked herself on her little stool by the fire, chuckling quietly. "Ah, this Sasha. Insolent. But works hard, pays his way. Don't you? You better not make pain for Sasha, *balame*."

"I won't." The words startled Laurie, falling from him half-involuntarily. He felt as if a priest had demanded the assurance from him at some unimaginable altar. He didn't mind; it was what was in his heart. "I promise."

The wizened old face became surprised and then approving, though Laurie could see an ironic glitter there too.

"What's a balame?"

"Just gajo in Mama's dialect, I'm afraid," Sasha said. "She's Greek Romani. Sorry, Laurie. There's so few of us, almost everyone's a stranger. Mama Luna, will you let this balame visit? I'll answer for his good conduct."

She nodded. "Yes, you will. Give me your hand, boy."

Once more Laurie responded unquestioningly, reaching down to accept her grasp. She was extraordinarily warm. Her fingers tangled with his. The feel of it was pleasant and oddly soothing—the sounds of the encampment around him seemed to fade out, and the anxieties he carted helplessly with him—about Sasha, Clara, his father—all seemed suddenly to lift themselves out from his chest. He took a deep breath, filling the new space inside himself.

"Ah, yes," she said at length and turned to Sasha with a peaceful smile. "This one, Sasha. *Mulo. Dadro shee mulo.*"

Sasha went white. Laurie turned to him curiously. The old woman's grip on him was firm, but he could have pulled away if he had wanted. He felt too serene, as if nothing could hurt him or anyone he loved anymore. And it was all right here, in this place, to follow up an impulse. He need not hide here.

He stretched out his free hand to take Sasha's gently in his own. "What is it?" he asked him, then looked back down at Mama Luna. "I promise," he repeated. "I won't hurt him. I love him."

Sasha's grip convulsed around his. A shocked, disbelieving pleasure blended with the fear in his eyes. "Oh, God. Laurie…"

"What did she say, Sash?"

The old woman was shaking her head, rocking herself slightly. She released Laurie's hand and intoned the strange, resonant words once more, looking straight up at Sasha. "Yes, *chiavala*. That one. Don't be afraid." Then she straightened up and blinked, as if shaking off cobwebs. "What are you both standing here for? Yes, your balame may visit. Gunari, see that no one gives them any trouble."

They made their way through the encampment, still hand in hand. Laurie wondered if Sasha had simply forgotten. He seemed lost in thought, and maybe the warm grip in Laurie's was only subconscious, the same lead Laurie automatically gave to Clara on dangerous ground. He didn't mind. He would take what he could get. How long had it been since he had brought Sasha in off the street—since their one night? More than two weeks, throughout which Sasha had been to him forbidden fruit, a beautiful presence he could see but barely touch, until a kiss on a clattering Tube that had gone on until their heads were spinning, and they had broken apart before it turned into something not publicly acceptable, even in twenty-first century London.

Laurie burned for him. Any touch was intoxicating. He tightened his clasp. Glancing around, he saw the men and women of the camp getting on with their business as the old woman had bidden them. Such a range of faces, skin tones—many dark like Sasha, but others who looked as ordinary as he did himself. Setting romantic preconceptions aside, Laurie supposed there was as rich a mix of bad and good here as in any other population, but he did not feel ashamed of holding Sasha's hand, as if, whatever their prejudices, a people so hunted and disregarded might not bother with that one.

Children and chickens dashed about between the vans, the kids warmly wrapped up in bright, modern fleece tops. Laurie smiled. Had he expected them to be in rags? Only Mama Luna looked the part. Thinking of her, Laurie abruptly remembered her words and his own, as if they had made their exchange in a dream from which the chilly air and diamond-pale sun were only now rousing him.

"Oh, God, Sash," he said as they approached the last caravan in the group, a battered two-berth with its tow bar propped on a crate. "Did I…did I freak you out back there, saying what I did?"

Sasha halted. He looked at Laurie wonderingly. "Did *you* freak me out…?"

"Oh. Right. *She* did."

"Mama Luna makes people speak the truth. If that's your truth, what you said to her, then…" He trailed off, and Laurie saw his eyes brighten with tears. "Then I don't know what to say, I'm so bloody happy. All right?" He gave Laurie's hand a brief shake, so tight it hurt, then shook his head as if these things were obvious and he needed to leave them behind to attend to more pressing business. "Laurie. I want you to think, clearly and seriously, about getting out of that house. Finding somewhere of your own. Do you understand?"

"Yes," Laurie said, startled. It was true enough. Since meeting Sasha, he had thought every day of making his escape. But he accepted, looking into the grave, lovely face raised to his, that the thoughts had been fantasies—air castles into which he could pull up Sasha and retract the ladder. "At least… It's hard for me, Sash. You know it is."

"Well, try. I know how hard it is, but believe me, you have to try."

"For God's sake, what did she say to you?"

Sasha let go of his hand. He opened the caravan door and leaned inside. "Come in. My fellow lodger's out. I'll make us some tea."

"Sasha, *what*?"

Sasha turned back to him. He shoved his hands into the pockets of his water-stained parka. He said reluctantly, "It was like she was expecting you. She said, 'This is the one. The one whose father is death.' Now I don't care how you do it, ves'tacha—you can come and live here if you like. But get out. Get away from him. Find a way."

* * *

They sat opposite each other at the little melamine table. The caravan had a living room of sorts, defined by the table and the two bench seats on either side of it. Other than that, there was a tiny galley kitchen and one bedroom, whose open door displayed a neatly made but solitary bed. Laurie stirred his tea and finished off the tinned chicken soup Sasha had provided for their lunch. They had been silent for a while, although Laurie had inadvertently made Sasha laugh till he choked with his assumption that the soup would have to be heated on some outdoor cook fire rather than in the perfectly efficient microwave hidden behind a panel door.

The space beneath the table was so tight that they could not have avoided contact if they'd tried—and neither was trying. More to break the tension than anything else, Laurie shot a sly glance toward the bedroom and said, "Tell me about this *lodger*, then."

Sasha snorted at the faint suggestive emphasis. Laurie was relieved. Apart from Sasha's burst of amusement at the balame's stupidity, he'd been quiet, as if angry with himself for translating the old woman's words. "He's a fifty-five-year-old bank clerk from Southwell. His wife left him, he had a breakdown, and he fell through the net. He doesn't say much, and he doesn't snore. I'm not sure he even knows I'm here."

Fell through the net. Laurie cradled his mug between his hands, looking thoughtfully at his companion. How bloody easy it would be to do. You lose your job, your mortgage payments, your house. You're too middle-class, too old, to trigger social services alarms—no one helps you, and you don't know where to go to get help for yourself. You fall.

Or you're young, rich, and stupid, and the net tightens around you till you drown.

"Poor sod," he said quietly. "Sash, do you believe her? The old lady?"

Sasha sighed. "She's a good woman. She did everything for me when I got here. But…don't let her scare you. She's old. Maybe a little crazy."

"Maybe. Doesn't change the facts. The old goat probably *is* death. And it was you who looked scared, love." He watched while Sasha absorbed the last word. Laurie ran one sock-clad toe up along the arch of Sasha's foot beneath the table. "Hey. Did I hear you offer me a home here a few minutes ago?"

"Well, why not? At least I've got one to offer. That bench you're sitting on folds out, or you could bunk down with Cyril." He waited until Laurie had stopped laughing and was searching his face to measure his seriousness. "*Please* tell me you'll try to get out."

"Look, he's not some kind of murderer, you know." Laurie felt his throat dry out. He could scarcely bear the intensity of Sasha's regard at the best of times, and now, when the midnight eyes were full of fear and longing—a boy who had nothing, trying to offer the millionaire's son a refuge and a future… "Yes. I promise. Oh, Sash." He shivered. “I don’t want to think about this anymore. I just want you. Is Cyril due back anytime soon?”

Sasha grinned. Apparently he’d found the right distraction. “I don’t know. But I tell you what. To avoid giving him a stroke, shall we…” He stood up and put out a hand to Laurie across the table. “Let’s go for a walk.”

On their way out, Sasha ducked into the bedroom and took out from a bedside drawer one packet Laurie knew well and another that he didn’t, though he thought he’d seen the logo in the coyly marked family planning section when he went to buy toothpaste and aspirin. Emerging, putting the things into his pocket, Sasha gave him a shy, warm glance. “Come on, then.”

It turned into a run, a wild dash through lowering light. The back of the encampment gave out onto open heath, miles and miles of it, bordered only in the very far distance by the glimmering streetlamps of Amersham. From here they looked like jewels, just beginning to shine out as the December day faded. Laurie sucked in great breaths of the frosty air and chased after Sasha, who had broken his sedate pace by his side as soon as they were clear of the settlement. God, he could run! Laurie—who sometimes forgot he was only nineteen years old himself, and lightly-made and strong from all his backstage work—watched him with a kind of envy for a moment. Sasha was nothing but a shadow, flying out ahead of him, caught in the wind.

“Laurie!” he yelled, spinning back to face him, hardly breaking stride. “Come on!”

They ran and ran. Laurie stopped thinking about their destination or anything other than the air, the great open space all around them—bigger here somehow than in the wildest countryside, a sense of its vastness conveyed by its limitations, the far-flung city tendrils that held it. Freedom defined by emblems of captivity, the whispering highways and suburbs they were leaving behind. Laurie ran, always in Sasha’s wake but gaining on him, almost ashamed of the fragmented laughter that kept rising up in his throat. Clara did that—helplessly laughed while she ran, and it was okay if you were eight years old…

"Laurie, ves'tacha! This way!"

Brambles caught and tore at them both unnoticed as they pelted into the outskirts of low woodland. A tangle of oak and beech, remnant of the great Buckinghamshire forest that once had clothed the heath. It was colder out here, the leaf litter beginning to crisp up with frost. Their breathless arrival sent wood pigeons clattering up from their roosts. Watching their wild ascent, Laurie missed his footing, slipped, and crashed down with a yell into the undergrowth. Reflexively he turned the fall into a roll, and by the time Sasha had stopped and come dashing back, face a pale blank of concern, he was ready for him—grabbed him, laughing, and dumped him into the ice-patterned ferns at his side.

Sasha surged up straightaway. He propped himself on one elbow and stared down into Laurie's face, laughing and struggling for breath. "Oh, clever," he panted. "All right. I'm caught. What do you want to do with your prey?"

Laurie swallowed. His chest was still heaving, the air like glittering light in his lungs. He knew, of course. He had played it out a dozen times in his head, but in those yearning fantasies had glossed straight over certain details because… "To fuck you," he whispered, then shuddered at himself. "Christ. That sounds awful."

"Does it?" Sasha kissed him gently on the mouth, as if to redeem the word. "Not to me. Not from you."

"And I've never done it before."

"Well, I've had it done to me twice. Once I was stoned, and the second time was business. So you don't have much competition, and even if you did, I want you so much—" he stopped as Laurie struggled up to kiss him, then to roll him onto his back, covering Sasha with his warm weight—"so much I could come from just thinking about you. I want you to do it. It's okay. I'll show you how."

Laurie felt Sasha's arms close around his neck. Laurie seized him in his turn, and they briefly fought, a gentle, impassioned struggle. Cold scents of crushed grass rose up, and a deeper tang of earth and their own warming bodies. When Sasha twisted in his embrace and rolled to lie on his side, Laurie sat up and stripped off his long winter coat. "Here."

"What? Don't be stupid; it'll get filthy."

"It'll wash." Laurie spread the coat and guided Sasha to stretch out on it. "Don't you understand?" he asked unsteadily from an aching throat. "I'd pull the bloody sky down for you if I could."

"The old star-eaten blanket?"

"Yes. Yes, love."

"All right. Take mine off too. I want to feel you when you..."

"Oh, don't. You'll be cold."

"You'll keep me warm. In fact..." Before Laurie could stop him, Sasha had struggled out of the parka and his sweater too. Underneath it was one of Laurie's own T-shirts, the remains of his ambassadorial disguise, left behind in their hurry to escape the house. Laurie watched, entranced, as he stripped this too over his head and sat there, skinny and lovely, warm brown skin catching sunset light through the trees.

Gooseflesh started to rise. "God, come here." Laurie gasped and pushed him down onto the coat. For a moment all he could think about was fending off the cold from the exposed flesh, but Sasha writhed under him, taut backside pushing up. Their hands met under his belly, and they fumbled for the buttons of his jeans. Sasha moaned in assent as Laurie got hold of the waistband and hauled them down. "Sash, are you...are you sure?"

"Gonna kill you and bury your body out here in these woods if you don't. Right. Pull my coat back a second. In the pocket: condoms and some stuff to make it easier."

Reaching for the parka, Laurie pulled out the packet and the tube. Yes, this was the part he had glossed over in his dreams. He was ashamed that he had left it to Sasha.

"Will it hurt you?"

"Not if you just get me ready a bit first. Listen, ves'tacha. I had my tests. A doctor comes out to the camp. I'm clean—God knows how—but the rubbers are there if you want them."

"I feel so bloody ignorant."

"Don't. You're not. It's just a first time." He put a hand back blindly and seized Laurie's for a moment. "Here. The tube. Open it up and put some on you, then some on your fingers, and…" But here even streetwise Sasha ran out of words and instructions. He lay flat and buried his face in the crook of one arm. "Please, Laurie. Just do it."

And, after all, it *was* easy. Laurie lay for a while, listening to the calls of roosting blackbirds—the cry of a first twilight owl, haunting and wild across the heath. Wind in the trees, although down here among their roots, the air was still. He could hear Sasha's ragged breathing and his own. The rest of the world had stopped for him. It ended where the woodland melted into dusk, a few yards away all around them. Everything he needed was here. He uncapped the lubricant tube, clumsily covering the fingers of his right hand in the sticky gel. Sasha twitched as he slid the touch into the cleft of his backside, and Laurie reached up his free hand. "Sasha."

"Why am I frightened now? Been screwed over a car boot by a six-foot skinhead; why—"

"Ssh." Laurie pushed an arm over Sasha's shoulder, down across his chest. Sasha inhaled softly as if surprised at the embrace, then seized it and hung on. He opened his legs, drew one knee up a little, and in the space his movement opened up, Laurie suddenly found the tense little circle of his entrance. It felt too small to admit anything. Holding his breath, he rubbed the tip of his middle finger across it, circled it, pressing gently in, until Sasha shuddered in his arms and the tiny muscle ring gaped. Fighting disbelief, Laurie kept up the pressure, closing his eyes in Sasha's hair as he slipped his finger inside. All the way. The boundary broached, Sasha did not resist him, and he groaned in what sounded like relief when the penetration increased. Lost in wonder at the feel of it, the strangeness—that tight, guarding circle, then beyond it, the heat, the silky space rippled through with muscle contractions—Laurie pushed at him, and then when Sasha bucked against his hand and made a frantic sound of encouragement, did it harder, bringing his index finger into the hole. A firm movement and that went in, his anus fluttering wide to admit the inward thrust—then closing, clenching hard, tearing a cry out of both of them. Terrified that he had hurt him, Laurie tried to withdraw.

But the convulsion ceased, and Sasha was suddenly warm, melted satin beneath him, around his hand. He let go his bruising clasp on Laurie's arm. "That's it," he whispered. "I'm ready, ves'tacha. I can take you. Fuck me now."

Laurie shuddered, but his cock had come up so hard inside his jeans that he could hardly breathe, and there was no denying that or Sasha's slow, sensuous shift onto his hands and knees. Laurie knelt behind him, easing his fingers out of Sasha's backside. Awkwardly, gel-slicked grip slipping, he undid buttons and zip. Did not dare touch himself. He was close, hot electrical flashes running down his spine, so ready he knew his own grasp would melt him to orgasm. His shaft sprung straight and hard for the target, and he wondered with his last coherent thought what the fuck was meant to be *unnatural* about this. Glancing down, he saw in the silvery, uncertain light how the head came to engagement, how Sasha eased back against it, a movement of welcome, as if Laurie had been lost and was at last coming home. He thrust, burying himself deep in Sasha's flesh. Now the rippling contractions that had squeezed his fingers ran up and down his cock, the muscle ring clenching and releasing with his movements, the pressure at once almost painful and unbearably sweet.

Sasha, braced on his arms, swung his head around to look at him, whispered, "Laurie, make me come now," and seized the hand that Laurie had clenched on his hip bone to steady him. "Hold me. Make it happen now." He dragged the hand down, and Laurie got the idea, reached under his belly and seized his cock. A few more thrusts—half a dozen jerks of the rigid shaft—and he was there; they both were. Laurie threw his head back. Through a red haze, he saw stars blazing out in the treetops, caught in their stripped twigs. Sasha blazed out like a star in his grasp—climaxed in openmouthed silence, bursting in his hand. Laurie sobbed rawly, thrusting and spending inside him, until Sasha went limp underneath him, dropping them both down flat and gasping onto the rumpled coat.

When he could see again, Sasha was leaning over him, tenderly picking leaves out of his hair. Laurie lay flat on his back. His breath would not settle. Every time he found a pace for it, he would remember some detail of what they had just done and break into laughter or fractured gasps.

"Are you all right, ves'tacha?"

Laurie nodded. He wanted to lie here forever, seeing nothing but Sasha's glowing eyes and the treetops in the distance, filled now with stars. Something occurred to him, something he had been meaning to ask. "What does that mean?"

"Ves'tacha?" A flush stole into Sasha's face, just visible to Laurie in the near dark. "It means…it means 'beloved.' So you need not have been worried about freaking me out by what you told Mama Luna a while ago."

“Because you’ve been calling me that—almost since we met.”

“Yes.” Sasha swallowed audibly. “It didn’t take me long to know.”

Laurie reached up for him. He pulled Sasha down to lie beside him, then beneath him, covering his face and hair with kisses, reaching for the coat to shield him as best he could from the cold. “Can we stay here forever?” he whispered. “I know what you meant now, when you said it made it worse for you—to have known something different and to have to go back.”

“Yes. Because our worlds were bad. My world is better now, and I’ll help you change yours too, beloved. I swear.”

Time passed. Belatedly Laurie noticed that, in spite of his best efforts, Sasha was growing chilly in his arms, and he sat up, stripping off his own sweater. “Here. Put that straight on, while it’s still warm from me. And keep it, all right? You won’t get beaten up for it here.”

Sasha nodded, shuddering in pleasure at the touch of the flesh-warmed cashmere. “No. It’s a good place. Safe. Can you come back with me for a while? We’ll get warmed up, and Friday’s a festival night. Mama Luna will have some good food on the go for everyone.” He helped Laurie up, and they both stood unsteadily, helping one another rearrange clothing and button up coats. “Come on.” He put an arm around Laurie’s waist. “Look. All the way over there, across the heath. I can see the fires.”

Chapter Seven

Laurie spent that weekend sleepwalking, locked in an open-eyed dream. The walls of the Mayfair house rose around him just as they always had, but they felt transparent to him—or as if he was, as if he had slipped between dimensions and could, if he wished, just walk through them. He came down to family breakfasts on Saturday and Sunday, went through as much of his weekend routine as would keep him under the radar—corrections from the week's tutorials, the cinema with Clara—and other than that, retreated to his aerie to turn over memories and be alone with his own altered state.

He did not just have a lover. When Laurie had thought about it at all, he had assumed there would be some kind of routine—a girlfriend, and then after maybe a couple of years, he would feel so unimaginably different that he would want to marry. This was what he had observed from the young men of his acquaintance. He had not envisaged finding someone he was fairly sure he loved before he'd laid a hand on him and now, after a couple of weeks, could not bear the thought of living without.

The odd thing was that, for all these large dramatic truths, he was calm. He'd spent the past two weeks in a blaze of anxiety, afraid that Sasha would never come back, that every time he saw him out the stairwell door would be the last. He wasn't sure what was so different now. The encampment could move on and vanish; Sasha could be swept up in a raid, deported overnight. The difference was Laurie's new conviction that they would find one another, no matter what happened. They had stumbled back across the heath, exhausted, arms wrapped around each other's waists. Just outside the encampment, Sasha had stopped him and kissed him so yearningly that Laurie could still feel the burning impress of his mouth. Laurie felt as if he'd know now if anything became of Sasha, as if he would be able to walk to him, like a fire in the dark, from any distance.

Two long shifts at the car wash would keep Sasha busy all weekend, and anyway, they had agreed it was best not to try to see one another outside their established routine, at least until Laurie found his way out of his father's labyrinth. That was Sasha's benign way of putting the thumbscrews on him. The last thing he had said to him, as they had parted at the bus stop. "*Get out of there, and we can be together*." It ought to be the best incentive in the world. Their carefully staged meetings in Sanderson's tutorial group would hardly allow for any more of the exchanges they had made on the twilight heath, and unless Laurie made a special effort, he could think of little else than that. He burned for the chance to do it again—not clumsily this time, but powerfully, slowly, showing Sasha what a good lover he could be. Imagined having a place where they could lie together undisturbed, their own door locked behind them.

So what was holding him back? *Clara*, came the usual answer. My mother. But these old safety belts were getting worn and useless to him. Sasha was right—he was doing no real job of protecting them by lurking here. Laurie had even gone so far as to look at the adverts for staff in the *Stage*. But even the lowliest of these seemed to require years more experience than he had, and the salaries were tiny.

Laurie, if he allowed himself to admit it, was for the first time thinking about who he was—or who he would be, once the old man was gone. Sir William was way too young and hale, and his wealth too much a source of discomfort as well as support to Laurie, for his son ever to have seriously considered what he would inherit. Now, though, despairingly weighing up his skills against the realities of independent life, Laurie found himself indulging the odd fantasy. He'd sell this old house—his mother had never liked it—and he'd set her and Clara up in a seaside château in the Languedoc, where her family came from. It would be warm and sunny all day long, and he and Sasha would visit them—Sasha, well fed and strong, living safely with him in their beautiful Bloomsbury penthouse; Sasha, whom poverty could never touch again. Maybe everything would be all right anyway. Sir William was not the monster he could seem to be. Laurie remembered when he had been a kind father. Perhaps he could talk to him. Perhaps when he saw Laurie was in love, that nothing could change him, he would relent.

Sitting back from his desk in the attic room, Laurie grinned. Okay, that was a wilder fantasy than the Languedoc château. But he still did not despair of finding some escape route between that and the plunge into the dark he'd have to take alone. No, the old man was not a monster. Not—what was the word Mama Luna had used? Not mulo. Not, for God's sake, death.

The old servant's bell over the bedroom door pinged faintly. Laurie got up, stretching. That was a summons Mrs. Gibson sometimes shyly availed herself of when Laurie was wanted downstairs and she was too busy to run up and find him. She hadn't liked the sense of role reversal, but Laurie had told her to go ahead whenever it was convenient. Usually it meant dinner was ready, or someone had come to call for him. Laurie sighed. He was far from in the mood for the formal and lugubrious Sunday evening meal that Sir William insisted on, but until he got himself a job as a minimum-wage props handler or runner, there was no help for it. Anyway, tomorrow was Monday, and Sasha would be here; Laurie thought he could get through almost any amount of overcooked vegetables with that light on his horizon.

He took the stairs down from the attic four at a time, warmed by memories. God, they had been a hard lot to crack, that Romani mob around Mama Luna's fire. They'd looked at him as if he had just crawled from under a rock with an immigration officer's badge in his hand. Laurie had supposed being admitted to the camp was one thing, but the old woman's invitation to join in their spiced-broth supper had raised some hackles. He'd been allowed to eat in relative peace, cross-legged on the ground at Sasha's side, but then, out of the tense silence that had followed, a missile had suddenly flown at him, striking his upper arm.

A leather juggler's ball.

Laurie had plucked the second one out of the air without even looking. Sasha had started to his feet, growling an imprecation in Roma, but Laurie knew there was only one way to return such fire, and had tossed the second ball high in the air, retrieved the first one from the ground before it could fall, and added an empty bean tin into the equation. He'd casually thrown all three in a tall arc above his audience's head. Plenty of call for juggler's tricks in his seasonal pantomime stint, and a good way of amusing himself during long waits backstage. He'd chucked out a few good ones and then fired both balls back into the darkness, in the exact direction from which they'd come. A yelp, and a rasping cackle from the old woman, and after that they had left him alone. Later one of them had struck up a song, rocking himself and patting his knee in time, in a language Laurie did not think was Romani, sounding more like Irish Gaelic with odd scraps of reversed-sounding English thrown in. Anyway, by the second verse, he'd caught the sounds if not the meaning, and Sasha had turned to him smiling as he'd joined in with the others at the chorus.

He could hear the strange, chanting melody yet. Lost in his thoughts, Laurie crossed the great hallway, trying to recall the words. *Shelta*, it had been, Sash told him afterward, a language of wanderers, of Romani blown as far afield as America.

The dining room was brightly lit, but there were no signs of supper. The table's polished surface was blank. Around it, sitting bolt upright in the uncomfortable chairs, were arrayed an unexpected group of people. His mother, out of her usual place of dignity at the far end, huddled in a seat she seemed to have chosen at random, with Clara on her lap. Hannah beside her, looking terrified. In the master's seat at the top, his father—with, incongruously, the tutor Sanderson sitting at his right hand.

For one second Laurie allowed himself the fantasy that his father had decided to relax the habits of a lifetime and invite the staff to dinner. Then he came to a halt. "Hello, Sandy," he said levelly. "Are we making you work Sundays now?"

Sanderson, already the yellow of curdling milk, went a shade paler. He was pressed so far back in his chair that Laurie wondered if the old man was holding a gun on him underneath the table. Not that it was necessary. The dead-eyed look, the huge passive bulk, would do. "L-Laurence," he stammered. "You'll have to forgive me. I…"

"I do," Laurie interrupted him, smiling. "I shouldn't have asked you to keep a secret. It was my fault."

"No!" It was a desperate, high-pitched wail. Laurie, spinning around, saw Clara scrambling off her mother's lap. Her face was a mask of grief. "No, it was my fault! I told about the gypsy prince. I just forgot!"

Laurie took three strides toward her. He put down his arms and scooped her up, feeling her scrabble like a monkey to get hold of him. "Listen," he said to her, calmly as he could across her sobs. "Nothing that happens here is your fault. Okay? Can you put that in your head and keep it there? Nothing."

He looked about him. So far the old man had neither spoken nor stirred. Well, that storm would break soon—and before it did, Laurie had some damage control to perform. From a long way out, he wondered why he wasn't afraid.

Shock, he supposed. His heart was thudding steadily under his left collarbone. He could see its vibrations faintly shaking Clara's hair. He also knew he hadn't really come back to earth since his encounter with Sasha on the heath. He was still out there, if he closed his eyes for one second and let this questionable reality slide.

"Hannah," he said, surprised by the calm of his own voice. "Come here. Take Clara."

"You stay where you are, you little bitch."

The old man at last. Hannah, who in her whole life had never been called anything less affectionate than *darling*, burst into tears and fled for the door. Laurie put out one hand and caught her by the wrist as gently as he could. "No," he said softly. "No, stay for a second. I'm very sorry, Hannah. Please just take Clara down to Mrs. Gibson; then you go straight home. Okay?"

Sir William lurched to his feet. He topped six and a half feet when he stood erect, and the drink Laurie could smell on him swelled him out too. No, he'd never laid a hand on his son. He'd never had to. Something in Laurie still believed he would not. Hannah, shaking and sobbing, was nevertheless holding out her arms for the little girl, and Laurie handed her over blindly, keeping his eyes fixed on the old man. He wasn't sure what their locked gaze indicated, but he tried to make his part of it *you'll have to go through me.*

"You don't order the staff in this house, boy. You don't tell my daughter what to do."

That low growl. Laurie had heard it all his life and obeyed. It still had power to command him now, and a sudden flare of rage at his own weakness stiffened his spine. Aware that he had stepped in front of Clara and Hannah to shield them, he waited till the dining room door opened and closed. "If you treated her like a daughter," he said coldly, "I might still respect that." He paused. His throat had gone dry and his palms correspondingly damp, but it still wasn't fear. "You'd better let Sandy go too, unless you want him to hear the details."

The old man went gray beneath the mottled purple that had risen in his cheeks. Laurie held his gaze mercilessly, daring him to try to bluff it out. To try to misunderstand. But after a moment he swung around on poor Sanderson, who flinched so hard he nearly went back over out of his chair. "You," he grunted. "Don't expect a bloody reference. Get out."

I'll give you a reference, Laurie wanted to tell him. *Not your fault if you thought your gypsy pupil was a prince*. But Sanderson was a fish-pale flash, squeezing past the heavy dining furniture and making for the door. All Laurie could do was open it for him to aid his escape.

Peripherally he saw his mother was on her feet too, one diamond-glittered hand pressed to the surface of the table as if she could barely support herself. Pity and anger went through him.

"No, Ma," he said reluctantly. "You have to hear this. Sit down."

"Damn right she has to hear it." Sir William was getting over his fright. Laurie could read it in the restored redness of his face. Laurie had been lucky, he supposed, to get him off balance even for a second—but the room was clear now, the only people left in it the ones who should be there. "She needs to hear how her son dragged a grubby gyppo tinker into her house and passed him off as some kind of diplomat's son to get Sanderson to teach him."

Laurie didn't think his mother was too interested. His rare clashes with Sir William had always terrified her, and she was herself so quiet, so restrained, that Laurie had usually restrained himself for her sake, bent his head into the storm of the old man's rage so that at least only one person was shouting. She had not sat back down. Abruptly compassion won out in Laurie. If he tried to pin her down here, who would it be for? Clara, whose protection had been out of those frail, glittering hands for years—or for himself, because he burned to shove into her face all the realities she had been avoiding? He could not keep her here, looking so fragile and sick.

"Ma," he whispered and, when she did not budge from her frozen half stance, shook his head and went to her. "Come on," he said, taking her arm. "Go and find Clara and Gibson. That's all I wanted to say to you anyway. Make sure Gibson's with her. Don't let her be left alone. Not with him." He wondered if he would be able to get her to the door with any dignity; she was leaning on him as if she would fall, and the old man, who had twitched at his last words, was beginning a nightmare-slow lumber toward them. But after a few faltering steps, she broke from him, pushed away with a whimper, and staggered out faster than Sanderson had done.

Laurie turned to face his father. He knew that a time came, for some young men, when they understood their fear of a brutal parent was hollow—just a habit, a memory, a lingering trace of childhood—when they understood they were stronger and one good punch would do the trick, send the shadow monster crumbling to dust.

Reed slender, much shorter, he knew this epiphany could not be his. Nevertheless he stood still. He said very clearly, watching Sir William devour the space between them, "Yes, I let the gyppo tinker in, sir. Not only that, but I'm fucking him. I love him."

And still the first blow came as a surprise. Perhaps some remnant of trust had stayed with Laurie after all. He was down on his knees, staring at the elegant claw foot of one of the table's central legs. He was not certain how he'd got there—had briefly seen his father move, and then the air had left his lungs. One side of his rib cage was dully exploding. He coughed and retched and heard the breath come back into him in a kind of sucking groan he could not control. He had a moment in which to reflect that maybe this was the price he paid for never having received a mild slap or a cuff from the old man. That, having finally broken his restraints, his father was going to jump the preliminaries and kill him.

And yet still he wasn't afraid. He had to get up; that was all. His father said, close and hot against his ear, "You perverted little bastard." But it hardly mattered to Laurie. The old man was dragging him onto his feet, an assistance he couldn't have expected. He tried to twist around. The vast grip upon his shoulders tightened. Sasha, Laurie thought, the word in his mind like a cry, and he wondered if Sasha knew how completely he loved him. Sasha. It stayed with him as his father shook him like a rat, as his brow connected with the solid back of one of the precious old chairs, then the table's edge. He took it with him, deep into the dark.

* * *

Curzon Street. About eight at night, Laurie guessed, from the patterns of the crowd milling past him. Most of them dressed for the evening, on their way to restaurants or the opera. In this well-heeled backwater, there were a lot of lovely winter clothes, long swishing coats, and sumptuous collars. Laurie, shivering, reached to turn up his own, and found it wasn't there.

He was standing at the bus stop in his shirtsleeves. Drawing a deep breath—or trying to; there was a knot of pain in his side that tightened when he inhaled—he tried to fill in the gap in his mind between hitting the dining room floor and being here. He could, when he made the effort, though it was like looking through water. He'd opened his eyes, detachedly surprised that he had lived to do so. The dining room had been empty. He had lain, staring into the cathedral forest of chair and table legs, until his eyes had stung from want of blinking. The door had been open.

Through it came voices—raised and agitated, too distant for identification. All but one, anyway. Female, strident. Laurie, who had never heard Mrs. Gibson shout before in his whole life, had listened in fascination while she dealt out this appalling rating to whoever had deserved it. Then the voices had died and other sounds began to rise. Slamming doors, restless footsteps.

Footsteps getting closer. Laurie had struggled to his feet. He had done this in stages, he remembered—hands and knees, then a grip on the edge of the table, then one last shove upright so painful he had almost passed out again and had only stayed upright by slipping into the skin of a man in a play with one mission—to get out of this prison house or die, and that was how he had lost track of reality, entered the amnesiac fog.

It had worked, though. Laurie sometimes wondered if there was anything he couldn't do if he could just persuade himself he was playing the role of someone capable of doing it for him. The absurdity of this made him briefly shake with laughter, tugging at his ribs, turning heads to look at him. He supposed he was conspicuous enough anyway. The hero of this most recent drama hadn't had the sense to stop for a jacket, money, or Tube fare card. He felt in his pockets for change, and there was a handful, but nowhere near enough to take him out across the city.

He couldn't go back. Leaning against the bus shelter's smeared acrylic wall, Laurie reflected that this was how it had been for Sasha, how it still was for all the thousands of others caught up in the night. No warmth, no cash, and no means of getting either. He subsided onto the little plastic ledge that served as a seat but didn't allow you to get too comfortable and drop off there, a nicety of design he had never noticed till now. Christ, his head hurt. He could taste salt. When he raised his hand to dab at his mouth, it came away bloody. He stared at it dully.

Headlights strafed the shelter. At first Laurie paid no heed. The street was busy, buses and taxis crossing and recrossing one another in the road ahead. A door clicked with a familiar sound, and he got his head up. He blinked. His father's driver, out of uniform, hair rumpled, was standing on the pavement beside the Daimler. "Oh, thank God," Charlie said. "I've been driving around the streets. Come here, son. Come on with me."

So his situation bore no resemblance to that of the homeless thousands, Laurie corrected himself as Charlie helped him move, ashamed of having exaggerated his own little earthquake to that extent. He sat in a warm car. Someone—not family; Laurie was beginning to understand how very little family had to do with it—had given enough of a damn to come out and find him. Charlie was digging in his pockets. He produced a large white handkerchief and switched the map light on so that the Daimler lit up with a golden glow. "Here," he said. "Let's have a look at you."

No, not family. Laurie remembered now a thousand times when this man or Mrs. Gibson or one of the other household staff out in Suffolk had come running after him, to pick him up when he fell over, ripped his eight-year-old knees to shreds once again on the gravel, or lost control of the half-broken horse his father had thought was such a good joke to give him. Charlie, frowning so hard in the map light Laurie thought his face would crack, was reaching for him now, beginning to dab gingerly at his mouth.

"It's okay, Charlie," he said, managing a smile, taking the handkerchief from him. "I'll do that. I…I hate to ask this, but can you lend me a few quid? I've come out without any money, and…there's somewhere I want to go."

Charlie stared at him. "You're asking your own bloody chauffeur for bus fare? There's only one place you're going, young man—"

"Oh, Charlie. Not home."

"No. No, son. Mrs. Gibson and me, and the others, there's none of us can bear to stay there anymore. Gibson's already given notice, and...well, I'm taking you to the hospital, that's all, and we'll see what happens from there." Frowning even more grimly than before, Charlie leaned to start the engine. "I never thought I'd live to see the day."

Gibson. Laurie stared at himself in the visor mirror. The right side of his face was alien to him, the wrong shape. When he touched it, a strange, sick pain went through him. *Oh, God. Charlie, tell her not to leave*. But he could hardly beg anyone else to stay in the hell he himself was running from, could he? The Daimler was purring, beginning its stately departure. "Charlie. Have I ever...given you an order?"

Charlie glanced at him. To Laurie's dismay, there were tears on his face. "No, sir," he said. "You've always been a good lad. Kind and polite."

"I want to give one now. Never mind the hospital. Will you drive me out to East Hill?" That was as close as Laurie was prepared to let anyone come, even this good man, to his destination. He could get the bus from there. "I've got friends there. They'll look after me, I promise." He wasn't much at giving orders, he reflected, slumping back into the passenger seat, letting his skull fall back against the headrest. He just wanted to be away and, for a short while, to sleep. The need was overwhelming. "Charlie, please."

"All right." Peripherally Laurie was aware of Charlie gazing fiercely ahead through the windscreen, drumming his fingers on the wheel. "East Hill, though, son? I never knew you have a friend outside the Tube zone one."

Laurie smiled—or tried to. The effort sent a dull ache up into his eye socket. He thought about his friends inside the zone and tried to imagine seeking help from any of them tonight. Bleeding on their marble Knightsbridge floors. "More fool me, then," he muttered. "Been keeping mixed company, Charlie." He felt his eyes close and, a moment later, a smooth, deep shift underneath him as Charlie put the Daimler into gear.

Chapter Eight

He was alone, and in the dead of winter night, the lane stretched out forever. Laurie stumbled slowly along the verge. There was just enough demarcation there between grass and track that he could find his way.

He remembered sunlight and Sasha at his side. The crackling electrical snap in the air between them. He had known then that they were walking toward a union that would change his life. Yes, the lane had been a path between two worlds. It still was. The last shreds of Laurie's childhood lay behind him, drops of his blood on the richly carpeted floor of a Mayfair house. Sasha had said he should get out. Very well. He was gone. Sasha would help him to build a new life.

He had to stay alive to let him. Laurie missed his footing, crashed hard to his hands and knees on the verge. The impact sent stars of pain skyrocketing through his skull and his lungs. By the time he had forced himself upright once more, he no longer cared about any future more distant or complex than his next step. The night was moonless. The lights of Birchwood somehow did not reach here as they had when Sasha had walked him back to the main road. The fires of the encampment did not shine.

Perhaps they were gone. Up until eight o'clock that night, Laurie had believed certain things without ever fully articulating them to himself. That, if pushed, his mother would stand up to defend not only her small daughter but her grown-up son, as well. That he still had a place in his home, and that his father still loved him enough not to knock him unconscious on the edge of a table. Perhaps other things he believed were just as fragile, just as much products of his own need. "Ves'tacha," Sasha had called him, and Laurie had believed that too…

But who could possibly call *him* beloved and have it be true? He was nothing, wasn't he? Useless. Pathetic. The lights were gone, the encampment vanished. Sasha, who was kind but not stupid, had told him what he wanted to hear.

Oh, God. He was sobbing, off the path and caught once more in the fucking brambles. He stopped himself, mortified. The encampment was barely twenty yards away, over in the trees to his right. He had not seen it because his head had been down, his vision wiped out by self-pity. He turned, reorienting himself, tore himself out of the thorns, and headed for the lights.

Zaga the bulldog ran out like a bullet the second she heard him. Sasha had been right, though. She knew him this time and did not bark. "That's just great," Laurie whispered to her, dropping to his knees.

He couldn't take another step, had been relying on her commotion to draw someone's attention. That was it, then. He was out here for the night. Apart from his sorrow at being so near to Sasha and unable to make the last stretch, it didn't seem so bad to him. The packed earth beneath him was becoming oddly soft. If the bloody dog would stop dancing around him and sticking her great tongue into his ears, he could probably lay himself down here and sleep.

But the rattle of her chain had been enough. The door to the nearest caravan swung wide, emitting a rectangle of pale yellow light and the immense shape of Gunari, Mama Luna's son. Laurie looked up at him. On any other night, that vision would have scared the crap out of him—a six-foot skinhead striding out of the darkness toward him, baseball bat swinging from one hand. Now Gunari almost seemed like light relief. Laurie tried to laugh, but it hurt too much, and he doubled up, coughing.

Gunari crouched beside him. He dropped the bat and shone the torch he was carrying into Laurie's face. Squinting, holding up one shaking hand to shield himself,

Laurie bore the examination patiently. He heard Gunari fire off a brief, rapid-fire stream of Roma, then add at the end of it, as if in translation, "Fucking hell." He got to his feet and marched off as fast as he had come. "Mama! Fetch Mama Luna!"

Laurie drifted. He'd been propping himself on his arms, but when the softening earth rolled itself up like a warm wave to meet him, he felt he couldn't resist it. He saw, through a blurring veil, that as soon as he was prone, Zaga gave up her assault and sat herself down beside him, as if on guard. He closed his eyes.

Rustling robes and a faint chiming, as if of the little gold coins that Sasha had told him were called *galbi*. He felt a dry grasp close on his wrist, dry, warm fingers push back his hair. A faint scent of apricots reached him. An exchange of Romani, not loud but urgent, the voice he could just distinguish as Mama Luna's giving what sounded like a string of commands. Laurie tried to take an interest, but it didn't seem to concern him anymore. Nothing did.

The last thing that held him out of the pit was another rush of footsteps, light and fast. Another grip on him—sweet, familiar, cold with shock. An embrace that closed and lifted him up off the earth. "Oh, my God. Laurie! Laurie!"

* * *

He could not pinpoint a moment of waking. In a way, he felt as if he had always been here—lying on his side in a room he slowly worked out was the bedroom of Sasha's caravan. The bed, a small double, was covered by two blankets and an unzipped sleeping bag. At the moment these were turned down. Laurie's shirt was tucked up to expose the left side of his rib cage. He wondered if he should tell Mama Luna, who was perched like a gaudy sparrow on the bed beside him, of his return to awareness. Certainly he should tell Sasha, kneeling in the tiny gap between the bed and wall, watching with one hand clamped tight to his mouth, his dark eyes bleak with horror.

He couldn't—not just yet. The old woman's palm was pressed flat to his ribs. She was exerting a pressure which, while he somehow knew it was good, diagnostic, and would not harm him, was at the same time imposing on him such extraordinary pain that, if he opened his mouth, he would wail like a child. And he'd made enough of a fool of himself already. He had a vague memory that Gunari had picked him off the ground and carried him here. He concentrated on breathing and keeping silent.

The old woman finished her probing and lifted her hand after a little caress, as if to tell him she was sorry. She looked at Sasha. "He's hurt inside, chiavala."

Sasha took his hand from his mouth. "Christ. You mean like internal injuries? I told you we should have called an ambulance."

"No. No, not like that. Inside. People like him don't heal fast in the places where they trust. You must be careful of him."

"I will. I'll do anything to help him."

"You don't understand. Careful of yourself around him, Sasha. Dadro shee mulo."

"What? He'd never hurt me." Sasha swallowed audibly, and Laurie tried once more to get enough safe breath past his larynx for a reassuring sound, but it wasn't going to happen yet. "And I know his bloody father is death. He's nearly killed him tonight."

"No. Balame will live a long time. The ribs are cracked, not broken. I can treat him here, good as in hospital anyway."

"Okay. What about his face?"

"Oh, face." Laurie felt the thin mattress rock as the old lady emitted a short chuckle. "Lovely again soon enough.

No harm to the skull or eyes. Very well—poultice for ribs, arnica for face. And now he's awake, *darozha* for all that pain he thinks he's hiding. English boy, why don't you cry out? You think I don't know?"

"Is he awake?" Sasha leaned toward him, reaching out to brush his the hair from his brow. "Laurie? No, he's still…" But Laurie, for whom being seen through amounted suddenly to permission, flinched back, buried his face in the pillow, and howled. He shot out a hand, blindly groping, and felt Sasha seize it. Sasha's other hand went into his hair. Laurie felt his warm breath on his cheek. "Laurie, it's okay. You don't have to hide." But Laurie did. Drilled from infancy to put a stone mask over pain, he could not just put it aside, and after a moment he sensed Sasha accept this and lean over him, shielding. "All right. I'll hide you."

"Good," Mama Luna said. "Good, keep him still there." He felt her weight shift. A few seconds later, a wet heat landed on his exposed ribs, as if she had dropped boiling mud on him. The heat was briefly unbearable. He convulsed under it and felt himself restrained by a grip stronger even than Sasha's, shoulder and hip. "No. Lie still, balame. Let it do its work."

Christ, what was it? Lava, it felt like, consuming his side in three bites as more of it landed on him. Aware he must be crushing bones in Sasha's hand, he tried to loosen his grip but could not; Sasha was holding him more fiercely still. He heard his own breath coming and going in anguished rasps—then, abruptly, the fist in his lungs unlocked. It was as if his rib cage had relaxed enough for him to get air into it for the first time in hours, and the heat, instead of boiling his skin off him, became a distraction from the pain. He sucked in an enormous breath. He'd been slowly suffocating—not just from the blow but the memory of getting it, as if the old man's fist had remained buried in his side. "Good," the old woman crooned again. "Good. Let it work."

The substance seemed to be drying on his skin. Laurie heard it crackling, like mud in the sun, imagined cracks as deep as Giant's Causeway appearing in it, down through his insignificant flesh and into the heart of the earth. He breathed and breathed, and the pain became bearable. Slowly he returned to himself—became properly aware of his surroundings, of the fact that he was on his side in a gypsy caravan and showing his rescuers very little appreciation. Breathed again—so deep that the gathered mass on his side, only warm now, seemed to break apart and fall away from him.

"Sasha," he whispered and kissed the hand still clenched on his. He got his head up out of the pillow. "Mama Luna, I'm so sorry."

"Sorry?" The old woman was calmly gathering up broken pieces of what looked like dried clay from the mattress. She folded these into her apron and briskly brushed away the dust. "You needed us; you came. No sorry."

"But I haven't got any… I can't pay you for any of this, not now…" He tried to sit up, Sasha moving to help him, the old woman pushing a pillow behind his back. He looked around him, taking in the tiny, cramped room, the view beyond it to the kitchen Sasha had said he shared with… "Oh, God. Am I in Cyril's half of the bed?"

Sasha broke into startled laughter. "No. You'll never believe this, but Mrs. Cyril turned up on Friday night to take him home. She'd tracked him down somehow. You never saw a happier man."

"Really?" Laurie thought he was seeing a fairly happy one now. Sasha's voice was still unsteady, but some of the terror was leaving his face. He supposed he had made a dramatic arrival. "That's good. Really good. I'm sorry I frightened you, Sash…"

"It's okay. You'll be okay now." Sasha slid an arm behind his back. He gave an odd, short gasp, and Laurie saw that tears had gathered in his eyes. "Fuck's sake, though, Laurie. He did it, didn't he? I *told* you to get out."

Laurie pressed their brows lightly together. Whatever his reply might have been—*well, he's done his worst now* or *never again*—it was halted in his throat by a sharp rap on the caravan's outside wall. Sasha restrained his bone-deep jerk of fright. But Mama Luna got calmly to her feet and shuffled over to the door, as if she would meet a whole army of men like Sir William without flinching. Laurie got a glimpse of Gunari's huge shape in the night outside, incongruously holding up to the old woman a little bowl, in both hands, as if whatever it contained was precious. She took it from him, nodding and chuckling, and took the opportunity of being three steps above him to pat him on his crew-cut head. Gunari said proudly, "Darozha, Mama."

"Yes. Darozha. Good boy. Go back to bed now." Turning, she made her way back into the bedroom, the bowl cupped between her two palms. "Sasha," she said, setting it carefully down by the bed. "This balame seems to like you. See if he trusts you enough to take that."

Laurie frowned. He wanted to tell her he trusted Sash enough to take anything from his hands. He remembered now, words heard in the ice storm of his pain: "*careful of yourself around him, Sasha.*" The old woman had no reason to put faith in him, he knew, and he didn't suppose his kind had ever helped her in the past, but still it hurt him that she could think him dangerous to Sasha, for whom he thought he could die happily tomorrow if asked.

"Mama Luna," he began but somehow forgot the thrust of the thought between one instant and the next. The bowl was steaming lightly, filling the room with a bitter scent. It should have repelled him, but instead it seemed to soften his returning memories in comforting veils. What had he been so concerned about? Oh, yes. Trust. He yawned massively. Sasha's arm was tight around his shoulders now, his warmth so close that Laurie felt him chuckle. "I told you," he said to the old woman, whose name he could not now quite recall. "I won't hurt him. I love him."

"That's good," she said, brushing down her skirts and rearranging her scarves to glowing magnificence. The little gold galbi danced and shimmered on her brow. "See how much you love him after he's poured darozha down your throat. Sleep well."

She was gone. Laurie, who hadn't seen her leave, rubbed a hand across his eyes and raised a puzzled glance to Sasha. In the silence she had left behind, he could hear his own heartbeat, and a brief spike of adrenaline returned him to the surface. Involuntarily he saw again the dining room in Mayfair, the first step—unknown to him at the time—in his journey here. When he thought about the whole of that journey, his mind balked from its totality. His last glance of the hallway through a haze of blood.

God, it had been just that, hadn't it? A last look at his home.

He couldn't go back. For an instant, panic touched him. Breath heaved in and out of his chest. Then Sasha's hold on him became a bruising hug. Why the hell should he care? Look what he'd won, in the midst of his night's losses. He was alone with Sash, curled up by his side in a room which, though frail, he felt was inviolable. Nothing could hurt them here. He felt his respiration settle enough that, after a few seconds, he could ask, "What's darozha, then?"

"I don't know." Sasha brushed a tender kiss to his right cheekbone, then withdrew with a hiss of sympathy. "She swears there's no frogs or newts in it, but… Ah, ves'tacha, he did make a mess of you, didn't he? Before you take your poison, let's see to that."

Sasha reached down, and Laurie saw with amusement that as well as her steaming, mind-altering mysteries, the old woman had left a perfectly ordinary tub of arnica on the bedside table. Sasha seemed to read his smile. "She doesn't reinvent the wheel, Mama Luna. Here. Sit still." Laurie did his best. He hadn't looked in a mirror since his one glimpse by the Daimler's overhead light, but Sasha's gentle touch with the arnica seemed to be mapping out a landscape unfamiliar to him, unexpected crests where pain flared like lightning. "Why did he do it to you, Laurie?"

"Poor little Clara dropped the ball about our lessons. She forgot you were a secret prince, and—"

Sasha went still. "Tell me you didn't get a beating like that because of me."

"No!" Laurie thought about it, memories returning in painful slow motion. "Actually, no. That wasn't it. I mean, he wasn't thrilled, but...he only really lost it when I told him I was..." The word stuck a bit, but he'd come this far, and he brought it out bravely at last. "When I told him I was gay."

"Oh." Sasha finished dabbing the arnica onto his bruises. "I'm pleased he took it so well."

"Ah, he's just worried I won't provide him an heir to his plutocratic bloody empire. And I didn't exactly put it like that, I..." He fell silent, a cold grip closing in his chest. How could he have forgotten? "Sasha...Clara!" Jolting forward, he tried to get out of the bed. "I've got to go."

"Wait," Sasha commanded him softly, pushing him back. "Do you think she's safe enough—just for tonight, anyway?"

"I... I'm not sure. I think so, yes. But I've got to get her out of there."

"You will. Tomorrow you can take on the world, love, start doing the things you need to do to get you and her clear of that place forever. But you're not going anywhere tonight."

The darozha, for all its bitter scent, tasted sweet. Laurie, who'd cupped his hands around Sasha's on the bowl to share with him responsibility for administering the dose, made a face of surprise. "It's not that bad."

"Ah. You must really need it. She gave it to me the first night I came here, when I was sick from the cold and couldn't sleep. I tried a bit the next night, when I was feeling better, and it tasted of rancid goat."

Laurie nodded. He was picking up a tang of that. It was the texture more than the taste that was strange to him, as if he were drinking barely dissolved leaves and bark. A faint sliminess. Nevertheless he obediently downed the lot. Sasha took the empty bowl from him and sat watching him as if he expected something to happen. Laurie waited too. He was about to say sorry—for what, he wasn't sure; possibly his balame impercipience—when Sasha suddenly reached past him and pulled a pillow flat on the mattress. Laurie thought there was no need for it. He could sit up all night, talking to Sasha like this. The pain in his side and his head, the pain in his heart, was not just fading but gone. He felt ready for anything.

A peace like nothing he had ever experienced before swept down on him from the van's rust-flecked roof—a wild, rushing release of tension. Laurie fought it—he had things to do, didn't he, people to care for?—but there was no chance. Tears of relief suddenly spilled down his face, and he had no more control of that than the softening of rigid muscle all down his spine and limbs. "Jesus," he whispered, and through rainbows saw Sasha reach for him, tenderly cupping the back of his skull in one hand, clasping his shoulder with the other, so that when he fell, it was gently, and his impact with the mattress—and it felt like falling in slow-motion through a thousand feet of sunny air—knocked him unresisting into sleep.

* * *

Thin curtains letting in a thin gray light. For a long while, Laurie watched it, only breathing. He felt as if he had been unstitched and rewoven. As if all the meshing threads that made up his being had been gently untangled, laid out flat so that the grit, the dirt and broken glass had fallen out from them, and then unhurriedly put back together.

As if his senses had been washed clean too. When he listened, he could hear with crystalline purity the early-morning sounds of the encampment. The burr of a generator coming to life. In the very far distance, the silvery slither of Zaga's chain. Oh, and he could feel… A shudder ran through him, deep and wonderful: he could feel Sasha, warm and naked, curled around his back. Sasha's arm was tucked under his head. The other was tightly holding his waist, and Laurie remembered that in his strange dreams of that night, this living safety belt had held him clear of monsters. "Sash," he whispered, the word a feather brush to skin in the pale light.

"Laurie?"

He put back a hand. He didn't even want to look yet—just to feel the plane of Sasha's hip. The bone was less stark now, the skin like damp silk. He moved his hand down and felt his palm brush Sasha's cock—quiescent but responding instantly to the touch. "Yes," Laurie murmured, smiling against the pillow, taking a blind hold on him.

"You're not even awake."

"I don't need to be. Please just do it. Like we did…like we did on the heath."

Sasha kissed his ear. "You're still stoned from Mama Luna's rotgut."

Laurie, turning, gave him a look which he hoped conveyed full lucidity. Sasha's shaft was now stiff and heavy in his hand. He couldn't imagine how it would feel inside. "Maybe a bit," he admitted. "But it wasn't Rohypnol. Sash, don't mess about."

“I have to—just for a second. Hang on, love.”

Laurie closed his eyes. He curled right over on his side, drawing his knees up. Sasha must have undressed him after he’d fallen asleep, and he was glad of it. By the time he’d reached the camp last night, his clothes had been damp with cold sweat, acrid with fear. Now he was only warm skin beneath the sleeping bag. Ready. He heard the crinkle of foil and recalled for the first time that, finally, he had not put a condom on for Sasha the other night on the heath. That Sasha was doing so for him tightened his throat with love and shame, and he drew breath to say something but lost the thought as warm fingers parted his buttocks. “Sasha…”

“Yes. Yes. It’s gonna hurt a bit, even with the lubricant.”

“I know. It’s okay.”

“Oh, ves’tacha. You don’t know anything.”

Sasha put his arms around him again, that sacred safety belt, and he had been right. Laurie knew nothing at all. He groaned and fought as the pressure at his entrance became tight, then huge, then unbearable, and then just as he thought he would rip apart or have to beg Sasha to stop, some spasm of his straining muscle ring, some part of his struggle, suddenly opened him up. He sank his face into the pillow and felt Sasha move to cover him. His warm weight was absolute. Laurie heaved up against it in relief, choked cries tearing from him. “Don’t let me go!”

“I won’t. Laurie, that’s it.”

Laurie seized the hand Sasha had pushed under his neck to support him. He kissed it, sucked at its fingers, finally turned his face into its palm and sobbed as the hot spear pressed deeper and higher inside him. Convulsions shook him, reflexive efforts of repulsion, but these only carried Sasha farther in—Sasha, with infinite gentleness, pinned him and began to thrust. Curled up tight, Laurie lost himself in the rocking dark. The tidal movements hurt him for a short while longer, then, as Sasha groaned and drove into him harder, found a place in the depths of him that responded with uncontrollable pleasure. Laurie could not speak, could not get a word out to tell Sasha not to stop—that his life depended on that motion continuing, deep and fast—but then it wasn't necessary; his orgasm boiled up without warning, a detonation that took place as much inside him as in the place where his cock was caught and squeezed between his thigh and belly. He felt Sasha wrap himself tight around his body. Heard him whisper, hot against his ear, "God. Now!"

Their voices lifted and wove incoherently together in the caravan's damp air. Laurie thrashed, climax drawing out long, white-hot with the knowledge of his lover exploding and spending inside him. He twisted the pillow in both hands, feeling a bloodred darkness threaten, the edge of overload. Then the pressure inside him eased, leaving him sobbing in loss and satisfaction and release, returning him slowly to earth.

He wanted to see his lover. Without thinking of anything else, he twisted over onto his back. The movement tugged Sasha out of him awkwardly and hard, and both dissolved into pained laughter. "God!" Sasha said rawly. "Are you all right?"

"No. Ow. Yes, fine—better than anything, better than…" Laurie fell breathlessly silent, and they struggled into an exhausted mutual embrace.

* * *

An alarm clock buzzed, jolting them both back to the surface. Laurie groaned as Sasha reached to switch it off, breaking the warm, damp interlock of their limbs. The room was brighter now. Had they slept? He wasn't sure. At the moment he was sure of one thing only. "Sash?"

Sasha burrowed back down against him. "Yes, love?"

"I don't want to sound like a kid at the fairground, but can we do that again?"

Sasha broke into laughter. He kissed Laurie's brow, then for good measure, his eyelids and mouth. "You liked the ride? I'm glad to hear you say so in daylight, because"—he hesitated, then finished into Laurie's waiting silence—"because to fuck you while you had a skinful of darozha was questionable at best."

"Oh, no," Laurie said. "No, I wanted it. I want it now."

"Ah, ves'tacha, we can't."

"We can." For all his difficulty with the word, to hear that soft-voiced *fuck* from Sasha's lips was a powerful turn-on to Laurie. He was getting hard again, and when he pushed up, he felt the pulsing heat of Sasha's response. "Can, Sash."

"It's not that. I have to go to work."

Laurie blinked. The quiet statement of necessity—of reality, falling like a stone into their sealed-off world—had given him a shock. For just one instant, on reflex, he became his father's son. *Bugger work. Stay here. I've got plenty of money. I can make it go away.*

But he couldn't, could he? As for money, he had nothing. Sasha was regretfully untangling himself from the bedclothes. Laurie watched him, the truth of his own self and his resources slowing descending upon him. It was a mix of joy and fear. Freedom and cold-blooded terror. But if Sash looked pale and tired beneath the weight of his obligations, they conferred on him a dignity as well. His own money, honestly earned. Laurie could tell he was proud. "Yes," he said quietly. "Yes. Me too."

Chapter Nine

Laurie stood outside the Rayne's End theatre in East Hill. A thin December sleet was falling. Already it had penetrated the jacket Sash had loaned him, and he was cold.

He didn't really mind. He had just left a coffee shop up the road, where Sasha had bought them both breakfast before heading off to his shift at the car wash. Sasha had paid for their bus fares from Birchwood and a copy of the *Stage*, which he had folded and smilingly left by Laurie's plate. He hadn't leaned across the table and kissed Laurie good-bye in the middle of the crowded café, but the look he had left him with was somehow better yet. It had stayed with him, as warm and real as the lingering soreness inside him.

The Rayne's End Empire was a million miles away, in style and purpose, from the plush little Twilight on the Strand. All he had wanted of that place was a refuge, somewhere to be that wasn't home. What he wanted from the grim redbrick in front of him now was a job. The chill sinking down into the bruised bones of his ribs and face was a friend to him, repressing the jump of his nerves.

He'd thought he had to apply, when he saw an advert in the paper for auditions. Apply, fill in forms, supply full personal details, then wait. The process had been so daunting—and, he now knew, his own motivation so slight—that he'd never got further than putting a red marker ring around the ad. He was still fairly sure that formal application was the protocol, but he couldn't wait.

He tugged up the collar of Sasha's coat, drawing comfort from the scent of him. Then he climbed the concrete side steps that led to the door marked AUDITIONS—just a sheet of A4 in a plastic folder, felt-tip letters starting to blur in the damp—and pushed it open.

Beyond it lay a small office, empty at the moment, though he could hear a buzz of conversation in the next room. Deciding to take his chances as he found them, Laurie did not stop to find whoever was meant to be fielding the candidates as they arrived. He padded silently into the corridor and listened, taking stock.

If Laurie knew nothing else, he knew theatres. The darkness that descended on him as soon as he was well away from the outside world was reassuring to him rather than disorienting. This corridor, with its slow curve, must lead around the auditorium. Good. Offices behind him, so stage to the front. A few steps into the half-light confirmed it. Voices, one patiently reading and the other chiming in for all it was worth. A little closer and Laurie could pick out act, scene, and players. A pair of double doors was ahead of him, their peculiar heaviness familiar to his hand. Accomplished at opening and closing these in perfect silence, Laurie let himself into the auditorium.

Seven young men of about his own age were gathered in the fifth row back from the stage. An eighth was up there, making a mess of Hamlet's first dialogue encounter with poor bewildered Ophelia. The reader, an unlikely maiden in his fifties, was doing his best to prompt as well as provide Ophelia's lines, but it was plainly slow going, and Hamlet was starting to sweat. Laurie raised an eyebrow. The weaknesses of others were not ordinarily pleasing to him, but the moment might be opportune. He went and sat down, very quietly, at the end of the fifth row. The boy in the seat next to him gave him a polite, puzzled glance. *Who are you*? Laurie, who would normally have told him, with full background and apologies, simply flashed him a smile and settled to watch the performance as if he owned the place, actors, furniture, and all.

Bristling, the other boy turned his attention back to the stage, where the director was thanking the would-be Hamlet with a don't-call-us politeness Laurie knew well.

He took his moment. The stage assistant stood up, clipboard in hand, and gestured for the next candidate. "That's me," Laurie said, getting calmly to his feet. Peripherally he saw the young man on the far end of the row turn a startled look on him, but he ignored it. "Laurence Fitzroy, here for Hamlet or anyone else you need."

The director took the board from his assistant and ran his finger down the page. "Well, we're only casting Hamlet this afternoon, son, and…" He paused, frowning. "Furthermore, I don't have your name here. Did you register?"

"No. I can do this play, any part, start to finish without looking. You don't even need to rehearse me. I'm here to save you some time."

That last had possibly been a bit much. The director came to the edge of the stage and raked a repressive gaze over Laurie and the other hopefuls who were now gaping in outrage. "I see how you came by those bruises," he said conversationally. "Sorry, Mr. Fitzroy. There's a process, or you don't step on this stage."

Laurie shrugged. "Okay. I can do it just as well down here."

He picked up from the point of the scene between Hamlet and Ophelia where the other boy had trailed off. For his first few lines, he made no shift of stance or expression, not even taking his hands from his pockets, and he was vaguely aware of the assistant laying her clipboard aside and vaulting down into the pit as if to meet and restrain him bodily from the impromptu performance. Equally calmly, he saw the director's expression slowly change, saw him gesture to the girl to wait.

A few lines in, Laurie paused. The reader, off-kilter, frantically began looking through his copy for Ophelia's response, but Laurie lifted a silencing hand to him. He left it a beat or two, then, once more without movement or gesture, shifted roles. He could not have explained how he did it if his life had depended on it. Rehearsing dialogue in mirrors, he had seen that he still presented his outward masculine self. And yet, as if by an effort to look through shifting veils or water, a girl would be there too—or a woman, or a man three times his age and weight, or whoever else was required.

So Laurie became Ophelia. He folded up the fabric of Hamlet in his mind, found its remembered connections and punched through it to achieve coherent passage between parts. He became, in rapid succession, Polonius, Gertrude, a frazzled combination Rosencrantz-and-Guildenstern. Claudius was easy, the shambling and lecherous old king a simple memory of his father, shining from his flesh like a sickening beam. *How like Hyperion to a fucking satyr…* He continued until he was exhausted, and then he stopped.

The director stood on the edge of the stage, hands on his hips, his frown made terrible and comical at once by the upward-blazing footlights. He waited for a while as if to be sure Laurie was quite finished. Then he said, "I can't decide if you're a genius or a freak. But either way, Mr. Fitzroy, you must apply. Actors need discipline as well as talent."

Laurie nodded. He wholly agreed, and he could see that what he had done wasn't fair to the other boys waiting their chance. "I don't have time," he said. "But thanks anyway."

He got as far as the aisle before the whispering began. The acoustics were good, and theatrical people were rarely capable of holding a discreet argument, even sotto voce. Still he knew his best bet was to keep walking, and his hand was on the door when the assistant, panting from her dash across the auditorium, ducked under his arm to block his exit. "This casting's to replace a dropout," she said. "We open in three nights' time. Can you start straightaway?"

“Yes. I’d have to.” Laurie looked past her shoulder to where the director was studiously trying not to take an interest in the outcome of the conversation. His projection was excellent too, and he didn’t need to raise his voice. “I’d have to be paid in cash, and I’d need the first week in advance.”

The director’s head jerked up. “What?” he boomed. “Do you think we’re running some sort of sweatshop here? National Insurance number and Equity card, or the deal’s off.”

Laurie’s second retreat was as genuine as his first. He knew he was good, but had no experience of his power to turn talent into cash. To make people drop everything to get him. He made his way out of the Rayne’s End Empire, head down, hands in his pockets, because he knew another company in the area needed a Torvald for their *Doll’s House*—a Dora too, and Laurie was prepared to give them either—and after that he had a whole day’s worth of hunting mapped out, circle after numbered circle in the *Stage*. He knew that getting knocked back was part of the business, and that his list of demands would—should, anyway—preclude him from almost everywhere. If all else failed, he had made Sasha promise to help him find a niche in the car-wash trade.

A faint metallic rattle behind him. Halfway down the Empire’s steps, Laurie glanced back. This time the poor assistant was struggling with the heavy exterior doors. On an instinct less of hope than habitual courtesy, Laurie turned around and went to pull one open for her.

“Come back,” she said. “Come in.”

She led him to an office off the reception hall, where a flurried-looking woman in her fifties was sitting down behind a desk, putting on her glasses and reaching for a file. A cash box was open at her elbow. Laurie politely ignored this and sat down on the chair the assistant pointed out to him. “Alison, are you sure about this?” the woman asked. “It’s very irregular.”

“It’s a bloody outrage,” the assistant agreed. “But Mr. Jacobs insists. He’s sent the other boys away.”

The woman raised her eyebrows. “Oh, God. You’d better be good, son. And watch your back on your way home.”

* * *

Laurie shook hands with Alison on the theatre steps. The rain had stopped, and a dull silver sunlight was struggling through the overcast. He had a hundred pounds in cash in his coat’s inner pocket, carefully zipped up. Laurie had been known to go out partying with that much casually shoved into the back pocket of his jeans, in that other world, where money, from its very superabundance, had ceased to matter. Alison said, “That lady who paid you is Mrs. Jacobs. They run the whole concern, and they take everything very personally. This better not be some kind of weird con, Mr. Fitzroy.”

Laurie thought about it. He supposed he could, at a far stretch of imagination, go and trot out his talents at the next venue, squeeze advance wages from them too, and move on. God, it would be easier just to mug someone. He smiled. “No. And call me Laurie, please.”

“Laurie.” Laurie watched her tuck a strand of hair behind her ear and blush. What had he done to bring that on? He had kept his sternest mask in place till now, he supposed, a shield for fear and disappointment. He could feel his own smile melting the ice. “Well,” the girl continued, helplessly smiling back at him. “You have to understand this is temporary. Mr. Jacobs runs everything aboveboard, so…”

“I understand.” It had been a relief to Laurie to be able to hand over his Equity card, his one solid credential. He’d had it for years, although he'd never got as far as using it. The one problem he'd never had till now was paying membership fees. "Just for a couple of weeks, till I get myself turned around. I really appreciate it."

"Okay. We'll see you at rehearsal tomorrow. And…we really do need an address."

"I know." Laurie straightened his shoulders. "I'm going to get one now."

* * *

And Laurie found his first accommodation as easily as his first job, and by much the same technique. It took much less time, which was just as well. The adrenaline wave he had unconsciously been riding since his audition was losing momentum, and whatever Mama Luna had used to ease out the pain from his ribs was wearing off. He stared at the unpromising Victorian terrace for a long time before crossing the road to keep his appointment with the landlord, whose name and number he'd selected more or less at random from a board in the café. There was a small and dingy park, whose bench was apparently some kind of pickup point. Laurie had to fend off two leering hopefuls before he could gather the courage and energy to go on.

After all, what the hell was he doing? He looked around the two-room flat in a daze, responding automatically as the landlord pointed out its dubious assets. Convenient for bus and Tube. At the back of the block, so shielded from road noise. Laurie smiled as an eastbound passenger train shot by with a shriek on the tail of this assertion, followed by a commercial one in the opposite direction. External charms were as good as it got. Otherwise, a grim, unloved little space with peeling fifties wallpaper and nonvintage furniture of the same era, saved from being a studio only by the afterthought bedroom wedged in at the back. The kitchen was a two-ring gas hob, bathroom facilities shared down the hall.

And this was where he proposed to live. If asked, Laurie would have said he did not depend upon the luxurious surroundings in which he had been brought up. His university digs were simple enough and smaller than this.

They were also clean, serviced once a day by college staff, and surrounded by the sounds of bustling student life. This was a real-world dwelling place, where people who worked for a living laid their heads at night. This was the choiceless bare minimum.

No. Staring at a patch of sunlight on threadbare carpet, Laurie drew a breath. He was tired, that was all. A blanket on the steps of the Hungerford Bridge was the bare bloody minimum, and Sasha had survived that. This flat, bleak though it was, met all basic human requirements. It was on the third floor and had a view of wintry trees across the railway line and telephone wires where starlings were gathering in the fading light. He told the landlord he would take it.

The landlord asked for references, two months down and a month's security. Laurie offered two weeks, and such character as could be gleaned from his face and the clothes he stood up in. This time, walking down the stairs after the outraged refusal, Laurie was not at all sure what had brought the landlord running after him. He was clean, he supposed, and not on welfare, and the rent he was prepared to offer was in cash. He handed over all but twenty quid of his advance from the theatre and found himself abandoned on the first-floor landing with a set of keys in his hand.

He made his way slowly back to the top floor and let himself in. Closing the door behind him, he tried to feel some of the exultation he had once supposed would come with finding freedom. He leaned his back on the door. At the moment he was only cold. Well, there was a lethal-looking barred electric fire on the far wall. That could be his first domestic triumph. He straightened up, and a strange metallic thud resounded through the flat, like a fuse-box tripping. Glancing up, Laurie saw that his power, far from being included in the rent as he had naively supposed, depended on the meter screwed over the door. Perhaps the landlord had shoved a pound coin into it for the purpose of his viewing… Well, whatever, it had run out now, the meter's dial flipped to red. He should have asked, shouldn't he? Caveat emptor—lesson one. Laurie felt in his pockets, but all he had left was the twenty-pound note and a handful of silver and coppers.

He went and sank down on the sofa, which creaked beneath him and gave off a sad scent of dust. Laurie put his head into his hands: for this, he had walked out on his baby sister, whose safety he had sworn himself to guard? Had he honestly somehow thought he could bring her here? And that reminded him… He didn't dare call the house, but the staff had their own private phones in their quarters. Perhaps Mrs. Gibson would have cooled off and relented: her number was on speed dial on his mobile.

Which had run out of credit. Laurie stared at its blank little digital screen in disbelief. It didn't really matter, of course, or never had done before—all he had to do was walk out of here, find a shop and top it up with his bank card, which he'd found in the pocket of his jeans that morning. He seldom checked his account. There was always a floating couple of hundred quid in there. Sir William didn't put him through the humiliation of asking for pocket money; his allowance, an unspecified but adequate amount, came in by direct debit.

From the same hands that had beaten him half to death the night before. Laurie fished the card out of his pocket, stared at it blankly for a minute, then snapped it in half. Briefly he considered slitting his wrists with the pieces.

Then he got up and left the flat, locking up carefully behind him.

At a pay phone across the road, he punched in Gibson's number and rested his aching brow on the metal while the line rang and rang. Christ, she *had* gone. And no chance that poor little Hannah would have come back, not after last night's scene. What the fuck had he done? Cutting the line, he punched in Charlie's mobile number and watched in panic as the voice mail ate forty pence of the fifty he'd put into the slot. Was that how much it cost from a landline? He'd never had to count or care. The lessons were coming damn hard and fast now. Scrabbling in the depths of Sasha's coat pocket, he found a twenty-pence piece and shoved that into the phone, mentally adding it to the long tab he now owed him. He struggled to remember the number for Charlie's quarters—he rang the mobile when he wanted a ride, didn't he, never thinking about Charlie's life outside his chauffeur's uniform and duties?—and swallowed dryly in relief when the call was picked up on the second ring. "Charlie? It's…it's me," he began and then felt so strange to himself that he added nervously, "Laurie."

"Oh, thank God. Mrs. G wanted me to start ringing around the hospitals when you didn't come home today."

Laurie repressed a smile. He was ceasing to be surprised at the sources of affection and concern in his life. He decided he would not bother asking if his mother had been worried. "Is she still there, then? Gibson?"

"You know her. Bark's worse than her bite. She's put her notice in, but…" Charlie paused, and Laurie could almost hear him trying to think of a tactful way to put it. "She knows the little girl needs looking after."

"Yes. Yes, she does. Thanks, Charlie."

"So do you, son. Where are you? Do you want to be picked up?"

Laurie closed his eyes. The wind that had sprung up with the sunset slipped its chilly fingers through the kiosk's broken glass, mitigating briefly its stench of urine. Yes, he thought distinctly. Yes, come and get me. Lift off from my shoulders this deadweight of adulthood. I can't survive out here—take me back to my cage. He heard, with weary surprise, his own weary voice declare, "No. I'm okay, thanks. I'm staying with friends for a few days, keep out of his way."

"Not a bad idea. He's away, actually, until the middle of next week, so…" Charlie hesitated, and Laurie listened with a pang of sympathy to the things he was trying not to say. *So you probably won't be missed. So you don't have to worry about Clara until then.* "Are you sure you'll be all right? The old bastard made a mess of you."

"Yeah. Yeah, fine, Charlie." Laurie watched the last few pennies of the last coin count down, felt them draining from him like blood. He didn't want him to hear the beeps, to get cut off midsentence. "Bye," he said softly and hung up.

Somehow night had fallen between the start and the end of the call. Laurie shoved the kiosk door open and half fell out into a street belonging to the city that had been his home all his life—and which felt to him entirely alien and hostile now. He saw that the long terrace facing his, with its array of shabby shops and launderettes, would block out daylight early every night, bring down the night too soon. Blank-faced strangers strode past him. Someone else wanted the pay phone; he felt himself shouldered aside, and he subsided on the low wall that bordered the park, grasping at its iron railings. His mouth was dry, heart thumping. He had the number to Gunari's mobile, his one frail link to Sasha, but that would mean going into a shop with his twenty-pound note and buying something to get change, and just at present this simple plan felt beyond him…

"Laurie?"

Laurie jerked his head up. He felt the odd inner clash in his skull, between wanting something desperately and finding it near to him—within arm's reach, almost, dodging through the crowd Laurie had suddenly found impenetrable. "Sasha," he whispered, mouth too dry to give the word sound. The most beautiful bloody sight in the world, dark eyes seeking him out as if somehow he was too. Laurie dragged up a smile and scrambled to his feet. "What are you doing here?"

"Finished my shift at the wash. It's just around the corner from here." He took Laurie's arm and guided him out of the rush on the pavement, into the park, and onto the bench Laurie now felt he could occupy in safety and contentment forever. "And I knew you were booked to see that flat, so I came this way to see if I'd bump into you. God, Laurie, sit down. You look awful. You didn't get it, then?"

"What?"

"The flat. Look, don't worry. You're welcome with us for as long as you need."

"But I did get it. I…got the flat, and a job. I start at the Rayne's End tomorrow."

Sasha grinned. He leaned forward to examine Laurie's face by the lamplight. "Bloody hell. I'd hate to see what you look like when you've had a *bad* day."

"I know. I'm sorry. It all went fine, and then…I called home, and…" He paused. His head was spinning. Now that he came to think about it, he hadn't stopped to eat since his breakfast at the café, so long ago it didn't even feel like this same day. "And I think I fucked up about the rent. Gave him pretty much everything I had before buying any sodding food. I'm broke, apart from…" He reached into his pocket. "Apart from one last twenty."

Sasha stared at the note he'd produced. His grin broadened, and he shook his head. "You really are new at this, aren't you? I thought you meant *pence piece*. Come on, love. Come with me."

Sasha proceeded to show him that he wasn't broke at all, not by a long shot. He took him into a grocery store—not the chain one, with its brightly lit windows and automatic door, but the Indian corner shop, where dodgy-looking little kids hanging about on their bikes scattered under the force of Sasha's black-eyed warning glance. He steered Laurie gently up and down the aisles, showing him what could be bought cheap and made to last, and where he should invest a bit more in fresh stuff to sustain him. Tinned soups, knocked down to nothing because their labels were ripped or their sides dented in. Bread a day past its sell-by, perfectly good but going into Laurie's bag at a quarter of the price when Sasha and the owner had finished amiable debate in several languages concerning its quality. "Old bread won't hurt you," Sasha informed Laurie, casting his eye over fruit juices and long-life milk. "Old rice will, and don't eat green potatoes." They came back out onto the street with two bulging bags, at which point Sasha handed his unceremoniously to Laurie and told him to go home and wait. "I'll be there in five minutes."

It was less. Laurie had not even had time to find pound coins among his change and the flat was still sunk in cold darkness when the soft tap came at the door. Ashamed, shivering, desperate to see that the act of faith he'd performed in the street by letting Sasha out of his sight had been justified, Laurie pulled open the door and hauled him in.

"Easy," Sasha protested, laughing. He let Laurie capture his mouth for one unsteady, cold-lipped kiss, then pushed him back. "Mind my takeaway."

"What? Didn't we just do economic shopping for the sensible young bachelor?"

"*You* did. I bought this big pile of burgers and chips to reward us. Anyway"—Sasha glanced around the shadowed rooms—"looks like cooking might be an issue. Is the power off?"

"No, but it's coin-op, a meter. I just need to find a few quid."

"Hang on a second." Sasha deposited the aromatic takeaway bags on the table and hooked out a chair from beneath it. He scrambled up onto it, ignoring its wobble, though Laurie seized the back of it in a steadying grasp. "Good. It's an old meter. Hand me a pound coin and a bit of paper. The receipt from the grocer's will do."

Laurie obeyed and watched in fascination as Sasha folded up the paper, tucked the coin into it, and eased it a little way inside the meter's slot. "What are you doing?"

"Magic coin. Old gypsy trick." Balanced on the chair, he flashed Laurie a wicked grin. "This'll stop the dial from tripping back to empty."

"Sash, no. That's—"

"What? Cheating? Did he tell you electricity was extra?"

"No, but—"

"Well, he should have." Sasha gave the meter a calculated thump and stepped lithely down from the chair at the same time as the lights came on. He surveyed the bare living space revealed by the unshaded bulb overhead. "*Latcho*, Laurie!" he exclaimed, eyebrows rising. "This place isn't bad!"

"Isn't it?" Laurie asked weakly. To him, the yellow electrical brilliance was harsher than daylight, bringing unseen stains blossoming out of the carpet and walls. Then rain rattled on the dark window, and he tried to see his surroundings through Sasha's eyes. Roof and walls. Warmth at the touch of a switch. Sheltered, all his own… "No. I suppose it is okay, isn't it?"

"Better than." Sasha put out a hand, brushed it down the side of Laurie's face, barely touching. Mindful of his bruises. "You did really well to get it, you know. And the job. You did brilliantly."

Laurie turned away. He went over to the sink. He supposed that in the cupboard beneath it there might be some plates and glasses, and, if not, at least crouching down here gave him temporary cover for his sudden and complete loss of control. He opened one cupboard door at random and knelt clutching its handle, muscles in his arms and shoulders locking tight with the effort to suppress his sobs. *God almighty, why now*? The food would be getting cold. His throat clenched. Hot tears half blinded him. Yes, there were plates in there. He reached for one, and it slipped out of his grasp, hit the tiles, and cracked in two along its dirty hairline fracture.

"Oh, Laurie." Warm hands on him, detaching his death grip on the cupboard door. Laurie closed his eyes as Sasha crouched beside him—made a despairing effort to lurch away, cracked his brow on the edge of the sink, and fell into the waiting embrace, the comprehensive catch that closed around him tight. "Oh, my Laurie. You'll be okay, ves'tacha. Everything will be all right."

* * *

The burgers and chips were good, even served almost cold. Laurie, half mortified, half laughing at his own collapse—his recovery and ravenous hunger in the wake of it—piled everything up on the one remaining plate and took it to the fireside, where Sasha was waiting for him, smiling.

"You all right now?"

Laurie sniffed and pulled his sleeve across his eyes. "Never better." He put the plate down on the bit of carpet that served for a rug and held his hands out to the fire, which although it smelled of dog hair while heating up, threw a good amount of warmth into the room. And Sash was right; it felt a hell of a lot better, knowing he wasn't paying for it. "I'm sorry."

"What for?"

"Falling apart at the first tap. Thought I was stronger."

"Oh, you're strong." Sasha pushed the plate toward him. "You need to eat, though. You think I haven't curled up and cried some nights?"

"I don't know." Laurie grabbed a handful of chips and watched Sasha thoughtfully while he demolished them. "You know, I really *don't* know. We've spent so much time together, and I've never given you a chance to talk."

"Well, we've been…busy."

Sasha's eyes glimmered, and Laurie, despite his exhaustion, felt a sudden wild desire to be busy again, right there on the rug. He pushed it back. "Stop it. I want to hear—all about your life, how you've survived. Tell me."

"I already have." Sasha reached for the carton of fruit juice they were sharing and, to Laurie's surprise, knocked it over—the first clumsy gesture Laurie had seen him make. He looked uncomfortable for the first time. "Container truck, yogurts, Hungerford Bridge. You."

Laurie reached for the napkins that had come with the burgers and helped him mop up. "Come on, Sash," he said gently. "More to it than that. I know about your parents, but… Well, who else came over with you, or…or tried? Do you have brothers and sisters? Did—"

"Laurie." Sasha's hand descended on his. It still had an outdoor chill in its palm, a tang of chemical damp from the car wash. "No," he said. "That is, no to the brothers and sisters. And as for the people who came with me—my friends, or if I *did* have family who stowed away with me… Think what you're asking me."

Laurie drew a breath. His head was full of his own day. He knew, to his shame, that his effusion of curiosity about Sasha's origins had been just that—an outburst, brought on by the relief of finding safety, food, and shelter. He shivered. All of that was meaningless, wasn't it, unless he had Sash by his side? He played back his question, imagining a cold morning on the Dover docks, border patrol agents opening a refrigerated van onto a scene of the living and the dead. "I'm sorry," he said. "I didn't mean to…"

"Shut up," Sasha said, smiling. The flicker of—what? anger? dismay?—had died from his face, and he was busy unwrapping another burger, handing it to Laurie.

Laurie thought he understood. They would have time, he thought. Time in the future, when he had built a safe world for them. Sasha would tell it all then. He reached forward and kissed him, making Sasha groan in mock disgust and swipe with a serviette at the ketchup on his mouth. Sasha asked him what role he'd landed, and Laurie, who for all he loved him and was growing up in huge unsettling shocks, was first and foremost an actor, with ego and benign self-obsession to match, beamed in pride—here with Sasha, in the warmth, he could take in his achievement for the first time—fell for the evasion, and began to tell the story of his day.

* * *

They lay together in the single bed, entwined. They had begun the actions of loving, and Laurie had so very nearly fallen asleep in the middle of it that Sasha had commanded a postponement, laughing, drawing the exhausted body close to his. Once Laurie had got over the embarrassment of that, he had settled in Sasha's embrace with an almost overwhelming relief. The bed—ungenerous even for a single—threatened to pitch him out with every move, but what he wanted was to remain…to stay very still. From where he lay, he could view his new world across the arm Sasha had wrapped around his chest, a slender, lean-muscled horizon that rose and lightly fell with his breathing.

He could bear it, from here. The floodlights that lined the railway track cast a pale luminescence into the room, filigreed by the bare tree branches outside his window. The rumbling from the lines was almost constant, but apart from the punctuating Doppler shrieks of the express, it was a sound he could get used to, more akin to music than machinery. Sometimes the overhead cables flashed, picking out each fine hair on Sasha's arm, bleaching his skin for an instant to diamond white. Yes, he could bear it. "Sasha," he murmured. "Move in with me."

He thought for a few seconds that Sasha had fallen asleep, although the rhythm of his breathing was shallow, still alert. Then he stirred and lifted his head to look at Laurie, dark eyes uneasy. "What?"

"Move in. Live with me."

"Jesus, Laurie. Wait till I'm half-asleep, then…"

"Sorry. Did I stealth bomb you? I mean it, though, Sash. It'll solve…oh, it'll solve all sorts of problems, won't it? For you as well as me." Laurie heard the scrape of urgency in his own voice and tried to back down. "I…I know I just got here."

"Yeah, you did. Though"—Sasha paused, and Laurie wriggled around so he could see the smile he had heard breaking in Sasha's voice—"though I like the nerve of the man who'd try to sublet his sublet on the first night."

"I wouldn't be. Not technically. I…I wouldn't want rent off you. I've got a job. You could just—"

"I have a job too."

The smile was fading. Laurie, who for one instant thought he had put his hand to this fruit he so badly wanted and pulled it straight down off the tree, felt a pang of dismay. "I know," he said. "But I'm gonna be earning more, for a while. And it isn't about that anyway. I owe you everything. Please stay with me."

"Laurie, wait. You want to find a safe place for your sister, don't you?"

Laurie swallowed. He ran his fingers through Sasha's hair, its luxuriant warmth a contrast with the cheap nylon sheet they were lying on, the chill of damp in the air. "Yes, but this isn't it," he whispered. "I don't know how I thought I could ever do that anyway."

"You couldn't—not with an illegal living here."

"That's just what I don't understand." A voice inside Laurie's head told him to shut up, but fear was at work in him—and the hopeless desire to make one thing fixed and certain in his shifting world. "There was nothing legal in anything I did today, and look how far I got. And you're smarter than I am. I…I still don't understand why you don't ask for asylum."

"I told you. Things aren't that simple for me."

"What things?"

"I'll tell you one day. You…you took my word for this before."

"I know, but—"

"Laurie." It was soft and flat. Sasha's hand spread out on Laurie's chest. His eyes had filled with pained shadows. He said, very quietly, "Don't push."

The air left Laurie's lungs. He held himself carefully still. He could not speak: his shame was acute, and cold shock was rippling through him. To incur even this much reproach from Sasha was terrible to him, worse because he knew he'd deserved it. His eyes stung, and he quickly closed them to hide the reaction. In the burning dark, he heard Sasha whisper his name, voice rough with remorse. He heard Sasha's hoarse apology and wished he could speak to tell him there was no need for it. He *had* been pushing, unable to accept the miracle of Sasha here in his bed with him.

A warm, anxious mouth brushed his. "*Laurie*. I wish I could tell you every fucked-up thing that had happened in my life. But I can't. Some of it hurts too much, and the rest..."

Laurie opened his eyes. He was wide-awake now. He shook his head, denying to Sash the necessity. Laurie seized him as he leaned to kiss him again, and they went at one another fiercely, hard enough to drive off this new demon. It was just the frantic shove of cock to cock—echo of their first encounter, in a bed as strange to Sasha as this one now was to Laurie—but the fire leaped high, running hotter for their moment's discord.

The bed began to creak rhythmically beneath them, forcing both to brief laughter. Sasha shoved the one thin pillow behind the headboard to prevent it from slamming. He twisted back down into the bed and rolled under, dragging Laurie on top. Laurie felt the intoxicating lift of Sasha's thighs, embracing his hips and then his waist, and suddenly understood how they could fuck like this. But that was for another time, if God sent them one, and from now on he was making no assumptions. Sasha was emitting choked cries, writhing up against him. He clasped at Laurie's backside, pulling him into place. Laurie thought they would come over straightaway, but on new instinct both of them held off, gasping and struggling, clinging to the safe side of climax, where thought was impossible and the world a dream.

* * *

Laurie began life in this real world. On the first morning, he had barely taken his jacket off in the spotlit dark of the Empire before Mr. Jacobs appeared at his side, expression anxious. "Well?" he said to Laurie, trailing him down the aisle. "Mrs. J nearly had me convinced last night that I'd hired a fluke who just happened to have learned a few good lines. And, incidentally, rejected half of northwest London's real young acting talent."

Laurie came to a halt. He loved the smell of velvet and dust that filled old playhouses like this. He thought of all the time he had spent, breathing this natural atmosphere, the only one that really fed him, hiding in the shadows. He wondered at the transfiguring force of necessity. He turned to Mr. Jacobs, one eyebrow on the rise, not at all minding his qualms. "Is that what you think?" he said.

"Well, you did get a tiny bit of warning yesterday of where to shine in." Jacobs shrugged half-apologetically. "But suppose I were to say to you now—oh, I don't know—the ghost scene, for example, or—"

"The ghost scene." Laurie smiled. Already he could feel the chill in the air, the shiver in the roots of his hair as Elsinore's bleak halls prepared to unveil their secret. He put out a courteous hand, gesturing to Jacobs to sit down, then dodged through the orchestra pit and vaulted up onto the stage. Mr. Barnes, retired accountant, was leaning on a crate in the wings, drinking his coffee and having a glance at the *Guardian*. Laurie seized him gently by both shoulders. He was meant to be Claudius, but Horatio's lines at this point were short and memorable, and Laurie was willing to bet he'd have a go. He swung the man out onto the stage, coffee mug and all. "Angels and ministers of grace defend us!" he cried, pointing to an empty space in the air with such utter conviction that Barnes gave a genuine shudder. Laurie skipped and abridged through to the end of Hamlet's horrified observations on the ghost—reduced Shakespeare again—and delivered Barnes his prompt line, clutching him in terror, as if both their lives depended on it. "It beckons you to go away with it," Barnes gasped, pointing too, knees buckling a little, "as if it some impartment did desire to you alone!" He stopped and looked at Laurie, plainly pleased with himself. "I didn't know I knew that."

"You probably know it all," Laurie told him, grinning. "It's just a case of being passionate—or scared—enough to get it out." He glanced around to Jacobs and saw that half a dozen actors and a lady with a mop had also arrived to stare in apprehension at the apparition he'd called up. Jacobs gave him a small bow, which he briefly returned. If they had been soldiers, Laurie thought, they would have exchanged a salute, one to another. He released Mr. Barnes and stood quietly. "What would you like me to do?"

Jacobs set him to work for the next three days with those whose personalities did not unfathomably hive off into separate Shakespearean entities upon demand. Laurie knew how it felt, to be frozen with terror in the wings, and, aware that his own gift for learning dialogue was almost preternatural, was willing to pass long hours on the prompter's stool, showing his talented but high-strung little Ophelia how best to string concept to concept, line to line, to get herself through her scenes. Even such nobles as Gertrude and Claudius—hairdressers and solicitors by day—were not too proud to drop by for these lessons, and Mr. Jacobs watched in wonder as his hard-worked troupe began to give him back so nearly accurate a version of *Hamlet* as to make him believe they might actually be ready for their opening night.

Each night Laurie made his way back to the flat. He walked. Bus fares across even that distance were expensive, and he was spinning out the remains of his advance. Sasha had been right. Twenty pounds was not broke at all, and something in the action of walking home began to reconcile him to the street, the approach to it through the maze of others just like it a route that could only be learned by experience. Now he was part of the crowd that forged up and down its pavements. Each night he told himself that he was not expecting Sasha to appear, and this became his talisman, a silent mantra. If he did not expect, he could not be disappointed, and his solitude would not get the chance to consume him. He wouldn't expect. He wouldn't push.

On the first night, the faint, hesitant tap at the door came after he'd been home for half an hour, diligently warming the place up and cooking himself a sensible meal from a recipe suggested on the rice pack. Sasha stood outside, a rucksack over his shoulder, which turned out to contain more groceries, as well as the dried herbs from which Mama Luna made her poultice. Laurie tried to pay but was only too happy to accept Sasha's suggestion that they share whatever he was cooking up instead. There was certainly plenty. Laurie tried to tell himself that the excess was only down to his incompetence, not a hopeful doubling up of ingredients. Sasha stayed till late that night but, just after eleven, broke from their heated tangle on the sofa and excused himself to catch his last bus with a fierce restraint that Laurie did not dare question.

Did not want to question, he told himself. Sasha was a free agent. He had never promised Laurie anything. And Laurie—or at least he told himself so, settling alone into the chilly single bed—had never expected Sasha to make himself responsible for him. Sasha had urged him to leave home, but the decision to do so—or at any rate, not to return—had been Laurie's alone.

They had never talked about what they were to one another. Laurie had never even thought about it, till loneliness and fear had begun to make him yearn to have some tangible thing to call his own—a boyfriend, a lover, whatever labels the world might choose. He could see the world's need for them now, and he was ashamed. On the second night, he made even less of an assumption and did not start cooking at all. He was fine, tired enough to sprawl on the sofa and not mind one way or the other if he did so all night alone. He was doing well, he thought, and that illusion lasted him until the soft rap at the door brought him off the sofa and upright in one barely voluntary pounce, convinced it was almost midnight, dismayed to see that only one bloody hour had passed since he had sat down.

This time Sasha had clothes in the rucksack—T-shirts, underwear, and the cashmere sweater Laurie had given him. Being asked to accept this disturbed Laurie's composure; it had been a gift. But he could see the sense. He had been getting by in the shirt and jeans he'd left home in, washing out his boxers and leaving them to dry by the fire each night. Sasha, reading his face, kissed him and told him the sweater was only a loan—he'd never owned anything so lovely in his life and damn well wanted it back—and Laurie's ice melted in a rush that knocked them both to the mildewed carpet.

But outside of passion, he would not push. Over breakfast that morning, he offered Sasha one of the free tickets he'd been given for that night's opening performance. Sasha went pale and told him hesitantly that large crowds in enclosed places scared him. Laurie only nodded. They were elbow to elbow at the little kitchen table. Sasha said, "Laurie, if ever I…needed to go away, if I wasn't here…you'd be okay, wouldn't you?"

Laurie swallowed. He looked around the room. Sasha had brought a potted plant along with his supplies the day before. It sat on the kitchen windowsill, a green splash in the gray morning light. He didn't know if it was just habituation, but the place didn't seem so sordid to him anymore. It had begun, in some plangent, sharp-edged way he had never known before, to look like home. "It wouldn't be for long," Sasha said, "and I'd come back to you, I promise. Can you trust me?"

"Yes," Laurie whispered. He locked his hands together under the table, where Sasha would not see. He wouldn't even ask a question. "Yes."

* * *

The opening night of *Hamlet* brought a fair crowd to the Empire. Jacobs had a reputation for getting a good show out of his semi-amateur troupe, and the area was in that state of gentrification which could bring large numbers conscientiously away from their TV sets on a cold night for a new show.

Padding about in the wings, automatically helping out with props and backgrounds despite Mr. Jacobs's efforts to make him behave a bit more like his lead actor, Laurie watched them gather. They were not like the languid little groups that used to accumulate in the Twilight, all cocktail frocks and tuxedos, on their way to late suppers at the Ivy. *Earnest* was the best word Laurie could think of to describe the crowd filtering through to their seats now. Middle-class, well-intentioned, determined to support community drama. Dressed much as they would be for the office, and most of them probably came straight from there. A lot of them had kids in tow, something Laurie seldom saw in the West End, for Shakespeare at least.

He saw his fellow cast members watching their arrival too, and noted pale faces and nervous sweats with compassion. For himself, he wasn't bothered. He had a kingdom in the balance. His mother had barely waited till his father's corpse was cold in its grave before taking up with that noble creature's shuffling toad of a brother, something that struck him as bordering on incest. He was filled with unease and disgust and wonder at the strangeness of the world.

Mr. Jacobs, watching his makeup artist begin work on Laurie, had stopped her after the first few dabs of greasepaint. Whoever he had hired on the off chance four days ago, the man sitting in the chair surrounded by glaring bulbs and mirrors now was, apparently, the young prince of Denmark, and to paint him would be the gilding of the strangest lily Jacobs had ever seen. As for the bruising—well, the director had always found Hamlet a sufficiently annoying young man that he might well have got in a ruck with the other Wittenberg students before returning to

Elsinore. Budget restraints kept costume to a minimum too, and so when Hamlet took the stage with Claudius and Gertrude for his first scene, he was simply Laurie in black shirt and jeans, nobility suggested by a thin gold coronet that was one of the Empire's few authentic and valuable props. But Laurie was gone. Hamlet walked quietly to the stone bench, sat down, and delivered his first line, and the audience, still a little restive with arrivals, coats, and cough drops, fell silent.

Only for one instant did he return to his flesh. He had given his spare tickets to Ophelia, and her proud parents were beaming at her from the second row. Laurie understood Sasha could not have sat there, damp from the car wash, all on his own amid the doctors and social workers. What he had not predicted was that he would look up and see him standing in the back, at the auditorium's farthest reach, leaning on a pillar and smiling. Hamlet muffed his line—just one, and a kind of sympathetic exhalation left the crowd's collective lungs, a relief that this eerily good unknown was human after all, just a boy, not the reincarnation of a prince they had been brought up to believe was fictional. Laurie smiled back at Sasha—one bright flash—and picked up the beat.

* * *

He searched for Sasha after the show. Throwing a jacket on over his shirt, he ran down the back steps into the car park, then up again to see if he was in the foyer or caught in the crowd on the main steps. He saw occasional faces flash surprised recognition at him—felt his sleeve caught, kindly words he could hardly remember deserving following him in the air. "It's him, Mum. Look, it's Hamlet." He paused to throw a smile back at a little girl whose resemblance to Clara placed a new knife in his heart, but he did not stop. Only when the theatre and its surrounding streets were almost empty did he come to a ragged, breathless halt by the box office, wrapping his arms over his chest.

Soft footsteps approached him from behind, and he whipped around. But it was only the director's assistant, Alison, her sweet face creased in a puzzled smile. "Laurie! What are you doing out here?"

"Nothing. Er…looking for someone. Why?"

"Because he wants to see you. They all do."

"Who?" Laurie asked stupidly. His mind tried to twist the universe into the shape where Sasha had somehow made his way backstage to find him. Sent the cast and crew out to look…

"Mr. Jacobs," Alison said. "He's bouncing off the walls. You'd better come on."

"Oh, dear."

"What?" She glanced up at him, then shook her head and smiled. "Oh, no. Not like that. He's wildly excited." She took his arm and began to lead him off across the foyer. "Laurie, don't you know how *good* you are?"

* * *

Many people that night told him the same thing. Laurie heard them with a distant pleasure. After all, this was what he had wanted all his life, and he wasn't immune to admiration. But the means by which he had come to this place were dreamlike to him tonight, and dreamlike the men and women who clustered about him backstage. Mr. Jacobs, flushed and drunk on half a glass of sherry, kept seizing his hand and pumping it up and down as if they had just met, and Ophelia, damp flowers still wilting in her hair, clung to his arm, attracting thunderous looks from Alison, which Laurie for a long time could not understand, then could not bring himself to care about when he did. The idea of himself as attractive to anyone but Sasha was dreamlike to him too, and irrelevant.

The heat and the chatter seemed to pitch around him. Walking away from the questions of a young man whom Mr. Jacobs informed him later—with some asperity—had been a reviewer, Laurie slipped down to the dressing rooms and got changed into his street clothes. The production didn't run to a dresser. He hung up his own costume carefully, ready for the next performance, and went out into the night.

Not to expect, not to hope. These had been his mantras. All the way home through the chilly streets, Laurie repeated them to himself. The long terrace by the railway lines was almost empty, only the occasional late bus and taxi disturbing streetlamp flowers forming in the freezing mist. His building's communal hallway was empty, silent for once of TV chatter. The stairs and the landings, the doorway to his own flat, all empty. The flat itself, a patchwork of shadows. Not one of Laurie's careful denials this time served to bring soft footsteps padding up the stairs, to make the sullen chipboard door vibrate under a cautious, flat-palmed tap. Curled up on the sofa, Laurie methodically strangled hope, and Sasha did not come.

Not on the next day or the next. No skinny figure threading a way through the crowds or smiling at him from beside a pillar in the standing-room-only section. As long as Laurie was Hamlet, his absence hardly mattered—served, in fact, to improve his performance, making it imperative for him to slip into another skin—and he barely noticed that the empty rows that had remained on his first night gradually filled, until on the Friday, just before curtain, Mrs. Jacobs startled all of them by dashing through from the box office hissing, "Full house! Full house!" It was a first for the company, and the curtain came down on tides of applause Laurie heard with the same detached enjoyment he'd have felt for the sound of the sea.

It was Hamlet's last night, and Mr. Jacobs found him in the dressing room and saw with wonder how the dashing, tragic prince became a tired-looking boy with the removal of the coronet. He watched in approval while Laurie boxed the precious prop and shook out his costume before hanging it up. He said, "I hope the flash didn't bother you."

Laurie looked at him inquiringly. Jacobs might as well have said *I hope the roof falling in didn't bother you.* "That reviewer you gave the brush-off to the other night was here again. I let him take a couple from the wings."

"Oh."

"Just *oh*? Most of my young men at this point go becomingly pale and turn into Laurence Olivier."

Laurie smiled, trying to picture it. "No," he said, sitting down to tie up his shoes. "I'm glad he came, though. I…I'm pleased it all went well."

Jacobs sighed and came to sit on the edge of the dressing table. "It did," he said. "Very well. Is this your only job, son?"

Laurie nodded, and Jacobs went on. "You'll need another one, you know. Something with flexible hours that's not too draining. Some of my young actors with stupid degrees put in hours at the adult literacy college in Shawcross. You could try there."

"I don't have a degree, sir." Laurie shrugged, a small, tired movement. "Not even a stupid one."

"Well, you can read. Try it. It beats flipping burgers." Jacobs watched him thoughtfully, riffling the pages of his prompt copy. "Listen, Laurie. You need to pay council tax. You need to give me your National Insurance number so that I can take a chunk of the pittance I pay you and hand it to faceless government drones to make warheads. So that, when I start rehearsing our Christmas performance of *The White Devil* next week, I don't have to jump every time the door bangs."

Laurie gave a faint snort of laughter. "Webster? Very festive."

"Well, you can wear some holly in your doublet."

"Oh. You want me to come back?"

"Very much. But I'll tell you truthfully, son, I think you should look around. Get the *Stage* tomorrow and see what else is rehearsing. You forced your way in here unqualified. Imagine what you could do with an actual theatrical review behind you."

"No. No, I love Webster. I'd rather come back here."

"Well, good. But mind what I say about the tax man."

Laurie shrugged. It was plain to him by now that no great seeking hand from his old life—his old home—was going to reach out to find him. This was, of course, a huge relief—and part of him was desolate. He reached for a pen and scribbled his NI number and new address on the back of a flyer. "There you are, sir."

"Laurie, where are you from? Don't call me sir. It makes me feel like a Victorian papa. I don't suppose you'll be joining us for the last-night party, will you?"

No hopes, no expectations. But I have to go home. "No. I'm sorry."

"And no chance I can tell poor Alison you'll join her for whatever raucous jaunt around the nightclubs she's got planned for afterward?"

Laurie smiled. He met Jacobs's eyes ruefully for an instant. "Sorry, sir. No chance at all."

"Didn't think so. Well, sweet prince, I hope you get yourself sorted. Meanwhile, go out by the box office. Mrs. J has a week's wages for you, and the take was so big tonight I'm splitting profits up between the lot of you, ten percent extra for Elsinore royalty. Okay? Hope I see you on Monday."

* * *

It wouldn't be for long. And I'd come back to you, I promise. Can you trust me? If I had to go away.

On the bus out to the heath, Laurie asked himself why it was a matter of trust. Because it was; in the cold, lonely gap between his last sight of Sasha and now, Laurie had felt faith falter. It occurred to him that he had never had a friend, not one he cared about enough to exercise the gift of letting them alone when need be. He had always been able to take people or leave them, accept them as they were, with nothing but mild, detached interest in their myths and their masks.

But what the hell were Sasha's? This refugee who wouldn't seek refuge, a boy who had known his mother well enough and long enough to be perfectly, idiosyncratically bilingual and yet who would not or could not talk about her beyond the barest facts of her existence. He told himself that he had never doubted Sasha, and a hot rush of anger went through him that he even need do that much.

God, no. All Laurie's incertitude, his lack of faith, should be reserved for himself. What right had he ever had to approach Sasha, disturb the dignity of his survival with his easy handouts? Something in Sasha must have despised him for it, sweeping through the underworld and picking out what he fancied, like Madonna choosing African babies. Sasha had never shown him contempt by a word or a look, but he must have felt it. Laurie felt it. Even now, what was he? A fraud, playing at poverty, while not five miles away, his father's house glimmered like a ship of diamonds in the night.

The people of the encampment knew him for what he was, at any rate. Sasha had been his passport, his key to the city there. Without him, he was nothing but an intruder. Mama Luna was nowhere to be seen, and Gunari only grunted negatives to his hesitant questions. Gunari lumbered after him like a bear all the way through the camp to Sasha's caravan and leaned in the doorway, face a hostile blank, while Laurie looked hopelessly around the cramped living space. For what? A note, a sign like the ones he had read of in childhood, made of leaves and stones? *Patrin*, Sasha had told him those were called. Not a myth at all, but rather a sophisticated messaging system still in use today. Even if he had, Laurie could not have read it. In every way that counted, he was utterly ignorant. They came from different worlds. Sasha's visits to his had been short-lived miracles.

Laurie missed the last bus home and walked back to East Hill, a trip that took him half the night and left him so footsore and exhausted that the other half was not a trouble to him; he fell facedown onto the sofa and slept still wrapped in Sasha's jacket, the lingering scent of Sasha's skin and the greasepaint on Laurie's own combining to send him lurid dreams, where he and Sasha met as lovers in a lost Shakespearean play, ran like deer through the Forest of Arden with ruthless hunters on their heels—leaped, despairing, hand in hand off the Hungerford Bridge. He woke with the taste of the river in his mouth, and Sasha was still gone.

On Sunday morning, he walked down to the Tube station. He had to collect some of his clothes. He had to see Clara. Telling himself that these were his sole reasons, he got onto a train bound for the city.

Chapter Ten

A fine snowfall was beginning in the Mayfair streets. Falling on last night's frost, it was causing London's heart to go into its usual palpitations. Already a taxi had skidded into the back of a bus, and a truck was slewed at forty-five degrees across Chesterfield Hill. No one was hurt. There were just a lot of muted British expostulations, and only the cabbies were rude enough to sound their horns in the ensuing jams. Laurie walked through the chaos, barely seeing. He felt like his own ghost. He could hardly claim, after two weeks away, to have gained a new perspective on this world, but still it struck him deeply—the sameness, the infinite difference. The crowds on the pavement: much the same mix of faces and races, most of them subtly transformed, lit up, padded out, made sleek by good diet, by the leisure to be out here in the daylight engaged in their Christmas shopping. This had been Laurie's world twelve months ago.

He remembered that his biggest concern then had been Clara's desire for a kitten, and his own half-child, half-adult plots to ransom one of the pedigreed darlings from its cage in Harrods' pet store and plan out a life for it on the Mayfair upper floor, where it would never run afoul of Sir William's temper or his mother's allergies. The least of his problems had been affording it. His pocket money would have covered the whole litter. Now he was, he supposed, an independent man. He had a job and a lover and little else—although both job and lover felt so tenuous to him on the back of lonely nights and increasing forgetfulness about food that he could scarcely believe in even them.

The crowds that had once excited and scared him by their rich density were now simply obstacles. Once he had drifted in them, let them carry him along, but more often than not, as he struggled up the pavements today, the occasional knock or shouldering contact felt to him hostile, ready and willing to hurt. The same buzz of commerce was going on—but here, Laurie saw for the first time, the shopkeepers plied their trade from caskets of jewels, magical caverns that bore little semblance to East Hill's dingy grocery stores and charity shops. He found himself pausing outside windows he had sailed past, oblivious, all his life, putting a hand to their frames to steady himself and try to breathe. Every commodity he'd just begun to learn to fight for was spread out in wild abundance. Lights blazed. Food halls touted free samples of their delicacies on trestles outside the shops. Wide-flung welcoming doors spewed thousands of pounds' worth of heat every second into the street.

No one from Sasha's world was to be seen. In a way, Laurie couldn't understand it. Starving men and women should overwhelm this place, surely—sweep the trestles clear of fresh-baked marzipan slices, fill rucksacks and plastic bags. Stand beneath the hot-air ducts in blessed relief from the cold. He saw a woman take one bite from a mince pie, make a face of amused disgust, and drop the rest into the gutter.

His head spun. No, the underworld people could not come here. After one week away, Laurie could barely come here himself. No police were needed to man the barricades. No chance of revolution in London today. No tiny upper class to tear down—instead, a huge majority of middle-class souls, some good, some bad, most here spending hard-earned money, some living on the wages of sin. All of them with just enough to have forgotten or to be unable to imagine how it felt to have nothing at all.

Charity workers shook tins and were not ignored. That kind of giving came easy enough, Laurie knew. Palatable. At a remove. But someone like Gyorgy, with his stolen shopping trolley full of rags, could not push his way up these pavements and into this world's golden heart. Probably no one would stop him. But empty belly, unwashed skin quailed and grew faint in the face of it. After a few weeks, you would not even try.

He turned off Avery Row and into the quiet residential streets that led to his own. Once out of the crowd, he thought he'd be able to catch his breath, but the sense of mild suffocation stayed with him, as well as a headache and a needling pain in his stomach. He tried to think when he had last eaten. He still had his array of economical and nourishing foodstuffs in the flat, had even replenished them yesterday in Sasha's recommended grocery store, where Sasha's friendly shopkeeper had cut him a deal on his apples. What had been missing was the prompt of appetite. Without it, the boxes and bags were just abstracts. He had put them neatly away and forgotten them. He wasn't hungry now, though he knew he should have been.

Sasha had said, "*I'll come back to you. Can you trust me*?" And Laurie had tried. But Sasha had come to him from nowhere, and the nowhere that had swallowed him allowed Laurie no handholds, not even the possibility of imagining where he had gone.

The grand facade of Sir William's mansion rose up before him. Laurie had to stop for a minute, cold sweat crawling in his armpits. He clutched at the wrought-iron railings until the wash of vertigo passed. He could, he knew, find the key beneath the garage door and slip into the house through his old escape route. He could perhaps never encounter any of the denizens of this world, who had become like cardboard cutouts in his head: his father's misshapen and bearlike, his mother's made of tissue and like a doll's. Clara's…

No. Hers was real, three-dimensional. Flesh lit from within by unmarred spirit. He had to see her. He owed her. And he would walk through the front door of his own house.

To his surprise, it was open. Just a crack, as if company was expected, and beyond it, through the tinted glass of the porch, he could see signs of activity, human figures passing back and forth.

Perhaps his mother was having one of her interminable pre-Christmas sherry parties. Laurie found himself oddly thrown—not at the thought of all those tipsy Mayfair ladies, although that had been bad enough, determined as they always seemed to be to molest him as he tried to hand around the bloody sherry, diamond-loaded fingers ruffling his hair, playfully patting his backside. "*Oh, Marielle! Isn't he handsome? Isn't he getting big*?"

Laurie repressed a snort of laughter and looked at the unlatched door. Somehow, if it was open to him, he could not just walk in. Puzzled at himself, he rang the bell.

Mrs. Gibson appeared almost immediately, her portly frame coalescing at an uncharacteristic trot through the glass. Laurie smiled in relief. Charlie had been right; she wouldn't go. She pulled the porch door wide, then came to a halt at the sight of him. She said hoarsely, "Master Laurie. She isn't with you, is she? Oh, God. She isn't with you..."

Laurie pushed the main door open and stepped into the porch. He caught Gibson's elbow and guided her collapse onto the marble bench. He crouched before her and, when she broke into ragged sobs, put out his arms and held her as she had so often held him. "Gibson. Gibson, who isn't? What's the matter?" Fear beginning a slow slide through him, Laurie patted her shoulders and head, seeing with indefinable disturbance that her gray-streaked hair, normally impeccably brushed back into its bun, was tousled and escaping in strands. "Who isn't with me?"

"Clara. It's Clara. She's missing."

Laurie sat back on his heels. Gibson, after a moment, raised her swollen eyes to him. She looked terrible, as if she had been crying for days. He dug in his pocket and found a tissue from the Empire's makeup table, slightly smeared but usable. "Here," he said, handing it to her. Her words were clear enough, he supposed, but they wouldn't seem to go in. "What do you mean?"

"We tried to get in touch with you, but your mobile was off." Shakily Gibson blew her nose. "Oh, Laurie. She was upset when you left. We thought maybe…we thought maybe she'd gone to you, or you'd come and got her. That was our last hope."

Last hope. Laurie frowned. At the same time, he could feel an incredulous smile trying to start. Poor Gibson. She did love them, didn't she? Him and Clara both. All this, because the little bugger had taken a huff and hidden herself somewhere. It wouldn't be the first time. And she couldn't half hold out. It had been hours when she'd last disappeared, the whole house in an uproar. Well, it was tough. Time was up. Laurie knew all her hiding places: attics, wardrobes, even a disused bathroom where the side panel of the bath came off, a frequent lair. He pressed a kiss to Mrs. Gibson's wet cheek. "It's okay," he said, getting to his feet. "She'll just be upstairs somewhere. I'll flush her out."

He was halfway up the first flight of stairs when her voice tugged him back. In his run across the hallway—ten long strides across the black-and-white marble from porch to polished-oak newel post, time enough to reflect that this house was not just a different world but a separate fucking universe from the East Hill flat—he had seen strange things, but not taken them in. Faces he did not know. And he had heard—weirdly, it brought to mind the opening scenes of TV shows like *CSI*, when the camera was panning in, the atmosphere mic open—an electrical chatter, hissing, and truncated static. He stopped on the stairs, not yet turning.

"Laurie, love," Mrs. Gibson called. There was so much pain in her voice that tears stung Laurie's eyes, though he still could not grasp at the problem. "She's been gone for three days."

The crackling was the sound of police radios. Returning down the stairs, Laurie could see one of them, attached to the shoulder of a grave-looking young woman police constable waiting in the hallway with an older man behind her. The WPC put out a hand to him, as if he needed steadying, and Laurie automatically took it. She said, "Are you Laurence Fitzroy?"

"Yes," Laurie replied. He was surprised he sounded so sure. Something gave in the muscles of his legs, and he felt himself sit down hard on the third step. "Who are you?"

"PC Christine Foster. This is Detective Paul Gray. We're investigating your sister's disappearance."

Laurie tried to take this in. It was one thing for Gibson to look at him through her tears and say *gone*. That could almost have been an extension of the unreal life of this household, where hothouse games played themselves out behind sealed doors. But this woman was so real that he could smell cold air in the serge of her uniform. *Gone* was somehow less than *disappearance*; Gibson could not terrify him the way Christine Foster could, with her formality and her careful choice of words. For a moment he couldn't find any of his own. Then they came out—weird, barely voluntary. "Please tell me not just the two of you."

Foster almost smiled. "No. No, not at all. There's a citywide alert out, and children's services all over the country have been informed. Don't you watch the news?"

"Not lately." Laurie looked at his hand. It was still clutched around hers, and its knuckles were white. He must be hurting her. Quickly he disengaged. "Sorry," he said. Then once more, roughly, "Sorry. This isn't true. It can't be."

"Well, we're very concerned. To be honest, we didn't think this would come as such a shock to you. We wondered if that was why you'd come home. You've been away this week, haven't you?"

"Yes. But I didn't… I hadn't heard a thing…"

"Okay. Try not to be too frightened. Most kids turn up alive and well. But we'll need to talk to you, obviously, and…" She fell silent, looking at him more closely. "You're very pale, Mr. Fitzroy. You look underweight, and you have facial injuries. Who did this to you?"

Laurie opened his mouth. Then he closed it again. Brought up not to tell tales, schooled in the doctrine that it was better to suffer in silence than expose even the worst of bullies, he found he could not speak. Her question slipped away from him anyway. *She's been gone for three days. Three days. Clara. Gone…* "No," he whispered, vision clouding. "Christ, no."

A shadow fell. At first Laurie could not bring himself to notice it or to put it together with the banging door, the heavy footsteps that had preceded it. Then his nostrils prickled with the scent of familiar aftershave and expensive scotch, and he jerked up in time to see his father, an inexorable bulk arising between the two officers. He tensed, ready to hear the old man add his lies to his own silence…

But Sir William said, to Laurie's astonishment, "I'm afraid that was me. I did it to him, Officer Foster."

The admission broke Laurie's restraint like a well-placed hammer on an eggshell. He sprang to his feet. The old man's smell was a pressure in his lungs, threatening to crack his healing ribs anew. The voice hit him like a big hand. He lurched past PC Foster's grip. He could barely understand himself. He thought his instinctive movement upon seeing his father again would be away, away, not this scramble toward him, to do when he got there who knew what.

"You bastard," he heard himself yell, his voice cracking up out of its register as it had used to do when he was just a kid and it was breaking. "Next time you lay a hand on me you better finish the job and kill me, or—"

"All right, Mr. Fitzroy!" His shoulder was caught. When he tried to free himself, he felt his arm tugged up his back. The other officer had not moved, so he could assume it was Foster who was holding him back from his father in an efficient restraint grip. Incongruously, once she had stilled him and could spare a hand, she began to rub his other shoulder, her touch unfazed and soothing. "All right," she said. "He admitted he did it. You can press charges for assault if you want, but you have to be calm. Okay?"

Sir William, watching his son's struggle dispassionately, said, "As I recall, I punched him in the ribs, as well. How are they?"

Foster gave him a look, then nodded to her partner, who came forward and unfastened Laurie's coat. When Gray reached for the hem of his T-shirt, Laurie tried to flinch back, but the woman's solid bulk behind him held him still. The detective leaned down and examined Laurie's side in silence, without touching, then straightened up. "They've been treated," he said grimly. "But in my opinion, Sir William, your son could bring a charge of assault if he wanted to."

Laurie looked from one to the other of them. These were not the usual coppers—the cronies—with whom his father liked to surround himself when he had dealings with the commissioners' board. The sense of being seen and heard took the edge off his rage, and feeling Foster ease her grip, he swallowed and began to catch his breath.

"I know he could," Sir William said. He took a step toward Laurie, and Gray shot out a warning hand. "We…haven't been friends, my son and I. It's my fault. I have a hot temper, and I drink too much. But I need him to help me now. Laurence, I'm very sorry."

Now Laurie was quite frozen: Foster did not need so much to hold him still as prop him up. A huge sense of unreality descended upon him. Any second now he would wake in Sasha's arms, tell him about this hideous dream, and feel his kisses, sweet and clean as daylight, melt it all away. The hallway began a slow rotation around him. Hallway, stairs, upper floors, Clara's empty room… He said faintly, "Where's my mother?"

"Upstairs, heavily sedated. She can't withstand this, Laurence. You know she can't. Please help us."

"I…" Laurie shuddered. He wiped his eyes, unsure when the tears had come to them. "Yes, okay. Anything. What do need me to do?"

Sir William, unexpectedly, looked at the ground. After a moment, it was Detective Gray who cleared his throat and held out a hand to him. "We need you to look at some documents," he said. "Through here. Come on."

The other source of voices and radio crackle was his father's study. Laurie had not even noticed until now that the door was open. The blinds were drawn, blue-white light emanating from three computers screens that had sprung up around the old man's desk. A third officer, this one also in plain clothes, got to his feet as Foster led Laurie into the room. He put out a hand, and once more Laurie found himself taking it, as if they were meeting at a cocktail party. "Is this…"

"This is my boy, Laurence."

The voice came from an inch off Laurie's ear. An involuntary spasm of fright seized him—muscle and bone still reacting to the hurt he thought his mind had assimilated—and he pulled away from Foster, almost falling, grabbing at a chair for support. Gray reached to steady him. "All right, son," he said, then turned on Sir William. "Could you back off, please, sir? Give him some space. Laurence, this is Detective Sergeant John Kucharski. He works with us and for Interpol."

Interpol. Now I know I'm bloody dreaming. Laurie subsided into the chair that Gray had pulled out for him.

Distractedly he decided he liked the look of DS Kucharski. Not much older than himself, but Laurie guessed he'd turned the years to better account than prancing about on a stage. His gaze was broad and kind with experience, and he had what looked like a knife-wound scar to the side of his neck. He said, "Okay, Laurence. I'm the Interpol liaison for the central Met. These other officers and I have just been looking through records for anyone who might have had contact with your family recently, anyone who could give us a lead to your sister."

Laurie nodded. This seemed reasonable enough. Kucharski was handing him a sheaf of papers. He did his best to concentrate, though his brain felt like a balloon, drifting near the ceiling somewhere, attached to him by the most fragile of strings. He wanted to help. He wanted to look as if he did, and he tried for the expression of respectful attention with which he often convinced his tutor he was actually there in the room with him. Contact with my family, he thought, a ripple of shocky amusement clenching his stomach muscles as his memory picked through the parade of music teachers, Mayfair society doyennes and charity workers who made their way into his mother's living room. "Sorry," he said, pressing a hand to his cold lower lip to keep the quake of laughter from his voice. "I…I can't think of anyone who'd…"

"All right," Kucharski said. "But I believe you know a young man called Alexandru Petrica."

Laurie hardly liked to contradict him. Obediently he read through the data and statistics on the first of the printouts Kucharski had handed him, with its impressive Scotland Yard watermark. He didn't. He knew Sasha, of course, whose black-and-white photograph was paper clipped to the sheet, as if there were some connection. He knew Sasha.

Laurie didn't have a picture of him. This was the first thought that struck him, followed by an absurd desire to ask

Kucharski if he could keep this one. He smiled. Sasha could not be other than beautiful, even on a police mug shot. His dark gaze sought Laurie's across time, circumstance, celluloid. He looked calm and unafraid, unconcerned by the alien name he was being forced to hold across his chest for the camera. Alexandru Petrica… Gently Laurie unfastened the photograph, drew it toward him. He ran his fingers over its surface. "No," he said, softly. "No, I don't know him."

Kucharski took the photo carefully back from him. He put a hand on Laurie's wrist. The grasp was compassionate but firm. He waited till Laurie looked up, and then he said, "He'll have called himself Sasha or maybe Sandru. He'll have told you that his father was a poet, driven out of Bucharest during the Ceauşescu regime. Some of that's even true. But Alexandru's father, Stefan Petrica, is alive, Laurence. He's the lynchpin of a massive drugs and firearms cartel that runs out of the Roma ghettos in Sofia. Interpol wants Alexandru in connection with its operations in the west. Drugs, guns, and…human trafficking. Do you know what that is?"

Laurie did. The *no* that had fallen from his lips was unconnected with the question. He pushed up onto his feet, oblivious to the chair that clattered over behind him. Kucharski still had hold of his wrist. "No," he said again, trying to take a step back, tethered by the grip, by the officer's steady gray eyes.

"I'm not saying Alexandru is responsible for the loss of your sister. But he has dangerous, ruthless connections. We've been watching him, and we know he's been back and forth to this house. Your father's told us, and our surveillance bears this out, that…he came and went as he chose, to share lessons with you, and you weren't always there to let him in. You have to tell us, Laurence. Did you give him a key?"

Laurie choked. He jerked at Kucharski's grasp, which only tightened. He thought a wind must have risen. It was all he could hear, drowning the hiss of the radios, beating like wings against his eardrums. He couldn't get a breath into his lungs. PC Foster's voice made it to him through the storm, fragmented and broken. "You'd better let him go, John."

She was holding the study door open. Laurie went through it slowly, having to grab at its frame to keep upright. The windstorm continued. He heard her say, "Is there a bathroom downstairs?" and his father replying, "Yes. I'll take him."

"No, sir. Better let me."

"For God's sake. He's my *son*."

"The son you assaulted, sir. You can see he's afraid of you."

Laurie walked off from the argument. He got a few yards down the hallway and doubled up retching, spattering water over the black-and-white tiles. It was all he had. Thank God I didn't have breakfast, he thought detachedly. His sinuses burned, and his knees tried to melt out from under him again. Shame hit him. Coughing, he struggled upright and made a desperate run for the bathroom. Tried to slam the door behind him, but it bounced back at him, and he couldn't even make it to the toilet, instead collapsed across the edge of the claw-footed bathtub, banging his bruised ribs, knocking the last breath of air from his lungs.

"Laurence. Laurie, my boy."

Sounds of struggle in the doorway. Laurie couldn't get his head up, but he could picture the scene—his father, bulldozing through whatever resistance Foster or Gray was trying to put up. Laurie could have told them that it was no use. He heard, without surprise, "All right. But you be bloody careful with him, okay? We'll be right outside."

When was the last time his father had tended him—touched him at all, for that matter, other than with a blow?

Never. Laurie began to fight, driving an elbow back. He did not want that hand on his shoulder. Didn't want his head held. "Fuck off!" he rasped between anguished dry heaves. All he wanted was Sasha.

Sasha, who was gone. "*I'll come back to you, I promise. Can you trust me*?"

Can you trust?

"Listen, son."

He did not want his father kneeling heavily on the bathroom floor beside him, reaching for a washcloth and awkwardly wiping his face. He tried to bat him away, but despite his half-starved emptiness, his stomach was trying to wring itself inside out, and he was too disabled by the spasms to escape.

"I'm sorry for what I did to you. And I know what you think about...me and Clara, but I swear to you, I never harmed her. Do you understand?"

Oh, God. The memory of those great bear paws, the same ones manipulating him now, on that little body. That did it for Laurie. He choked and threw up the remains of a long-forgotten supper, shuddering and clutching at the side of the bath. "Fuck you," he repeated when he could. The old man was washing out the cloth under the tap, wiping his mouth for him. "Did you tell them? Did you tell the cops out there, about...*you and Clara*?"

"No. Because nothing happened. She hasn't run away, Laurie. She's been taken. Snatched."

"Christ!"

Laurie found he was sobbing. He knelt on the bathroom floor, brow pressed to the rim of the bathtub. He could feel his own hands reaching, starfishing on vacant air. His father's hands closed under his armpits, lifted him as if he weighed nothing. Deposited him on the toilet seat. And Laurie remembered. It wasn't the first time, no. The old man *had* taken care of him, when he was very small. Swung him around in the air for a game, hoisted him into and out of his playpen. Then something had changed. His father had never harmed Clara. Never harmed him, either. And nothing had happened.

Was that how he had stopped himself? By ceasing to touch Laurie at all?

Big hand on his head now, gently stroking back his hair. "Laurie. We've been enemies, haven't we?"

"I… Yes." Laurie tried to shake him off, but he was dizzy, nausea still roiling through him. "Stop it. Let me go."

"We have to be friends now. For Clara." The stroking continued. Laurie, suddenly unbearably tired, felt some last resistance give. He tried to get up—get out of here, anywhere away from this horror that could caress the child in him into thinking that it was a good—but his effort miscarried, and he crumpled forward into his father's arms. "Listen," the old man said. "My son would never choose to be with someone evil. I know that. But somebody this Alexandru—Sasha—knows…"

Laurie could hardly breathe. It didn't seem to matter anymore. "What do you want?"

"The police out there need to talk to his associates. Just talk. Maybe one of them knows something." The old man rocked him slightly, pressed a rough, tender kiss to the crown of his head. "Come on, son. You're my good boy. Just tell us where they are."

* * *

To make the journey this way was so easy. Brow resting on the glass, Laurie watched slip by the miles of streets and suburbs he had traversed so laboriously on foot or on the bus, which stopped every few hundred yards and started again with a bone-shaking roar. The Daimler was silent. Its progress through the night was smooth as a shark's. His father was not so good a driver as Charlie, but still they covered the ground in great effortless swathes. They would soon be there.

In the end, he had not told the old man. He had told John Kucharski, who had appeared in the bathroom door and asked Sir William to leave them. The doctor who had been attending his mother upstairs had come in and looked him over, and Laurie had scarcely noticed his attentions, not even the sting of a needle to his inner arm. While the doctor worked, Kucharski had sat on the edge of the bath, had given Laurie his nice smile and told him how much danger Alexandru Petrica was in. How Interpol could help and shelter him from dangerous men Laurie had no reason to help shield.

He had stumbled out of the bathroom. His father had hung up the phone at the hallway's far end and come to intercept him. Kucharski had hesitated, as if reluctant to hand him over, but PC Foster had called for him from the study, and he had hurried off. Sir William had put a warm arm around his shoulders and led him away, down through the kitchens and into the alley, where the Daimler waited in its garage. Laurie had wondered where Kucharski and the others were, but his father had said they would follow on if Laurie gave the lead.

Laurie had. His father knew the way out as far as East Hill. By then, a glassy calm had come over him. It was familiar. A far cry from the potent, vital effect of Mama Luna's darozha. This was just sedation, a chemical intensification of the false peace he had sought for himself in his mother's pill bottles. He wanted to sleep. The car was beautifully warm, its movements on its deep suspension soothing. Sir William kept putting out a hand and shaking him. "Which way now? Which way now?"

And Laurie told him. The streets gave way to open ground. It was so easy. The heath opened up all around them. Laurie could just see, through the reflecting glass, the rags of a ruby gold sunset. The long, straight road it had taken him the entire night to walk disappeared in ten minutes. Laurie saw the bus stop and the fence and the gap in it that led to the lane and the camp.

"It's here. Stop here. From here you have to walk."

His father pulled the car up smoothly by the side of the road. Put out a hand and caressed his son's face, as if wondering where the bruises had come from.

"All right. Good boy. You stay here."

He was gone. Laurie shifted in the passenger seat so he could curl up and lean his pounding skull on the headrest. He drew up his knees to his chest. He didn't know what the fuck had been going on in his life for the past few weeks, but it was over now. All over. Laurie closed his eyes.

He opened them. Why? Sleep was calling like a lover, like Sasha with arms outstretched and waiting for him. Blinking, he stared out through the windscreen, trying to see what had roused him. There were other cars pulled up near the Daimler now, in front and behind. Not police cars. Nor, Laurie thought, the type of vehicle plainclothes men would choose. All of these were noticeable, just as the Daimler was. Ostentatious Chryslers and Bentleys, a vast four-by-four Laurie knew from his father's semiofficial, quasi-Masonic nights in with the old boys' brigade of the commissioners' board. When Laurie thought of police, this was what he pictured. Not kindly, open-minded young officers like Foster and Kucharski.

Who were nowhere to be seen. Laurie sat up in the passenger seat. His mouth was dry, his head fuzzy. What had woken him? Rubbing his eyes, he wiped steam off the windscreen's cooling interior and squinted into the dark. Yes, flashlights, probing the dark beyond the fence, lifting and vanishing as the bulky figures that bore them clambered off the roadside path and into the woods. Shuddering, Laurie pushed open the door. These last ones were stragglers, he saw. He had lain, curled up and still trusting something, while the majority of the men who had arrived in these vehicles had set off down the lane to the camp.

He fell out of the car. He remembered sitting tamely, rolling up his sleeve when his mother's doctor—no, Sir William's pet doctor, who never made a fuss about continuing to feed Lady Fitzroy the pills that would keep *her* quiet and tame in her turn—had shoved a needle into his vein. The pavement was icy cold beneath his hands. Fragments of glass under his palms, a scatter of diamonds. He pressed down till they cut, but could not feel them.

Laurie, who thought he had found out what betrayal was in his father's study an hour before, staggered to his feet. He knew what it was now.

"*My son would never choose to be with someone evil. We have to be friends now.*" A kiss to the top of his skull. Everything Laurie had longed for in a father—faith, camaraderie, complicity; the tender, demonstrative aspect of love he had been taught to value by the absolute lack of it. Christ, he had left those needs so far behind he had thought they were dead. Dry soil. Still full of life, apparently. Only dormant, only waiting for a few drops of rain, however bloody toxic, to bring them bursting and flourishing through. Laurie, who had believed the old man almost a stranger to him now, was suddenly impressed.

And terrified. He took the fence in an uncoordinated vault that landed him painfully on his hands and knees on the far side. He thought—he hoped—his father would have stopped short of actually poisoning him.

Already, hauling great breaths of the night air, he could feel some of the mists clearing. It was enough. He didn't need to be firing on all cylinders to run a straight line through the dark, did he? This time he had guiding lights ahead of him, receding torch beams. And he had learned from his last visit that an unhesitating track was the best to keep him out of the thorns.

He ran. The first few strides were a controlled fall, but after that his blood began to beat, to shake out the drug in adrenaline. His legs gained strength beneath him. He was silent on the leaf litter, half in flight before he reached the last stragglers of Sir William's lumbering brigade. One of them turned on him. God, in the swaying light, Laurie knew him: a retired Metropolitan chief, commended a hundred times for harsh-but-fair methods of keeping the London streets clean. At his side, companion and helper, was no more or less than a thug. Laurie had time to pick out the swastika tattoos before the pair of them moved to block his path. The recognition was mutual. "Laurence!" the chief snarled, getting a grip on his sleeve. "You get your arse back down that lane and into the car, boy, or—"

Laurie tore out of his grip and ran again. There were the lights of the camp. Laurie could not distinguish the probing torch beams from the fires and the yellow gleam from caravan windows and doors—all were entangled, merging together, as if…

As if his father's band of mates and heavies were in among the vans. Laurie felt terror close tight in his chest. He dashed over the last twenty yards of open ground that lay between the track and the camp, seeing Zaga's broken chain but no sign of the dog. It was a Sunday night, wasn't it? The communal fire outside Mama Luna's van was burning brightly, casting tawny shadows. She lit it on a Sunday night, Laurie knew, not a Romani day of rest or worship but a chance for a feast, some singing and dancing before the drab balame week began. Sasha had told him that.

Beyond the fire was a strange sight. At first Laurie's mind would not take it in. As if to think of Sasha was to conjure him, there he was, on his knees in the flickering light. Laurie loved London's art galleries, had spent many hours over the years gazing at the scenes they called the pietà, wondering at the pain in them and what had caused half a world to require a broken, dead boy to be lifted from a cross and draped across his desolate mother's lap to save their souls. He dropped from his flat run to a ragged-breathed halt a few yards away.

Christ was holding the mother this time. Sasha, eyes wide and blank, was clutching the birdlike cluster of bright scarves and robes that concealed Mama Luna's tiny frame. Mama Luna was stretched out across his knees. Her face was contorted, limbs disposed awkwardly. Most incongruous of all, a wrongness that almost made Laurie start retching again—his father, standing off to the side, barely three feet from Sasha in a world in which Laurie had sworn he would never allow them to meet. Because it couldn't contain them both. It would tear itself apart.

"Sasha," he choked out, stumbling across the space that divided them. Laurie fell to his knees at his side. "Sash!"

Sir William was staring at the old woman on the ground. One of his big fists was bunched against his hip, the other running through his hair in a gesture of bewilderment. A pair of his colleagues came running back from the vans and also halted by the group by the fire. "I didn't touch her," he said. "I didn't lay a hand on her."

Sasha, who had not moved or blinked in response to Laurie's voice, suddenly seemed to hear him. He shifted a little to look at him. "Laurie," he said, as if just woken up. As if he and Laurie had never been apart and were carrying on a conversation from before. "That's what she meant. 'The father is death…' Not yours. Her own."

"No. She's not…" Laurie stretched out his fingers. The old woman was still warm, her skin soft and dry as a seasoned apple's. But there was no flicker of a pulse, in her wrist or at her throat. Laurie whispered, "Oh, no…"

"She had a weak heart. When they all came running in, she was frightened. She tried to jump up, and…" Sasha lowered his head. “She just fell. Laurie, what are they doing here?”

Laurie, shell-shocked, had nothing left in him but truth. “My sister’s gone missing. He…” He jerked a hand in his father’s direction, not looking up at him. He thought he would never look again. “He thought it was something to do with you. The police told me about your father.”

Sasha shook his head. “What? Dear God, no.” He swallowed and flinched as if a stone had struck him. “And Clara… She’s *missing*?”

“Yes. Three days.”

“It can’t be. Oh, Laurie. This is why I tried to stay away from you. But I couldn’t. I couldn’t be without you. I…” He fell silent for a moment. Laurie saw him losing his way among the pits and holes opening up in the world all around him, as Laurie had lost his own. “Look,” Sasha said suddenly, tenderly shifting the old woman’s body in his arms and reaching into his coat’s inside pocket. “I bought the *Stage* for you yesterday, in case you forgot. For next week. And there was this in it. Have you seen?”

He withdrew a newspaper sheet, carefully folded, and handed it to Laurie. Laurie took it from him in numb fingers. Opened it out and knelt staring at his own image. Or his own borrowed skin. He could not remember the moment from *Hamlet* in which the shot had been taken, could not recall his murderous advance on Laertes, sword in hand. It was a good photo. Dazedly scanning the page in the firelight, he saw that the article was better. *New talent. Huge potential. East Hill’s hidden star*. In another world, he would have been delighted. “I want that back,” Sasha rasped, eyes filling with desperate tears. “I don’t have a picture of you.”

A picture. A mug shot, height markings on a wall. *Alexandru Petrica*. Laurie handed the article back to Sasha, a sudden tremor making the paper vibrate. Laurie did not care who Sasha was. The only thing he knew now with any certainly was that he should never, not for one instant, have had the slightest doubt of him. Horror rose up in him, metaphysical in its intensity. The night filled with black, beating wings. He glanced up at his father, at the six or seven men emerging from the caravans where they had finished doing whatever their worst might be. "Sasha," he said very softly, not taking his eyes off the old man. "You have to go."

"What?"

"The police. They found out everything about you. They were meant to come here, not…not these bastards. Go."

"No. I haven't done… I'm not leaving her. But—" Laurie jumped as Sasha's grip suddenly closed on his arm. He turned, a pain like hot stone weighing in his chest. No point in looking away. Nowhere in the world for him to avoid this admission, this consequence. "Laurie, how did they find us?"

"I told them. I gave you up. Oh, Sasha. *Run*!"

Laurie didn't think he would obey. Sasha was on his feet, Mama Luna falling from his arms into the fireside dust. His gaze on Laurie should have turned him into stone. The brown eyes were lightless. He held still for one second, then another. Then he fell back by one step, and William Fitzroy stirred and snapped upright.

"Oh, no, you little fucker. We want to talk to you."

"*Run*!" The cry tore from Laurie's throat, so hard he tasted blood. He saw Sasha turn and, as if in slow motion, begin to retreat. He saw his father make a signal to one of his men. Saw both of them—his father and the burly crew-cut thug—begin the pursuit. All Laurie had was his position and his weight. Jolting halfway upright, he tangled with the crew cut, went down with him in a flail of arms and legs that knocked the wind from him but did not stop him scrambling back up to see his father setting off on Sasha's heels. He saw Gunari appear between two of the vans, his baseball bat swinging. "Gunari!" he yelled. "Stop him!"

The authority in his own voice was a mystery to him. He had lost everything. He was nothing. Some cold blue-blooded ghost rose up and spoke for him, and Gunari obeyed. Laurie had the dubious satisfaction of watching Gunari run, pounce, and tackle Sir William to the ground, an earthshaking effort, the two big bodies crashing down into the frost-shimmered grass. *The bigger they come, the harder they fall.*

But he was falling so hard himself, watching Sasha become a fleet-footed shape among the trees, then a shimmer, and then nothing. Watching Sasha run from him and flicker out to nothing in the dark.

Chapter Eleven

Paul Jacobs sat on the desk of the Empire's tiny office. It was ten o'clock on Monday morning, and he had only come in to tidy up the props and hand some costumes to the dry cleaner. To his surprise, East Hill's hidden star had been sitting on the steps outside, oblivious to the rain, apparently waiting for him. He had taken Laurie in, given him a plastic cup of tea from Mrs. J's office supplies, and waited in his turn for him to begin to talk. The office door was open, the cleaner cheerfully whistling as he plied an industrial mop across the foyer's tiles.

Not much of the star about Laurie this morning. The review from the *Stage* was proudly tacked to the board behind him, and Jacobs looked from the photo—all that flash and glamour, a haughty Renaissance prince with poor Laertes, who looked genuinely scared, at sword point—to the young man sitting opposite him. The bruises he had arrived with last week were fading, but he looked more life worn than before. Older too. Oddly calm, as if something inside that had been keeping him off balance had burned out.

Laurie took out his wallet. It was a very nice one, Jacobs idly noticed, far better than the usual accessories of those walking shadows who came to strut and fret their hour upon his stage. He was well dressed too, which was something of a relief to Jacobs, who had feared last week he was going to have to ask him to do something about that solitary T-shirt. Jacobs watched him count out a hundred pounds in notes. "What's this for?" he asked.

Laurie looked up. "What you gave me on Friday," he said. "That was another advance, wasn't it? Because you paid me in advance for last week."

Jacobs shrugged. "I suppose so. Apart from the take on the house. I wouldn't worry. You earned it ten times over." He glanced at the newspaper cutting and smiled. "Or you will, at any rate."

"That's just it. I can't be here this coming week to rehearse *The White Devil*. So I need to give you this back." When Jacobs did not immediately reach out for the proffered cash, Laurie laid it on the desk. "I'm sorry. I didn't mean to let you down. You should cast Laertes for Flamineo. He's pretty good."

Jacobs pulled a wry face. He looked from Laurie to the money on the desk. "I suppose," he began thoughtfully, "that…technically speaking, and based on experience, rehearsal may not be strictly necessary."

He watched. It was a silent challenge. Laurie picked it up in silence. For a moment, Jacobs wondered if whatever had happened to him between Friday night and now might have knocked his mercury, his transfiguring magic out of him.

As usual, Jacobs failed to see the shift. As usual, Laurie did nothing—nothing more than fold his hands into his lap and raise his face to look at him. "What is 't you doubt?" he asked him conversationally. "Her coyness? That's but the superficies of lust most women have." He shook his head, as in friendly wonder at the vagaries of the sex. Then he shifted a little in his seat, expression darkening. "Why should ladies blush to hear that named, which they do not fear to handle? Oh, they are politic; they know our desire is increased by the difficulty of enjoying, whereas satiety is a blunt, weary, and drowsy passion. If the buttery-hatch at court stood continually open, there would be nothing so passionate crowding, or hot suit after the beverage."

"Laurie, stop." Jacobs stretched out a hand to his shoulder. He saw Laurie take long seconds to come back to himself, and in the interval watched the departure of a scheming, lust-sickened nobleman from the court of the Medicis. He had never heard anyone, let alone a boy in his teens, throw the right degree of sexual revulsion into the metaphor of that vile buttery-hatch. And yet he knew that, regardless of his experiences in the outside world, Laurie's nature remained sweet as day. "I was thinking of you for Bracciano, but…clearly you can do villains too. Laurie, tell me something. Are you one of the Mayfair Fitzroys, whose little girl was snatched last week?"

"Yes, sir. She's my sister."

"I did wonder. You didn't know, did you?"

"Not until yesterday. I don't have a TV."

"No. I don't suppose Flamineo would." Jacobs folded his arms across his chest. "I'm very sorry. That's why you can't come. Have you moved back home?"

Never spend another night under that roof as long as I live. Laurie, medieval fires dying out from his brain, understood with relief that it was true. "No. I need to be there during the day to help search and be with my mother, but I'm living in East Hill. At the address I gave you."

"All right. I see you picked yourself up a change of clothes. That's good. Are they funding you otherwise?"

"No, sir." Another truth. Another great pang of relief, finding its way through the dull cloud of fear in which Laurie had been living since the day before. *Not another night. Not another penny*. "I just grabbed some of my things."

"Then for God's sake, take the money. Do you think you can make it over here at all?"

"I…I'll try."

"Good lad. I'll have Laertes understudy for you, be your placeholder for the others. Just turn up on the night."

* * *

Laurie sat in his mother's room, in a patch of pale winter sunlight. It was Tuesday afternoon on the fifth day after Clara's disappearance. John Kucharski had told Laurie that in missing children cases, this was the critical time. Kids who'd wandered off by accident normally turned up after three or so days, alive or dead. Kidnappers tended to issue ransom demands before the fourth—long enough, Kucharski had said, for the parents to build up a good head of terror. To be only too willing to pay.

No one had called in their price for his sister. Kucharski and the others were becoming puzzled and alarmed. Children not found or ransomed in five days tended never to be found at all. Kucharski had said all this gently to Laurie, at the end of a conversation in which Laurie, too, had set out his store of certainties.

Laurie would walk the streets to find Clara. He would post leaflets, canvas half of London, set up a Web site to get to the other half and the rest of the world. He would tell Interpol absolutely everything he knew about his whole family and acquaintance. But he would not answer any further questions regarding Alexandru Petrica, because Alexandru—his Sasha—had nothing to do with this. Never had, never would, and if Kucharski wanted to pursue his inquiries about drugs, weapons, and human trafficking, he would have to do it on his own time and quit using Laurie as some kind of human crowbar to get into his case.

Kucharski had not appeared offended by this declaration. He had looked at Laurie quite serenely and continued packing up his computers and files. There was nothing further he could do at the house, he had said, and he gave Laurie his contact numbers and the details of the room in Scotland Yard from which the investigation would now proceed.

In another conversation, concluded the night before, Laurie had told his father that his game of cat's-paw was all over too. Laurie understood now. Sir William loved his children, but the fallout from that love was lethal. Indifference would have been better—or outright hate. His outraged love for Clara had given him the reason he craved to smash at the foreigners he so despised, to try and crush the boy with whom Laurie had violated his sacred English walls. To crush Laurie while he was at it—or those elements of his son's nature he could not bear.

Laurie had told him all of this, and Sir William's reaction had not been as calm as Kucharski's. Bruised and humiliated from his encounter with Gunari as he was—deflated, too, by PC Foster's assurance that even the board of commissioners could not obstruct justice or deal out their own as they pleased, that he would in fact face charges for the death of Mama Luna—the old man still had strength to growl and rage.

"*You're nothing without me, boy. I changed my will when I found out you were buggering your little rent boy. I don't change it back, you're a pauper.*" And Laurie, who once had feared poverty, had experienced nothing but a kind of soaring, transcendent relief. "*You might as well leave it. You don't have a son anymore.*"

His mother stirred in the bed. Laurie, who was sitting on the end of it, turned to look at her. She was of a piece with her delicate white bedclothes, barely disturbing their outline in her little chiffon gown. He braced himself to talk to her. He had been doing so, between long hours on the streets, over the last three days. Normally it did not cost him too much. She seemed less grieved than detached, on the run inside herself.

He could easily become the calm and supportive young man who was not inwardly dying himself of terror and grief. Who was not subject to flashing images of all the fates that could have befallen the little girl who had been more his than Sir William's since the day she came home and he had fiercely assumed to himself the duties of brotherhood, knowing how much she would need them, loving on sight the little creature mewling in her fancy, uncomfortable cradle.

Yes, Laurie could do it. It was just that, at present, he could not decide if his feet or his heart were hurting him worse. He was exhausted. He thought that every pillar, caryatid, and lamppost in Mayfair now bore Clara's image. And, when not assailed by visions of her discarded body, all he could think about was Birchwood camp and firelit dark and everything he had ever wanted disappearing like a ghost into the night. Sasha, whom he'd betrayed and would never see again.

Did not deserve to see again, because even now, when the house became quiet, his treacherous logical mind would insist on trying to click two and two together: to place Sasha, innocent though passion's voice declared him to be, somewhere on the scene of Clara's disappearance. Oh, against his will—coerced, at the end of his father's long reach, but there, playing a part, involved…

Lady Fitzroy moaned and fell back into drug-assisted sleep. Laurie let go a shuddering breath and buried his head in his hands. A reprieve, then, for half an hour or so. He should probably stretch out on the striped satin sofa and try to get some sleep. He had made it, after all, to one of the East Hill rehearsals, which Jacobs had put off until the evening to give him a chance. There would be another tonight.

Laurie knew he had to go, all other possible duties discharged here. He had been given this week, out of trust and generosity, but after that—well, after that Laurie was nothing more or less than a man with a job, who had to hold that job down, like untold millions of others, no matter what crises were erupting around him. Half an hour would give him time to stretch out and cry for his losses, pick up his sanity afterward, and go out to work.

But the place in him where tears came from was hot and dry. Everything he had cried for in his life—

everything, he knew, including this horror over Clara—burned to ashes in the face of losing Sash. There were no tears for it. He could not even feel his way around its edges. He knew that, when he had time to take it in, it would consume him.

The bedside phone rang. Two tones: an outside line. Laurie made a dive for it. Gibson was on the alert downstairs to intercept calls, but she was moving slowly these days, grief putting years on her, dragging her down. He snatched the receiver and answered quietly, hoping his mother might still sleep through. He was expecting—what? John Kucharski, with news of the investigation? Clara's abductor at last, with a ransom demand?

Instead it was his father's secretary. Laurie knew her well. A nice woman, patient and efficient. Laurie listened for a few seconds. Unusually, he was having trouble understanding her. Her normally crisp Cambridge accent was broken up, choppy. "Ruth," he said, as softly as he could. "What on earth's the matter?"

"Laurie. I'm so sorry, dear…to tell you like this—"

Her voice dissolved once more. Slowly Laurie understood she was crying. He eased the receiver under his chin and looked out through the big sash window of his mother's room. It opened onto the little square that lay behind the house. In summer it was leafy and pleasant. Even now, on what Laurie belatedly worked out must be Christmas Eve, the branches of the trees made elegant patterns on the sky. He watched them, sitting on the edge of the bed, running a hand into his hair. It was possible, he supposed, that news concerning Clara had gone to his father in the office. That the old man had been—oh, Christ—too distraught to speak to him, had got Ruth to call.

"Sorry. To…to tell me what?"

"Your father. It was a massive heart attack. They need next of kin at the hospital straightaway, or I'd have come around and… Oh, God, Laurie. He was dead before the ambulance got here. He just went down."

Laurie watched the trees. Their infinite fractal branchings seemed a message to him now, one he could interpret if he just let go. *The bigger they come, the harder they fall*. Drifting from his flesh, Laurie listened to himself take over and conclude the telephone call. He was sensible and calm. He got the information he needed—the name of the hospital—and he reassured poor Ruth that calling him had been okay, that yes, she'd had to call. Yes, he was all right. He'd tell his mother. He would go as soon as he could to the Royal Hospital.

He would tell his mother. Gently Laurie set the receiver down. Yes, he'd tell his mother that, out of her family of four, only two of them were left. That—impossibly; Laurie did not believe it himself—Sir William was dead. He turned very slowly on the bed. He'd have to wake her first.

No. She was wide-awake already. She was bolt upright against the headboard, knees drawn up, clutching the fine lacy coverlet in both hands. Laurie, who had not seen or felt her move, stared at her. For once, she held and returned the eye contact. She said, "Laurie. What's happened?"

He told her. Somehow it was possible, while she was looking at him like that. It had been easy for Laurie to forget his mother was an adult. She had, over the years, abdicated more and more adult responsibilities, turning over to Gibson and Laurie the care of her daughter, becoming daily more like the porcelain French doll she resembled, tiny and exquisite and dead. She slept in her own room at the far end of the house from her husband's. Sir William, presumably, discharged his sexual appetites elsewhere. Laurie could not tell what had now caused her to emerge from her cloud of sedation and gaze at him like this. As if she had remembered she was his mother.

She put out a frail hand, weighted down by its diamonds, and took his. "Oh, my Laurence. What an awful thing for you to have had to break to me."

"It's all right, Ma. Are...are you all right?"

"Yes. He's dead, then? Quite dead? It's certain?"

Laurie shook his head, bemused. The dreadful thing was that he wanted to laugh. He said unsteadily, "It...sounds that way, yes."

"Oh, thank God." Lady Fitzroy clasped together her hands in a Catholic gesture of absolute devotion. "*Que le bon Dieu soit remercié*. Thank you, thank you, God."

Pity shook Laurie. How she must have hated him! All those endless days and nights alone with him, in a marriage that had turned into a life sentence around her. She was rocking herself a little to the rhythm of her prayers. He reached out. "Sorry," he whispered. "I'm so sorry. I didn't know."

"Now I can tell. Thank God, now I can tell."

Laurie frowned. She was holding him at arm's length, her fingers clamped on his shoulders with a surprisingly powerful grip. He said uneasily, "Tell what, Ma?"

"That poor boy! But it was convenient. I had to do it. You know what your father is like, Laurence. He would never have let Clara go. I knew he was going to harm her, and I couldn't stop it. He'd have pursued her forever. Never, never let her go. I had to do it!"

* * *

Laurie took the stairs down to the hallway five at a time. The phone extension in his mother's room had no memory library, and he didn't have the number in his mobile. On his way across the hall, he almost ran over Gibson, who turned as if in a dream and began to follow him—afraid of God knew what news, Laurie understood—and he smiled and held out a hand to her. There was a chair by the phone table. He told her to sit down. For himself, he knelt.

It took a long time for his aunt to answer the phone, and longer still for Laurie to tell her, in his passable but halting French, what had happened. She was hard to convince. Laurie guessed she had been coached to be wary of such calls. Eventually she told him to wait, and there was another long silence.

Then the line clattered to the sound of the receiver being eagerly grabbed, and a clear child's voice carried forth from it, vivid to Laurie as if they were in the same room. Yes, she was fine. She was a little out of breath; she had run up from the kitchens, where she and her cousins were making canapés for their *reveillon* Christmas Eve dinner. Her only concerns were that she missed her brother and she could not understand why *Tante* Elise, who normally allowed her to roam like a wild goat over her extensive Languedoc estates, would not let her out of the house.

He hung up the phone and went back upstairs. He didn't know what to say to his mother, who was where he had left her, curled up in the bed, clutching her lace. It didn't matter. Gibson pushed past him, rushed to her side, and seized her in an embrace Laurie knew from experience would leave bruises, powered by this much emotion.

The room was very warm. Laurie hadn't noticed before. It was stuffy, the temperature of sickrooms and hothouses. A place where impossible secrets could grow. He strode over to push up the sash window. Leaning his hands on the sill, he looked out into the light.

* * *

Laurie had found John Kucharski alone in the Scotland Yard ops room. He had had some difficulty making it to this point past the security desks. He supposed he hadn't made a convincing concerned relative, shaking finely as he was with reaction and joy. He wondered if Kucharski was having trouble believing him too. He had sat in silence through Laurie's news, staring at him across the desk. This was why Laurie had come to him directly rather than phoning: to see his face and let his own be seen, to be, as far as possible, accountable.

The ops room was lined with images of Clara. Of Sasha too, although from these Laurie kept his gaze carefully averted. Clara, Sasha, a handful of other dark-eyed, harsh-faced men he didn't know. *Stefan Petrica.* He fought a painful lurch of his heart. He had to stay calm, remain in the functional zone he had found between anxiety for Sash and this wild, unmanning release from fear over his sister. "I'm sorry," he said, for he thought the fifth or sixth time. "I…I know all the trouble we've caused. But she's okay, sir, really. She's found."

Kucharski rubbed his brow. He had in front of him, Laurie could see, a formidable array of files and photographs, and he looked tired. He said at length, "All right. I…want to believe you, Mr. Fitzroy, but I think there has to be a…well, a misunderstanding at best. This has been an investigation at the highest level. Partly because of your sister's vulnerability, of course, but also—I won't kid you—because of the men we think are involved. There just isn't any way it could have proceeded so far as it has without basic checks being done on family and…"

Laurie pulled out his mobile. He handed it across the desk, top flipped up, Elise Devereaux's details on the screen. He said, "I know. But—that's her number, if you want to…"

"You've spoken to her yourself? And the child? Directly?"

"Yes, sir."

The agent pushed the mobile away. He laid down his pen. It looked to Laurie such a gesture of defeat, the king going down on the chessboard. He could have smiled had not Kucharski's doubts—adult doubts from a world Laurie wasn't sure even now he had earned the right to inhabit—almost made him wonder if he had imagined his conversation with Clara in a happy dream. After a moment, Kucharski picked up the receiver of his desk phone. He tapped in an internal number and said, rubbing the bridge of his nose, "Foster? I want you and Paul Gray in here right now."

There was a brief, awkward silence. Laurie tried not to clutch at the edge of the seat in a gesture that would have instantly told Kucharski of his strong desire to be out of there. He wasn't sure where he wanted to be—France, possibly, shaking Tante Elise until her sapphire earrings fell out, or back at his own flat, waiting and hoping against hope. He felt a painful sense of responsibility toward Gray and Foster too, and swallowed dryly when they appeared in the doorway to the ops room, glancing at one another in apprehension.

"Oh, it's all right," Kucharski said, gesturing them in. "No little body washed up out of the Thames this time. Far from it. Mr. Fitzroy here has come to tell us that his sister is alive and well, under the protection of his aunt, who apparently owns the south of France." He paused for a moment, watching the effect of this news on his colleagues. "DS Gray, am I right in thinking you were responsible for initiating the check on the relatives?"

"Sir," Gray said, a touch of outrage in his voice. "I had MI5 *background* check the relatives."

"Yes, but"—Kucharski picked up his pen again and waved it wearily in Gray's direction—"did anyone *look*? *Physically* check? By which I mean, did anyone glance up from their psych profiling and DNA analysis long enough to send a gendarme out to the Devereaux estate?"

Laurie cleared his throat. He really felt for Gray, who looked relieved and mortified in equal parts. "I don't think there was any reason to," he said. "My mother packed Clara off pretty neatly. She had one of our Devereaux cousins come over to escort her, so she'd be traveling on a passport not in the name of Fitzroy. She even dyed her hair."

Kucharski did not look consoled. "I don't care if she gave her a Groucho Marx wig and nose. My officers just raised a full-scale child trafficking alert across the whole of Europe without checking in on Aunt Elise. Foster, Gray, this is what I mean when I tell you not to lose your basic police work in the joys of promotion and technology. I'm delighted that this had a happy ending, but…" He hesitated and glanced back at Laurie as if he had just recalled his presence, and that probably he should not rip a strip off his officers in front of a member of the public. "Well. We'll go over this later. For now…just get out of here."

Laurie watched them go. "It's not their fault," he said. "It's ours. My mother was determined to get Clara away."

"Mr. Fitzroy, leave me to deal with my staff. And, as for you, if I didn't think you incapable of sustained deception in a matter like this…" He hesitated and sighed, visibly relenting a little. "All right. She's found. Let's both thank our gods for that and be grateful."

Laurie nodded. He wasn't yet sure who his gods were, but he would happily have gone down on his knees to thank Kucharski's. "Yes, sir."

"All right," Kucharski said again. He had an air of a man rapidly rearranging his ideas and preconceptions. "Your mother wanted her away. Thinking about what he did to you—do I need look any further than your father to work out why?"

Laurie caught his breath. Not half an hour before, he had stopped off at the Royal Free Hospital's morgue to identify Sir William's body. Odd. After a lifetime of florid purples and scarlet, the old man's face had been gray. And much of his bulk had been Laurie's own fear of him. He was small on his slab. Diminished and gone. He said, a little unsteadily, "No. You don't. My mother was afraid of him. Not because he'd be violent to Clara, but…" He shivered, running a hand into his hair. "I'm sorry. It's hard to talk about."

"Okay. I get the picture. You don't have to. But, Laurie, when the child comes back from France, if she's gonna be in danger in her home…"

"She won't be."

"Why are you so sure of that?" Kucharski paused, frowning. "Does it…does it have anything to do with your mother's reasons for choosing today to give up the game?"

"Yes. Yes, it does. My father had a heart attack. In his office this afternoon. He's dead."

Kucharski sat up. "*What*? Sir William?"

"Yes. I've seen him." *Seen him; checked. Read the damn tag on his toe to be sure. If I hadn't, he'd become a bogeyman to haunt my mind forever.* "It was quick. He didn't have much pain."

"Oh. Good Lord, Laurie. I'm terribly sorry."

"It's all right. You…can't be thinking he was much of a loss."

Kucharski visibly considered pretending it was otherwise. Then he said, lacing his fingers together, "Well. He was still your father."

"Yes. And I know that should always be sacred, sir. But it's not." Laurie paused for a moment. He looked up at Kucharski, a half smile hitching. "Look. I know she's caused…a diplomatic incident, but will my mother get into much trouble for this? She's not well. At any rate, she's not strong."

Kucharski shrugged. "If you can forgive it, I suppose we can." When Laurie raised his eyebrows questioningly, he clarified, "She seized the opportunity of the Petrica boy having been in your house to make your sister vanish and try to set Petrica up for it. Am I wrong to suppose his loss meant—means—a great deal to you?"

Laurie could not answer. Kucharski watched him in silence for a minute. Then he closed the file that had been open on his desk. "With regard to your mother and making false accusation… We wouldn't normally pursue it, not in her circumstances. At least that's what I'll recommend in my report."

"Thank you," Laurie said. He got to his feet, feeling his head spin slightly. He was about paid out, events beginning to catch up with him. "I'd better get home, if there's nothing else I can do here." Suddenly he grinned. "I'll take a few posters down from lampposts between here and Mayfair."

"Well, that would be a start." Kucharski let him get as far as the door. Then just as Laurie was turning to bid him farewell, he said cautiously, "Speaking of the Petrica boy…"

Laurie stiffened. "No," he said. "I told you. There's nothing more I'd say to you about him, even if I knew. I don't care who he is or who his sodding associates are. He was good to me. He *is* good."

"Suppose I wanted to say something to you about him?"

"It wouldn't make any difference. Whatever it is."

"Well, maybe not. But as it happens, you're right, as far as our information guides us. You didn't listen to me the other day at your father's house. When I told you that Sasha was wanted in connection with drugs crimes and trafficking, that was all I meant. Not that he was involved."

Laurie took a grip on the door frame. He said faintly, "All right. Go on."

"Stefan Petrica is about as bad as he can be. I don't know if he was a monster before he fell into the hands of monsters, but Sasha grew up witnessing some serious deals and how his father dealt with the people who broke them.

When he got old enough, he tried to run. Stefan told him he'd not only have him killed, but that he'd activate people in Britain who would hunt down his mother, who'd fled here when Sasha was a child.

"So when he was scared enough to ignore the threats and run anyway, he ran in this direction, to find her and warn her first. Last week he thought he'd got some news of where she lived, and he went to investigate. But the trail went cold. We can't find her either. She may have changed her identity, emigrated farther west."

Kucharski paused and indicated the chair Laurie had just vacated. "That's why Sasha doesn't give his real name or stay anywhere for too long. He's afraid of leading Stefan straight to anyone he gets close to. He knows he shouldn't have come to your house, Laurie. You made him forget his own rules for a while, he says."

This time when Kucharski gestured at the chair, Laurie obeyed. He barely got there. "How…how do you know all this?"

"Your father and his mates inadvertently helped us out at Birchwood the other night. We were there, but on the far side of the encampment. They chased Sasha straight into our arms. We took him in and questioned him."

"What? You said he hadn't done anything wrong."

"Well, he's not selling guns or abducting children. But he entered the country illegally and remained here and worked."

"Oh, God. Where is he now?"

"In the Dover Immigration Removal Centre. We're not pressing charges. He agreed to deportation."

Laurie lost a breath. He could see—cold tiles, tiny windowless rooms. Sasha's face among a thousand others caught between the worlds. "No," he said. "You know what he's running away from. He's a refugee, not an immigrant."

"And if he'd seek asylum, we could help him. My department wants Stefan Petrica very badly. Sasha could lead us straight to him, and in return for that—well, God knows what deal they'd cut him. Refugee status at the very least."

"Then—make him tell you. Let me see him. I'll persuade him."

"Laurie. Listen. You didn't know Sasha very long, but you probably knew him well enough to believe me when I say that, although he was anxious for me to tell you the truth—to clear his name with you—he is equally unwilling to besmirch the name of anyone else. Even a monster like his father. He won't talk. Don't judge him too harshly. That kind of loyalty, even so badly misplaced as this, is incredibly rare."

"He's still your father." That should be sacred. Laurie closed his eyes. He didn't know Sasha. He had no idea at all of what it was like to be someone like that. To have inside him that undying fire of love and duty that did not alter according to its object's worth. To be someone who would love you no matter what you did. "I betrayed him," he said suddenly, harshly, voice cracking over the words. "Please, can I see him?"

"They won't let you near him. And…he asked me to tell you not to try. He has to go. Laurie, seeing you will only make it harder for him."

* * *

Kucharski was right. The Dover immigration facility was a sheer steel wall, impervious to Laurie's attempts to get past it. And he didn't give up easily. He phoned and e-mailed, then got on the coach from Victoria and went down to see for himself. He did not want to meet with Sasha. He had taken him and Kucharski at their word and would not inflict further harm on him. But he needed to impress on someone in authority his own conviction that, if Sasha were shipped back to Romania, his life would be worth no more than the time it took Stefan Petrica or one of his hit men to find him.

On a bitter day between Christmas and New Year, he stood at a counter in the Dover removals department and argued until his throat was sore with the official behind the shielding glass barricade. He would hire a lawyer for Sasha, he told her. Money no object—the best. In promising this, he didn't anticipate breaking his not-another-penny rule. Lady Fitzroy had told him, tears in her eyes, that she would spare no expense to help the boy she had come so close to destroying. But the official shook her head and told him Alexandru Petrica had been offered excellent legal counsel already, courtesy of the Interpol agent who'd brought him in, and had refused it. Further, there was little chance of intervention now. His deportation order had gone through. A flight to Bucharest was leaving in the morning.

So Laurie went home. Not to Mayfair, where his mother was being tended by Gibson and the private nursing staff Laurie had asked her to bring in when Lady Fitzroy's wild mood swings—from elation to weeping despair—seemed to threaten her sanity, and where his father still lay tucked away in the hospital morgue until someone found the time to arrange his funeral. He went back to East Hill, to the cold little flat, smiled at the meter where Sasha's magical coin was still bringing him light and warmth, and locked the door. He felt very calm.

First he called Clara, who was still safe in her aunt's château, only now given the freedom of the grounds as well. She still thought she was on her Christmas holidays and chattered away to Laurie in the patchwork mix of English and French she always acquired among her cousins, about the snow and *Pere Noël* and St. Sylvestre's night. Laurie responded in kind. There would be plenty of time to tell her about the demolition ball that had swung through her family since her departure—either that or no time at all, and either way there was no point in disturbing her now. Elise, although bewildered and not a little angry at the charade her sister had forced her through, had promised to keep silence.

Then Laurie packed. It took him hardly any time at all, he found, when he owned next to nothing. Everything he needed for a trip of unknown duration to Eastern Europe fitted nicely into one rucksack. With regard to tickets—well, those could fall under the heading of the *anything* Lady Fitzroy was prepared to pay to help Sasha, couldn't they? If Laurie could not protect him by law on English soil, all that was left for him to do was fly to Bucharest and intercept him there. He had no clear ideas about what he would do if this mission succeeded. No helpful ones, anyway—just a single thought of placing his own flesh and bone between Sasha and whoever might come to hunt him down. Just that. That would be enough.

He was scanning through the battered Yellow Pages the last tenant had left behind—having no Internet connection had knocked him back a couple of decades when it came to travel arrangements—when his mobile rang. He picked it up impatiently. John Kucharski was one of the handful of people he would have picked up for at all at this moment. "Yes?"

"All right, Laurence. Is he with you?"

Laurie gave the question thought. Kucharski's voice was an Interpol bark, not the humane tone of their last conversation. Then the implications hit him. Laurie leaned his back against the living room wall and did not fight the desire to slide down it in relief. "He got away."

"Yes. He slipped his bloody leash between Dover and Gatwick. Now, once more, son—and you should know that I am *not* pissing about—is he with you?"

"If he was, would you expect me to answer that honestly?" Laurie felt himself smiling, heard the sound of it alter his voice, and shut up. He liked Kucharski and had no desire to piss him off either. He waited, holding his hand over the mouthpiece until the agent stopped swearing and his own face was straight. “For the record, he’s not. Send someone around to check if you want.”

“Really? How very kind. His name is Anthony Ward, and I’m surprised he’s not already there. Cooperate, Laurence, and he won’t break your furniture.”

“I will. But you have to know, sir, if Sasha comes to me, I won’t inform you. I’ll hide him if I can, or do any other thing he wants me to do.”

“That’s great, Laurence. That’s really beautiful. Interpol is grateful for your entire family’s cooperation, believe me. Ward is there now. Don’t open up until you’re sure it’s him. One knock and then three, for future reference. I’m bloody certain you’re going to need it.”

* * *

Laurie stood aside and watched in silence while Agent Ward, who was built like a brick shed but astoundingly quiet and subtle in his movements, went patiently over his flat. It didn’t take long. Laurie, arms folded, fought to maintain a solemn mask while Ward looked in the few places a fugitive immigrant might hide, and then, diligently, in the places where he could not—under the sofa, in the kitchen cupboards. He checked the floorboards, glanced upward for access to the building’s loft. Looked at the meter and said, with apparent approval, “Ah, a magical coin, eh?” Then he picked up his raincoat and left, assuring Laurie he was sorry for the inconvenience.

Alone, Laurie stood for a while, resting his palms on the stainless steel draining board of his kitchen sink. It dawned on him that it was pretty dirty. There were things he had not yet got around to doing in this flat which he could see now needed to be done. He was very spoiled, he knew. He’d tried not to be a messy kid growing up—aware that, the more he chucked about, the more Gibson and her housemaids would have to pick up after him—but nevertheless, the staff had always been there. Basically he had no idea of what it took to keep even the simplest living quarters clean. Letting them get into this state was probably the best first lesson he could have.

It was late. The shops were closed, even Sasha's hardworking Indian friend's general store. Pulling open the kitchen cupboards, Laurie saw that either the landlord or some departed tenant had left a bottle of disinfectant and some steel-wool scrubbing pads in there. A duster too. Under the building's communal staircase, he found a vacuum he assumed might be communal too, and dragged its monstrous eighties bulk up the stairs, trying not to bump it off every riser and wake the house.

He worked until one in the morning. Not very efficiently, he thought, but the place did look and smell a lot better when he was done. He watered the plant. The electric fire was on, spreading such heat as it could manage. For want of a change of bed linen, he stripped what there was, shook it hard out of the window in the freezing small hours air, and put it back, turning the duvet cover inside out. Then, feeling that most of the flat's dirt was now transferred onto him, he padded down the corridor to the shared bathroom, where the unsocial time of the morning ensured that, for once, he could have a long bath uninterrupted.

Clean, hollowed out, he put himself to bed.

No hopes or expectations, Sash. But I'm here. I'm ready.

Chapter Twelve

Last day of January on the empty heath, it was hard to tell where the caravans had been. Turning up the collar of his coat against the knifing wind, Laurie tried to get his bearings. The track from the main road, which led to this clearing. On the horizon, that line of trees, in whose shelter he and Sasha had lain.

When the Romani left, they left completely. Sasha had told him this. It was not like a travel folks' camp, where a hundred traces of human habitation might remain—abandoned hubcaps and tarpaulins, old tether pegs for horses. They were too used to being hunted and moved on. Leaving a place came more naturally than staying.

And this camp had been wiped out. Eradicated. Laurie had crept back on that apocalyptic night. Shaken Sir William off when the old man had caught up with him and tried to get him back into the Daimler to go home. He had knelt in the tree line, watching men and women gather around the corpse of Mama Luna. Gunari had knelt over her, sobbing like a child. Laurie had wanted to help them, but he knew he had brought death on them and had no right to ever intrude on them again.

A circle of stones on the ground. Shivering, Laurie went to stand beside them. Inside them was the faintest trace of burning, a bronzing of the frosted earth.

"Laurie?"

He looked up. Clara had stopped her silent carousel circling of an ivy-covered oak and was watching him, eyes wide. He put out a hand to her, and she ran to his side. She leaned against him, pushing one mittened hand into the pocket of his coat.

She wasn't the same child who'd returned from France after Christmas. She hadn't come back to the same world.

Laurie had sat with her in the remains of her old one and tried to explain to her the things that had been changed. He was grateful for Gibson's presence, and his aunt's, but the words had had to come from him: that her father was dead, her mother incapable of looking after her. Conscience, strain, and overwrought nerves had met in Lady Fitzroy a week or so after her confession, and she was now repeatedly assuring the staff of a discreet private nursing home that she would do anything, anything at all for that poor boy.

Clara had listened to him. She had been very calm. She had said she was tired and wanted to go to bed. Laurie had carried her upstairs. Tucking her under the duvet, Laurie had asked her what she felt—just that, because he needed to know she felt something, that shock had not wiped her blank. She had said, "I don't really mind, Laurie. I know I should, but I don't, as long as I have you."

Laurie had tried. He had finished his run as Flamineo at the Empire to great acclaim, and acceded to Mr. Jacobs's insistence that he now move on and find himself a company that could pay him according to his worth. It hadn't taken long. Laurie, who detested musicals, hadn't wanted to go into rep with *Les Misérables*, but the money was good, even for the kind of bit part that was all he could swing for in a big West End show, and the juggernaut that was *Les Miz* showed no sign of slowing down or stopping. Ever. Regular work, a decent wage.

These things established, Laurie had put in a hopeless application for Clara's guardianship. A kindly social worker had come to the flat in East Hill. Laurie could afford something better now, but he could not move. How would Sasha find him? The social worker, who had seen children thrive in accommodations far more cramped and squalid than this, had told him that the flat was not the problem. He was an actor, wasn't he? He lived alone. No matter what he did, he could not guarantee to be at home when Clara needed him. And he was young. Give it a couple of years, some changes in his circumstances, and perhaps they could look at his application again.

Elise Devereaux, who was fond of her nephew and had not contested his guardianship claim, had waited until he came to her, pale and tired, and asked her please to take his sister in. She wanted to be near to Marielle, she said, and rather than disrupt Clara's life still further by a move to France, she would, with Laurie's consent, move with her family into the Mayfair house until things were calmer. That way Laurie could visit—she understood he did not want to move back in—and Clara could go and see him. Laurie had smiled at her in gratitude and told her it really was not up to him. Sir William had been as good—or as bad—as his word and had left his entire property to Clara, to be held in trust until she was eighteen.

He lived for Clara's visits. She came, face alight with the adventure of it, every weekend when he had both days off, and they slummed it, although Laurie's standards of housekeeping were now quite high, and they washed and recycled their tins when they'd eaten the beans directly out of them. They had long walks. The heath was the nearest big stretch of outdoors, and Clara loved it, flying around in its windy vacancies, forgetting for a while that she was different now. That she was sobered, shadowed, leaving childhood behind. Her hand in his pocket clenched and stirred, and Laurie stroked her hair. "All right, love," he said. "Let's go home."

"All right. Are *you* all right? What was here?"

Laurie couldn't tell her. Sometimes he thought the events of that night had broken him in ways he didn't yet understand. He was fine when he was busy, and he lived as good and regular a life as he could manage. But when he let his guard down, things were strange. Walking home from the Tube stop one night, he had picked up a tail—a couple of thugs who catcalled and jeered and followed him a block or two, long enough to make his heart beat fast, and yet when he'd turned a corner, they'd been gone. The Indian general dealer, one day when he'd been short of cash and gone in to do what he could with a fiver, had handed him a twenty, assuring him he'd dropped it on the floor last time he had been in. Laurie somehow never felt entirely alone.

But he was. Sasha had vanished as completely from his world as he had from off John Kucharski's radar. Laurie, always ready, had waited. Was waiting still. He took Clara's hand. The year's first snow began to fall, whirling in wind-driven spirals around them. Soon the edges of the world were blurred, the air a dancing chaos. Laurie waited until the flakes were coming fast enough that he could half convince himself the caravans were back again, and then he turned away.

* * *

February the second. Only just—Laurie heard his alarm clock beep midnight as he fell through the door. His *Misérables* nights seldom ended much earlier than this, but tonight he'd got entangled in an after-show party and barely caught his last train home. Counting on his fingers, he worked out what day it was and how many times he'd manned the barricades and danced up and down the streets of revolutionary Paris that week, and decided with relief that tomorrow had to be his day off.

There'd been food at the party, and since tomorrow was Saturday anyway, he didn't need to cook himself the dutiful late supper he seldom wanted but knew he had to have if he wanted to wake up the next day capable of getting out of bed. He hadn't foreseen—probably few straight-drama actors did—the sheer bloody effort of musicals. He was aching from his hip bones down to the balls of his feet. Flopping down onto the sofa, he kicked off his shoes and socks and inspected the damage. Not too bad.

His blisters from the first week had callused over, and his arches, though throbbing, were intact.

He let his head fall back. He wondered if he had the energy left to be lonely. If so, it was his own doing. He could have had company tonight. The boy playing Enjolras, who had been gently circling him for the last week or so, had made his move, emboldened by cheap champagne. Laurie, cornered in the cloakroom, had for a few seconds been too surprised to do more than stand there, pressed back among the coats, letting Enjolras kiss him and run hungry hands down his spine to his backside. The extrication had been hard. Enjolras had been embarrassed and upset. And there was nothing wrong with him, or with what he had done—on the contrary, for that first moment his touch, the press of his body, had been delicious. It was just that he wasn't Sasha.

Laurie lifted a hand to touch his lip. It was a bit sore. Enjolras, nervous, had been rough. Pressing the bruise, Laurie tried to conjure the mouth he did want there. Always warm. Texture of grape skin and suede. Often as not, smiling as it descended onto Laurie's, not just a kiss but a grace, a benediction. Shivering, Laurie rested a hand on the fly of his jeans and arched up against his own touch. But he was too worn-out even for that, and he closed his eyes, letting his hand fall away.

February the second. Candlemas, St. Bridget's day. He hoped she was looking after Marielle Fitzroy, other than whom she had no more devout worshipper. Laurie remembered being taken to the early morning mass at St. Patrick's in Soho Square and seeing the church full of snowdrops and candle flame, heralding the arrival of spring. Bride's day, too, the goddess of painters, poets, metalsmiths, and players. That had been the excuse for the party at the Queen's. Theatrical people were careful to placate all available deities. Laurie had heard whispers that Bride had been good to him and the director was going to ask him to try out for Marius. Laurie shuddered. He prayed not. The pay would be too good for him to turn it down, and yet he did not think he could spend six nights a week persuading Eponine in musical couplets not to die. Perhaps his indifferent voice would save him. Good enough for spoofing opera to Clara. Not, he was fairly sure, even halfway strong enough to fill the Queen's capacity-crowd spaces, vibrating the plasterwork and the audience's heartstrings like their majestic Valjean and Javert.

His thoughts became disjointed. He should get himself to bed, he knew. But he was suddenly too tired to move, and his sleepy brain had caught some trace of Sasha in its electrical flickering. Something so clear that Laurie, when he inhaled, could smell him, could feel his skin against his palms. Smiling, letting go, Laurie followed him into the dark.

* * *

Cold air woke him at dawn. Unwillingly he watched the vivid tapestry of his dreams bleach out to black-and-white, then fall apart in cobwebs. That was the trouble with passing out here on the sofa, he reflected, sitting up stiffly. Waking with a crick in his neck and chilled to the bone. The contrasts between his night world and this were sharper than if he'd at least come around in his bed, where combined lingering scents of his own and Sasha's allowed him a few seconds' cushioning fantasy. Well, it was Saturday. He could go back there for a while, drag the duvet over his head and slip away for a little longer, try to catch the tail of the dream the chill in the room had interrupted. With him on the heath once more—only this time it had been summer—Sash lying in the long grass beside him, trailing a fern leaf down Laurie's chest, over his solar plexus, and down his naked belly. Smiling, shivering, Laurie swung his legs off the sofa.

God, though, it *was* cold, even for a one-bar-fire flat. Glancing over, Laurie saw he'd left it on. Fire hazard as it was, at least it was free. It wanted to be, he thought. It was doing nothing. The living room was freezing, as if…

As if a window was wide-open. Laurie stared at the room's far wall, trying to make sense of its differences. What he could see of the sky beyond the railway lines and the terrace beyond them was stunningly clear. Only a first luminescence, not so much dawn as the distant promise of it. The nights were getting a bit shorter, he had begun to notice, though normally he did not see it until he was outside. The windows on the railway side of the building were gray with diesel. Now Laurie could pick out silver blue from the first trace of rose, and every single fading star.

Yes. The veiling glass was gone, the window shoved high as it would go. The other difference on that side of the room was the dim human shape occupying the space between the window and the sofa—dead still, as if watching in silence for God knew how long. Laurie's heart shot up in his chest, so hard he thought it would burst. His throat closed, squeezing his cry to a whisper. "Sasha!"

"No." The shape moved, and Laurie saw his mistake. Sasha's elegant silhouette would have fitted twice into the bulk now outlined against the translucent dawn. Too sleepy and astonished to feel fear, Laurie knew only the swipe—like a vast descending wing—of loss, of renewed sorrow. The voice was not dissimilar. Soft, loaded with velvety intonations. Romanian… "Why, gajo? Is that the way he lets himself in? Through the window, or"—the human darkness took a step toward him—"or do you open your door to him, like the little *polone* you are?"

Laurie barely had a second to begin to wonder what he had been called this time—let alone who this thug was, although *gajo* brought back plenty of memories. A fist like a lump of kebab meat fastened in his shirt. The room shot around him through a hundred and eighty degrees, window exchanging place with the door. The edge of the sink unit punched him in the stomach, and its metal draining board leapt up to smack the side of his face. Once, then again, as his assailant swapped the grip on his shirtfront for one at the back of his neck—and a third time, which made him care less about everything somehow. He was just vaguely glad he'd cleaned it. He could smell disinfectant, and the depressing tang of old food, eaten joylessly and lonely, which rose up from the sink no matter how thoroughly he scrubbed. Then connections formed in his ringing skull. The accent. John Kucharski's story of a vengeful father who would not let go. He heard himself say, with surprise that he could still talk and take an interest, "Are you…are you Stefan Petrica?"

Laughter shook his assailant. Yes, a vibration. Silent, but Laurie felt it through the hot bulk pressed tight to his back. The grip had moved again—from his collar into his hair, which the *Les Miz* director was making him grow for the sake of the revolution. Probably little suspecting how much it would hurt when grabbed and twisted. "Stefan!" the dark voice echoed, a harsh explosion up against his ear. "For a little fish like you? You're joking." Laurie's scalp burned as the grip yanked him upward. A thin line of cold, like a wire, stung suddenly against his throat—*but you need two hands to garrote someone, don't you? Just the blade of a knife, then.* Almost a relief. "Where is he? Where's Stefan's brat?"

"I don't know!" For the first time, Laurie was glad that it was true. Wildly glad—this thug could do as he pleased with him, and still it would not lie within Laurie's power to betray Sasha again. Some suicidal gleam of amusement went through him at the stupidity of Interpol agents and Romanian heavies, and he added, as he had to Kucharski, "Do you think I'd…bloody tell you, if I knew?"

This time his assailant laughed aloud. Laurie guessed he didn't like his victims too docile. "Oh, you will. You will, polone. You soft-skinned gaje never know how much pain you can feel, until you're shown. And I'm in no hurry. We can have a little fun while we wait." He shifted, and his grip left Laurie's hair. His movement brought the heated press of his erection up against Laurie's backside. "Come on. You're used to it, aren't you, little faggot? I know you let Stefan's boy fuck you. It's not like you don't know how."

And now fear struck at Laurie like a snake. Not of rape—although, Christ, he did not want the long, hot shaft now unzipped and shoving at him, could not imagine it tearing up into his flesh—but what it would take from him. What it would wipe out. He had been Sasha's in that way. Only once, but for always. Laurie didn't know when that resolve had burned into his mind, but there it was. He didn't know what life would bring. All he knew was that he had done with that part of it, until and unless Sash came back to him. A bed in a rusty, damp caravan. A sleeping bag spread out for warmth. "Sasha," he whispered—no more than a movement of his lips. A promise. A good-bye.

He felt, with an indescribable shudder of mind, flesh, and bone, the knife blade burst the skin.

A soft thud. Laurie caught his breath to silence it. Behind him, he felt the big man go still too. Laurie could not define it. It was as if a cat had jumped into the room. No. Larger. A panther or one of the mythical beasts that haunted English fields and started black beast panics in the countryside.

Then a sharp command in a language he did not know. In a voice he absolutely did. He jolted upright, suddenly able to—his assailant had jerked up too. He felt himself dragged backward, the knife following, searing its hot ice across his throat. His vision reddened and sparked, and through its glitter, he saw… God, he saw Sasha, poised against the brightening sky.

Sasha said, in English this time, "Luca, drop the knife. Let go of him."

Laughter rumbled against Laurie's ear. He wasn't surprised. He couldn't see how Sasha had a hope in hell. He was just as Laurie remembered him—upright, slender, beautiful. His dark eyes somehow full of their own light. Perhaps he was hoping to influence Luca—*Luca*, for God's sake, a name like a crown of daisies on a bear—by charm alone. Well, it should work, from Laurie's point of view. Joy seized him, despite the terror of the moment. "Sasha! Oh, God. Sash!"

"Yes. It's all right, ves'tacha. You'll be okay. Just stay very still."

Luca dragged him back another step. He was still laughing, but it had an edge to it, as if for some reason he was afraid. "Don't be stupid, Alexandru. Your father wants to talk to you; that's all."

"Fine. I'll talk. Just let him go."

The grip on Laurie slackened. "All right. Give me the gun, and he's yours."

The gun. Sasha shifted, and Laurie saw that his hands were not empty. There was a dull, blue-black gleam between them. Laurie observed, with nausea, how Sasha's fine-boned fingers curled around the grip. He knew bugger all about guns, but this was a serious one—heavy and large, with what he guessed to be a silencer thickening its muzzle. He swallowed, sucking in a breath as the pressure vanished from his throat. A foreboding seized him.

"Sash," he whispered. "No. Don't give it to him."

"It's okay, Laurie. Stand away from him. He'll let you go."

Luca did. Sasha advanced a couple of steps, his gaze on Luca unwavering. The gun clicked—the safety going on, Laurie guessed—and he held it out in one steady hand. "Take it. All right. Now, let's go."

Luca backed up toward the door. Sasha followed calmly after, smiling faintly. "Don't go with him," Laurie said, low and urgent. "Don't trust him. He's gonna hurt you."

"Don't worry, Laurie. I'll come back to you, okay? I love you."

Laurie watched the flicker of disgust pass over Luca's face. It didn't bother him, though he thought it pretty rich from somebody who'd been about to rape him. What bothered him was the grim smile that followed it. The hardening. Luca, to this point, had not had time to do up his pants, and the gaping fly lent an element of grotesque comedy to the scene. He reached the door. Laurie, whose job it was to read and reproduce human faces, to portray convincingly their million nuances of feeling and intention, saw what he meant to do. "Sash! No!" he cried, and reached out to grab Sasha's arm. "He's been sent to kill you."

Luca swung the gun on both of them, snapping the safety catch off. He accorded Laurie a glance of acknowledgement—almost respect. "Not bad, gajo." Then he turned the muzzle and his full attention onto Sasha, who had stepped to Laurie's side. Who was already trying to get in front of him, to shield him. "Come on, Alexandru," Luca said. "I'm not your father's fucking errand boy. I'm his assassin. You know that."

"Yes. I do. But not here, Luca, for God's sake. Not in front of Laurie."

"He won't have long to grieve. You've been on the run too long, Sandru. Told too many people our secrets. Too much pillow talk. I know you've been trying to watch over him, but it's no good. 'My son and his friends,' your father said. You know I have to take both of you—then anyone else you've been playmates with. Come on. Don't make this harder than it needs to be."

"There isn't anyone else! Luca, there isn't even him. I've told him nothing. Let him go!"

Laurie drew one breath. Sasha had moved right in front of him. Hesitantly, as if frightened, Laurie crept up close to him. He put one hand on his shoulder—passed the other around his waist. To do so, even now, was food and drink to him, sunlight at last on his skin. He pressed his face to Sasha's shoulder, as if hiding. Sasha gave a kind of moan and tried to reach back for him, blindly caressing. "Ah, love, don't be scared," he whispered. "I won't let him. I won't let him. Luca, for fuck's sake. *Let him go*!"

Luca would not. Laurie knew this. He knew nothing about guns, assassins, or the terrible world that had encompassed his, but he knew men's faces. And he knew how to act.

He shoved Sasha aside. He was a boy in a play who had been held at gunpoint too long and had cracked. He was the coward, the one who broke down and pleaded for his life. Sasha, caught off balance, had dropped to his hands and one knee by the sofa. Laurie lurched forward. "Oh, God, don't!" he wailed, flinging out his hands at Luca, seeing how the gesture brought the gun muzzle swinging in his direction. A defensive instinct. *Good.* "I don't want to die!" He allowed his legs to give. A proper stage collapse had to be done with care. You always hurt yourself a bit. Trying to guard yourself, to save yourself with an outstretched hand, spoiled it entirely. And yet the movement had to be controlled, impact absorbed in carefully tensed muscles. You had to be able to die.

He fell at Luca's feet. Heard his growl of contempt, and that was fine with Laurie too. Contemptible men were not dangerous. They clutched at your ankles despairingly—not to distract or unbalance you. They did not uncoil, drive one gouging fist into your balls, and snatch your gun.

Luca's reflexes were good. His grip closed on thin air an inch behind Laurie's exit lunge, his leap back and away. Laurie would have choreographed it better for the stage—so bold a move deserved a better coda, not an undignified thump onto the sofa as he misjudged his footing and the little table in front of it knocked his knees out from under him. Instantly he scrabbled back up.

He was lucky, he knew, not to have shot himself. He held the gun as he had been taught in props class, straight and true, pleased at least that he had the right end of the thing trained on Luca. "All right, you bastard!" he snarled. "That's it. Get the fuck out of my flat. If you ever come near me or Sash again, I'll…"

He trailed off. Partly it was an uncertainty about how on earth he should finish the threat. He could kill, he thought, but it would have to be in hottest blood. It would have to be a man who was attacking him or hurting Sash—not staring at him, disarmed, in absolute bewilderment. And partly it was that someone was laughing. Not Luca. This sound gave Laurie nothing but pleasure. He had seldom heard it. His dealings with Sasha had been too intense for much comedy. Laurie glanced at him without altering his aim.

"Sasha. What?"

"Give that to me." Sasha was getting to his feet, holding out one hand. His eyes were bright with laughter, tears beginning to catch in his lashes.

"Why? I'm okay."

"Yes. But you can't use a gun. And Luca knows it. You're not *that* good an actor."

Laurie swallowed. It was fair point gained. Already Luca was shifting, his own grim smile beginning. "Oh?" Laurie whispered, edging toward Sasha, keeping his fierce mask in place. "And you *can* use one, right?"

"That's right. I'm sorry, ves'tacha. So much I should have told you." He met Laurie's eyes, and carefully,

carefully, lifted the weapon from his grasp. He sobered absolutely. "Yes. I can use a gun. Forgive me, Luca. You should never have come here."

Laurie stared at the corpse on his carpet. He had not thought this was how violent death came about—so quick, so soundlessly. The gun's silencer was good. Only the faintest detonation, like percussion heard through someone else's headphones, had accompanied Sasha's squeeze of the trigger. All Laurie's attention had been on him, not on Luca. No terrible crunch of bone and blood. Even now, all he could see was a neat, dark hole in Luca's T-shirt, just over the heart.

Warm hands closed on both his shoulders. "Laurie. Laurie, come away."

That was Sasha. Laurie didn't think anything else could have broken his trance. He had seen death before. Luca, in his blank-eyed sprawl, had lost half his apparent bulk, just as Laurie's father had, laid out on the hospital slab. But he had not seen *dying*. He stumbled back a little, turning, and felt Sasha seize him and grasp him tight. "Oh, Laurie. Forgive me."

Laurie breathed him in. He smelled of the night, of frost. Of hard living, as if he had been forced back out onto the streets. Laurie closed both arms around his back, gulped down air, short inhalations, until he could speak. "Forgive *you*?"

"Yes. So much trouble and darkness. I tried…I tried to keep it away. I tried to keep away from you."

"It was me that brought trouble to you." That did not sound right. Sasha had once taught him an easy grammar rule for checking, but he couldn't remember it now. "I brought my father to Birchwood. I killed Mama Luna."

"Ah, no. No, love. She would never say that, I swear to you. Now, Laurie…" Sasha squeezed him ferociously, then pressed his hands to his shoulders, trying to ease him away. "Now I have to go. My people aren't like Mama Luna.

They're like *him*. And there'll be more, just like him, who come after."

He pulled himself away. Laurie, frozen with shock, for a moment could only stare at him. He remained rooted stupidly to the spot until Sash was almost at the door. He had arrived so suddenly—his absence before that had been so complete, so dreadful—that damaged emotional tendons inside Laurie, strained beyond elasticity, were failing to respond. There was an instant when he could have let him go.

But just one.

Sasha gasped as his exit was blocked. Laurie took him by his collar, then knocked him hard against the wall. "No," he snapped. "You don't do this to me again. Kucharski offered you a deal. You're a refugee, and neither of us owes our sodding fathers anything. Take it."

"Laurie," Sasha whispered. His eyes were wide, pupils dilated all the way with shock. "I ran. I've got an unlicensed gun. I just killed someone. All deals are off."

Laurie stood silently, taking this in. He glanced around the room. An unlicensed gun. Yes, there it was on the table, where Sasha had carefully set it down after shooting Luca through the heart, as if it had had one sole purpose and was now useless to him. "You don't have a gun," he said, releasing Sasha with one hand, reaching with the other into the pocket of his jeans. "What would you be doing with a gun? Your prints are on that one because you used it to defend me. Luca's are on it because it belongs to him. All right?" Sasha gazed at him. Laurie, who felt like a stranger to himself, was not surprised at the blank lack of recognition in his eyes. "As for running, Kucharski knows why you did that. And you've no idea how badly he wants Stefan Petrica." He handed Sasha his mobile and watched him take it blindly. "That's Kucharski's number. Call him."

Sasha wrenched from his grasp. He turned his back—walked away from him with his head down. Laurie shuddered and folded his arms across his chest. What had he done? By what right did he tell Sasha what to do? Christ. In exacting obedience from Sasha, what had Laurie sacrificed? Couldn't he have been content to love him and let him alone, even if that meant losing him?

Sasha slumped down onto the sofa. He propped one elbow on his knee and ran a hand into his hair. In his other hand, he clutched the mobile so hard his knuckles were white. He said, after a moment, "Is that DS Kucharski?"

A pause, during which Laurie thought he could hear frost forming beyond the open window.

"Yes. This is Sasha. This is Alexandru Petrica. I'm turning myself in. I'm in East Hill with Laurie Fitzroy. I want to seek asylum, and…I'm prepared to give up Stefan to you. My father."

There was a long pause. During it, Laurie could only imagine what John Kucharski had to say. The last part of it must have been *why now* or *why the change of heart*, because Sasha suddenly looked up. Tears were pouring down his face. He said, brokenly, all the ice gone from his voice, "Because of Laurie. My father sent someone, and…he was going to hurt Laurie."

Laurie stumbled over to him. The mobile clattered to the floor. Laurie knelt, said, "Here," and caught Sasha as he crumpled off the sofa and into his arms. He turned so that he shielded Sasha with his body from Luca's dead stare, and clutched him and kissed the crown of his head until the seizure of sobbing relented.

Laurie was half-relieved, half-afraid. He had known Sasha could cry, but Alexandru—son of Stefan Petrica, capable marksman, deadly in proportion to the world from which he'd come—Alexandru was new ground to him. Tenderness and pride racked Laurie at once. He was seeing—beginning to see—all that Sasha was; Sasha was letting him see it. "Hush," he said, rocking him. "You're okay. You're home now."

Sasha snatched a breath and choked. "That's the…problem," he said when he could. His hot brow was pressed to Laurie's shoulder, hands clenching in the wool of his sweater. "I was so close. Living in a squat in the next street. I was watching you."

"Heading off muggers. Leaving a deposit for me at the bank of Hassan Greengrocer." Laurie kissed wet salt off Sasha's cheek. "I know."

"But I couldn't come to you. I couldn't come home."

"God, Sash. Do you think I'd have cared? About the danger, or… I'd rather have faced that a hundred times than all those nights not knowing where you were. Is that why you wouldn't stick around after I'd moved in here?"

"Well, I did. Far too often. I'd thought we were safe, thought I'd shaken them off. When you left home, all I meant to do was look after you. And I wanted to live with you." He gripped Laurie's arms convulsively. "When you asked me to move in, it nearly killed me to say no. But I swear to you, the very day after you came here, I thought I saw one of my father's men near the camp. I should have cleared out then. But I couldn't. I didn't see him again, so I kept taking chances, coming back to you, then being so afraid…"

"And running back into the dark. Please, sweetheart. Never again."

"Oh—like I could. My father's mob would have killed me if I'd been deported back home, but it wasn't why I ran from the immigration police. I couldn't stand the thought of a sea between us. Thinking of that, so much distance—it was stones on my chest. I…I couldn't breathe."

"Breathe now." He was struggling, half-drowned in tears. Laurie sat back to ease it, to let him get the morning air coming in through the window. It was fresh—laced with petrol fumes, but somehow sweet. Full of light. They knelt together in the February sun. "After that night at the camp," he said quietly, "and what happened to Mama Luna, I didn't think you'd even want to come," he said. "I hoped, but—"

"Oh, Laurie. I tried to hate you, but it lasted not even ten minutes. Not even till I got out of the woods. Your father did that, love. Not you. I know what he can do to you. I know."

"Not anymore. Sash, once we sort out your stuff, we're free. Out from under. He died."

Sasha went still. He lifted his head and looked at Laurie in astonishment. "What happened?"

"Heart attack. Too many years of getting apoplectic with rage over foreigners, queers, and other vermin. I think the pair of us shoved him over the edge."

Sasha snorted with laughter. It wasn't a good idea, and he reached gratefully for the handkerchief Laurie produced for him. "For God's sake. John Kucharski told me that Clara was safe. That there'd been some huge family misunderstanding. Was that something to do with your father?"

"I'll tell you all about it soon, but his death solved it. Yes."

"Thank God." Sasha reached out a hand. He touched his fingertips to Laurie's cheekbone, his brow, as if seeing him wasn't enough.

Not enough for Laurie either. There was a corpse in the room, and Laurie had no doubt that at least one Interpol agent was burning up the road in their direction. If the world had been ending, though, he couldn't have kept his hands from Sasha's face, his mouth from falling softly on the swollen one lifting to find it. The tang of salt hit him first, then, in a rush, the taste he hadn't even known he'd registered, let alone missed. *Sasha.* He'd been starving without it. He pushed his fingers into Sasha's hair, feeling his gesture returned as they both measured the distance and the time they'd been apart. "This is beautiful," Sasha gasped, pulling back from the kiss. "Longer. Enough to bury my hands in."

"Yes. I've been in the eighteenth century. And you… This is shorter, like velvet…"

"Mm. Bloke in the squat with me had a set of clippers. Fifty pence for a grade one."

Laurie broke into shocked laughter. Sasha silenced him, warm mouth hungry, drawing him forward until the edge of the sofa stopped them. "Sash, not here," Laurie whispered. "Get up. Let's go into the bedroom, away from…"

He didn't need to finish. Sasha cast a glance back at Luca, then scrambled up into Laurie's arms with frantic haste. "We don't have time, do we?" he murmured, clinging to Laurie. "They'll be here soon—Kucharski or…"

"I don't know. But come on, love. Please."

No need to ask Sasha twice. He put an arm round Laurie's waist and led him through into the bedroom, whose tiny confines were ablaze with morning light. They fell onto the bed together, Laurie banging his head off the wall and barely noticing, though Sasha did, gasping and reaching out to stroke his skull. "I'm all right," Laurie assured him, hauling him on top. "You, though—even skinnier…"

"You can talk." Sasha's hands ran hard down his ribs, then his hip bones. "What've you been doing?"

"Missing you. Dancing."

Sasha looked up from the task of unbuttoning Laurie's jeans, a puzzled smile quirking. "Dancing? Hamlet dances?"

"Nn-nn. Not that gloomy bugger. Fourteenth chorus boy in *Les Misérables* does, though."

"Chorus?" Sasha sat up long enough for Laurie to help him struggle out of his parka. "What are you doing that for?"

"Money," Laurie said succinctly—the one clear word he could get out before Sasha plunged back down, driving the air from his lungs. He smiled. He'd encountered this pair of charity-shop combat trousers before, knew how to deal with their complicated fastenings. *There you are...*

Sasha groaned against his neck as the zip gave, and thrust down hard, shivering with passion. "God. Sorry."

"What the hell for?"

"Pouncing on you. I planned... I dreamed, every night, how I'd do it when I found you again, how I'd have you or let you have me, so slow, so sweet..."

Laurie pushed his hands under the fabric of Sasha's briefs. He seized his backside tight, thrusting up at him, beginning their rhythm. "Reckon we've got ten minutes max, love. So pounce away."

"Oh, Laurie—so hungry for you, so hot..."

It didn't take ten minutes. It barely took two. Laurie's mind flared with the images Sasha had painted—their first reunited fuck, alone in the soft-thudding heart of the world, sweet and slow. This was neither. This was the rough coupling without which both would die. Sparing a hand, Laurie clenched it in the nape of Sasha's T-shirt, dragging him down tight, locking him into a kiss. Laurie's cock rammed painfully against Sasha's thigh, and he shoved his hips up in brief, violent synchrony to meet him. Sasha unleashed a raw shout and came, bruising Laurie's ribs where he was holding him. Something tangled in Laurie—a need too intense to cope with its satisfaction, an emotional air lock—and he wailed, struggling on the brink. But Sasha, even done and beyond done, did not let him go. Would never let him go—stayed in place, soaked and panting, till Laurie's block evaporated, releasing him to shuddering climax.

Time passed in the sunny room. How much, Laurie couldn't tell—he marked it only in the slow return to normal of his own breathing and Sasha's. Sasha's head was pillowed on his shoulder. He'd taken one of Laurie's hands and spread the fingers, looking into his palm as if seeking answers there. At length he said, an odd note of apprehension in his voice, "So now your father's gone, are you…Lord Laurence of somewhere? Heir to his millions and ruler of all you survey?"

Laurie smiled. He cleared his throat and found he could speak. "I can disclaim my peerage. But if you mean what I'm surveying right now, yes. Rent's paid here till the end of the month. Other than that, nothing's changed. His will's with the lawyers at the moment, but I'm pretty sure he left the lot to Clara."

Sasha kissed his palm. Laurie had to wonder at the man who would suddenly give him such a look of relief—of exhilaration, almost—at the prospect of a life of poverty. "I don't know what you're grinning about," Laurie said, stroking back Sasha's hair. "I'll never make any money, you know. We'll be eating Hassan's discount soup for the rest of our days."

For the rest of our days. Well, he had said it. He could have wished they were on a beach somewhere, or at a nice restaurant, or anywhere really without a fresh corpse in the next room, but it was said. He watched Sasha hearing it and understanding. Sasha said softly, "I'm glad, love. I could never have given you anything, could I, if—"

"If I'd been Lord Laurence of somewhere."

"That's right. And I want to, Laurie. For the rest…" He paused and suddenly blushed up to his hairline beneath his weary pallor. "God. How *but guli*. How…what's the English word?" Laurie, who seldom knew him at a loss for one, waited with interest to discover what had given him pause. "Yes," he finished after a second, still blushing, with an air of satisfaction. "How *corny*, ves'tacha. But yes. For the rest of our days."

Laurie pressed his mouth to Sasha's. Now in their aftermath, he could do it without bruising them both, and their kiss became a slow, almost shy rediscovery. The room chilled around them. He should have got up and shut the window. He should have shut the bedroom door to seal out the smell of blood. He closed his eyes and interlaced his fingers with Sasha's and let the sunlit time drift on.

Footsteps on the stairs. The sound carried clearly through the flat, and they jolted apart. He held Sasha's shoulders. One knock came, and then another three in swift succession. Laurie smiled. A hell of a lot had changed in his life, hadn't it, for him to have a prearranged signal knock with bloody Interpol.

"It's all right," he said. "It's Kucharski, or one of his men. Don't be frightened. I'll be with you." He pressed his brow to Sasha's. "Not going to let you out of my sight."

Chapter Thirteen

A pine coast—a Cézanne coast of impossible blues and golds. Rocky inlets, new moon bays. A wild coast, backed by hundreds of miles of maquis and pine forest. You could walk for a day and not see anyone. A good place to hide a child.

Laurie had wondered, looking out to the sea from his room in Elise's château, how long his mother would have held out. Forever, possibly, though he was not sure that Elise could have tolerated her part for long.

A more robust soul than her sister, she had sat in the Mayfair house and listened in horror while Laurie told her how Marielle had tried to divert the focus of Clara's disappearance. Like her sister, she had felt the need to offer recompense, but while neither Sasha nor Laurie could accept financial help, they did not turn down her invitation to the Languedoc château. Elise was thinking of moving back there, she said, once Clara was more settled. Of selling the Mayfair house, with all its bad memories, if Clara's trustees would consent, and taking the girl and her mother back to the sunshine world poor Marielle should never have left. Clara could go to school with her cousins.

Could Laurie bear that? There would always be holidays. Laurie would be welcome, together with the young man who would probably still be referred to with a smiling, polite *ton ami* if he and Sasha lived to draw their pensions.

Sasha bore no ill will. He had talked to Marielle on his own quietly, both of them foreigners on strange English soil. Marielle could more or less take things in again now, certainly to the extent of knowing she had been forgiven. Better than that, *understood*, because Sasha, after all that he had seen and done, was not about to condemn a mother for loving her own daughter best. They hadn't known one another then, he told her. Things would be different now.

And so he and Laurie had come to France for their first holiday. It was Easter, three hard-strapped months since Laurie had been cut loose on the world. Sasha had ordered him, as soon as he had heard of his latest career move, to drop *Les Miz* and rediscover his inner Hamlet. He would rather they both starve, he said, than that Laurie should wear out his strength and his talents in any chorus, no matter how grand. Thanking him dryly on both their behalves, Laurie had obeyed him.

Starvation had not quite been necessary. They had sometimes come close—though not by Sasha's standards, who still considered himself almost guiltily rich if he had more than a tenner to dispose of at any one time. Laurie had landed the role of Biff Loman in a new production of *Death of a Salesman*, developed on the spot a perfect Brooklyn accent, and gone to work. The pay was twice what Jacobs had been able to give him, and his first night at the Bloomsbury Hall a vivid contrast to his debut, every one of his giveaway tickets eagerly taken—Clara and Elise in the front row, shoulder to shoulder with Sasha in his new, posh jacket, and Jacobs himself next to him, bearing no grudges, beaming and mouthing the lines in case Laurie forgot.

They were doing all right. Sasha, asylum status granted, was working too, translating for an outreach branch of the Romanian embassy in London, gladly helping teach newcomers what he'd had to learn the hard way. In September he would start at college. John Kucharski had set that up for him, pointing out the necessity for turning his various gifts into paper qualifications, after which, he said, Sasha should come to him again. Interpol and Border UK needed agents who'd seen the system from the other side. Sasha, who plainly felt that much of his allegiance still lay with that shadow world, could not imagine being part of the forces that controlled it, but had said he would consider it. At the moment all he wanted was to work and to learn.

And to live with Laurie. They had not spent one night apart since Sasha's very nominal three-day return to the detention facility, just long enough for Kucharski to draw up the paperwork to set him free. Kucharski, anxious to protect his witness, had tried to move them out of the East Hill flat, but both had refused to go. Sasha gave his evidence, and still they refused. By then they could have afforded something better, but their associations with the place—their meetings there, the refuge it had been, the life-or-death scene enacted in its living room—were too vivid. Even Luca's bloodstains on the carpet could not spoil it for them. They hired an industrial cleaner to remove them, but Laurie wondered if Sash thought Laurie didn't see how he sometimes crouched down to touch their shadows, as if they could avert further evil. They slept in a passionate tangle in Laurie's single bed.

The Languedoc had come almost as a shock to them. So much light and air—endless green spaces arched over with imperturbable blue sky, a climate as serenely different as could be imagined from that of London or Bucharest. Laurie had been here many times before but somehow hadn't seen it. It had taken him his first real-world winter to reveal to him the perfect sunlit fantasy this was. Drenched in scents of myrtle, in the tang of heated resin blowing in from the coast. The Devereaux estate was only three miles from the sea. They walked there and back almost every day, often with family, alone as often as they could without seeming rude.

Sasha had drawn a little ahead of him among the dunes. Laurie had let him, happy with the rear view. No one could have taken more rewardingly to sunshine and good food than Sasha. At the end of their two weeks in the sun, he was still whip thin but had filled out his hollows in lean muscle. His skin glowed. He hadn't owned much by way of summer clothes, but Laurie's fit him now, and the male Devereaux cousins, sardonic and friendly, lifting dark eyebrows at their shared room and declaring that, *bien sûr*, they'd always known about Laurence, were happy to share their wardrobes. Today, a white shirt worn soft with sun and washing and a pair of Lucien's jeans, whose fit left nothing to the imagination. Laurie, who remembered the torn parka, the huddle of sweaters beneath which he once had found the skinny refugee boy, watched him in unadulterated pleasure. A breeze was coming off the sea, making the blazing day bearable. It stirred Sasha's hair, made the cotton of his shirt flutter and flatten against him.

Almost unadulterated. Sasha did not run these dunes the way the Devereaux cousins did. Laurie felt an ever-present background note of anxiety rise up and blend with his desire. Stefan Petrica and his vast network of dealers and runners had been most efficiently rounded up, but Kucharski had warned them that such gangs were never truly stamped out. That they should get on with their lives—but watch each other's backs while they were at it. The warning hadn't come as news to Sasha, Laurie could tell. In the city, the care with which he moved, his caution, were not so apparent. Most people kept sharp eyes about them there. Out here, Laurie observed how his guard was never quite down. He chased Clara up and down the dunes but stopped before he broached their skylines, ducking down to scan the bright distances that glimmered all around. On pine forest tracks, he would keep to the tree line—or, more often, subtly make sure that Laurie did, placing himself on his other side, between him and the direction from which any harm must come. He had gone ahead now, Laurie guessed, because their path was widening out into a bay whose far side was bounded by a tumble of lichen-starred rocks, the only direction without a clear view.

Somehow Laurie had never seen this bay before. It was not far from their usual walks, just half a mile down a white sand track from the forest. Invisible from there, though. You followed the track on faith and emerged into the bay at the last moment. Sasha had slowed down as the turquoise sea suddenly revealed itself before him, flashing diamonds and purring up softly onto ivory sand. The beach was quite narrow, shaded all along its crescent by pines that had caught enough soil in their roots for a thick, rich turf to grow, scattered with wildflowers. "Sash," he said yearningly, holding out a hand.

Sasha stopped. He turned to him, and Laurie saw that he was ready too, eyes dark with passion even in the brilliant light, cock lifted explicitly beneath the worn denim as if he had been waiting for Laurie to end the pursuit. The pine shadows dappled his skin. "Yes," he said, taking Laurie's hand and pulling him in. "Where's Clara?"

"Gone back with Lucien. They've all gone back."

"Thank God."

Laurie smiled. Sasha kissed him with joint-dissolving intensity, holding his backside and gently shoving until Laurie was erect as well, moaning with arousal and discomfort at restricting fabric. "Thought you liked them," he said, when Sasha had let him go and was deftly unfastening his shirt.

"I do. They're perfect, beautiful people. But you can't do what you're about to do to me with family members present. Or even in a five-mile radius."

"Bloody hell," Laurie observed, grinning widely. He wasn't as tidy with buttons as Sasha and removed the white shirt the basic way, seizing its hem and pulling it up and over Sasha's head. The satin-skin chest and shoulders, the stomach beginning its adult musculature, snatched the breath from him as it always did. He said faintly, staring at Sasha, "What *am* I about to do?"

"Requires you to take my pants off. Completely, or..." Sasha hesitated, and Laurie saw in the drifting shade that he was blushing, as if unnerved by his own boldness. "Or I won't be able to wrap my legs around you." He swallowed audibly, looking down, and Laurie took pity even while the shuddering wave of need occasioned by the words washed through him. He drew Sasha forward, gave him refuge on his shoulder, running a hand through Sasha's hair while he finished in a rough whisper, "Around your waist. Over your shoulders. Or you won't be able to...fuck me face-to-face, down here on the sand."

Laurie groaned. His cock leaped. They'd tried most things, once reunited back in London, and with nightly diligence too. But not that. Not that, and Sash had been much too discreet a guest in Elise's house to be able to let go. They'd been almost chaste in their shared, lovely room. A fortnight could be a long time.

"Oh, God. Sash, I didn't bring anything. I—"

"I know. Saw you thinking about it; then Clara joined the party, and..."

"Well. You know what she's like. She'd have found the tube and tried to use it as lip gloss or something."

Sasha rocked with laughter, his movement and warm breath against Laurie's ear not helping. "We won't always be fully equipped, you know," he said, going to work on Laurie's jeans. "We don't need these off. Just...down a bit. Around your hips. Lovely... We might get caught short. We might need to be resourceful."

"I see," Laurie gasped, doing his best not to give it up and come at the touch of Sasha's fingers. Again, as Sasha sank to his knees in front of him, looking up at him with brilliant, sea-lit eyes. "Emergency sex, is it? Sex in the wilderness?" Sasha's mouth enclosed him, hot and slow, as Laurie braced himself on his shoulders, swaying. "Survival sex. Oh, love, be careful. I haven't got a tool on my Swiss Army for that, and you're gonna make me—"

“No, I’m not.” Sasha sat back, surveyed him for a second. His shaft was taut and straight between them, glimmering with saliva. Maybe not quite enough. Sasha leaned in again, without sucking or holding, just getting him wet. The rush of his tongue made Laurie tip back his head, buttocks involuntarily clenching, spine going stiff. If Sasha thought he could hold off, he was wrong, he was wrong. “Hold on to it, Laurie,” he commanded, easing back again, giving him a look of mischief, sharing a memory of a long-drawn-out tease. “We both know you can. The Swiss Army tool in this situation is just spit, I’m afraid, and now it has to be yours.”

Laurie looked down at him. He was still a bit naive, he knew, and Sash had been his guide in their more adventurous collisions. He could also be stupid, when his head was fogged up with desire. “Mine?”

“Yes. We need to…” But Sash could be shy too, and couldn’t finish. “I’d understand,” he whispered, “if you don’t want to, or…”

“Oh!” Laurie suddenly got it. Connections. Sasha had got him ready, and now… “Oh, God, I do want to. Yes. Completely, right now.”

Grinning, Sasha let himself be tumbled down onto the grass. Laurie pulled his jeans down, and together they made an awkward, laughing job of getting rid of them. Laurie wasted no time now that he knew what was required of him. Although he had never touched Sasha quite this way before, the thought of it was wildly compelling. He helped Sasha over onto his hands and knees, took his hips between his hands, and drew him up.

He tasted of salt from their last swim. He was exactly as Laurie might have imagined, here in the core of him, the deep-rifted cleft between the taut rounds of his backside. Skin silken and hot, scent an intensification of the rest of him, earthy and thrilling. He dropped his head as Laurie made tongue contact, hands clenching tight on the grass.

"Oh, God, ves'tacha. Are you sure?"

And Laurie said, "Never more certain of anything," pressed Sasha wide-open with his thumbs, and pushed his tongue as deep as it would go. Laurie held him open, held him up with strong fingers in the junction of his thighs and hip bones. Held him like a chalice and thrust his tongue hard past his pulsating ring of muscle, withdrew it and circled him. Lapped down to his perineum and back to the target. Again. Again, feeling his control begin to break down. Again, and Sasha gasped out his name and collapsed down onto the turf, rolling onto his back, reaching for him. "Yes! That's it, that's enough. Come here!"

Almost enough. Laurie crouched between his thighs and pushed into him, trying to be gentle, almost put past it by arousal. They were wet, but spit wasn't lube and the penetration dragged. Sasha moaned and writhed, trying to help him find a way. He guided Laurie's hands to the backs of his knees. "It's all right. This bit...always hurts. Open me up."

Laurie shuddered. He watched, fascinated, as Sasha took his own shaft in his hand and began to stroke it—diversion from pain and, Laurie knew, a certain way of keeping him in the game. No matter what Laurie's scruples were about hurting Sash, the sight of him jerking off would distract him completely. He had never seen him like this—not laid out in front of him, not while he pushed inside his body.

"Oh, love." He breathed and pressed gently forward with both hands, encouraging Sasha's legs wide, his backside to lift and accommodate him. The movement eased something. Sasha gasped explosively and masturbated hard until Laurie was all the way in, then let go, kept his promise, and wrapped both legs tight around his waist.

They rocked to sudden stillness. It was mutual, a natural hiatus, the silence between each rush of the surf.

Laurie, cradled, buried deep, looked into Sasha's face. He was smiling faintly, breath coming shallow and fast between parted lips. The shadows painted him, warm breeze swaying the pines, calling music from them. Ruffling Sasha's hair, which here in this paradise he had let grow a bit, as if one day he might, despite everything, forget himself and…

Yes. He was off his guard now. Laurie saw. His dark eyes were dilated, fixed only on what was in front of him. Laurie shivered and smiled to be the focus of such concentration, and he began to move again. He felt Sasha start to warm and relax around his cock, to reach for his impalement with small upward thrusts. Bracing on his arms, Laurie shoved into him, short and deep, over and over again.

And he knew it was seeing Sasha like this, laid out, undefended, that was now ending for him his long, absurdly painful scramble into adulthood, passing to him the torch he had let Sasha carry till now. In the back pocket of his jeans—he could feel it, as the fabric strained on his backside—was a knife. There always was. Until today it had been token, only a response to Kucharski's warning. Now he knew he would use it. That he would have learned to use a gun, had not Sasha's revulsion for them been so complete. If Sasha had briefly relaxed his vigilance over the skylines, Laurie would take it for him. Even now, thrusting so deep that Sasha cried out wildly, he was glancing to the forest above him, the rocks, listening in between breaths for any sound that was not the wind or the sea. He would keep the watch.

Sasha convulsed underneath him. He raised his thighs still farther, then hesitated as if scared or overwhelmed. "Yes," Laurie gasped, shuddering to a stop at the pitch of one thrust. "Do what you said." Sasha surged up against him, moaning. Laurie guided him. He put a hand to the back of each of Sasha's thighs, where muscle quivered under the satiny skin. Gently he pushed, at the same time leaning over Sasha, even deeper into him. Everything fell into place. Sasha lifted his knees up over his shoulders, the gesture one of such total abandonment that Laurie felt tears boil up. When he was caught, steady there, Laurie straightened his spine a little, raising him. Stretching him out, rejoicing at the weight of him. He could see him now—see everything in the wild, dancing sea light. His eyes wide and fixed on Laurie, his beautiful mouth giving up silent prayers. To be released. *Laurie, make me come, make me come*. Laurie caressed him. Down his chest, over the taut nipples, the muscles of his belly, to which sand adhered. Then he fastened the hardest grip he could on him, on his rib cage, holding him in place. It would bruise, but Sasha wailed and grabbed his wrists, adding his strength to it. *Hold me still*! He found his voice suddenly. "Christ, Laurie!"

His cry rang out across the lonely beach. Laurie heard it melt into the sky, and moved to follow it, pounding forward and up, in and up, until Sasha whipped his head back and forth and began to come, his shaft spilling wildly. Oh, Laurie would care for him. They would share all their dangers—watch one another's backs forever. But for now—for this one moment—he was only a man who had come to the beach with his lover, to fuck in the sunlight, thrust and thrust until he could drive Sasha no further and he was at last climaxing too. For a moment, they could have been shot where they lay and not have regretted it or thought themselves shortchanged.

* * *

They leaned against the roots of the great Cézanne pine that had sheltered them. Despite Laurie's best efforts, sand and lack of lube had made withdrawal painful, and they clung together, getting over it, recreating with hands and arms the passionate unity of sex. Tomorrow would see them back in London, a city now as unimaginable as this place had been to them from there. Tomorrow—work and long hours and the vagaries of an English spring. Raising his mouth from Sasha's sweat-dampened hair, looking out to sea, Laurie said unsteadily, "Paradise, isn't it, love?"

Sasha glanced up at him. He looked exhausted, and his breath was still coming hard. "Yes," he said, smiling. "But I can't wait to get you home."

About the Author

Harper Fox is the author of many critically acclaimed M/M novels, including Samhain's *Driftwood* and *The Salisbury Key*, and the bestselling *Nine Lights Over Edinburgh, Last Line* and *Scrap Metal*. Her novels and novellas are powerfully sensual, with a dynamic of strongly developed characters finding love and a forever future—after the appropriate degree of turmoil. She loves to try and show the romance implicit in everyday life, but she writes a sharp action scene too.

To find out more about Harper and see updates on her current writing projects, please visit www.harperfox.net.

If you enjoyed this novel by Harper Fox, you may also want to read Half Moon Chambers, a powerful police drama set in Harper's native city of Newcastle upon Tyne.

Excerpt from Half Moon Chambers

I didn't announce myself. You could sometimes learn more from a witness in the ten unguarded seconds before they knew you were there than in hours spent with them afterwards. Out of habit, I began to make my observations. The first thing I saw was that the surveillance picture hadn't been that good after all. Maybe Rowan Clyde was nothing special in the street, but here, intent upon his work, he sent a strange pang through me. I'd only experienced anything like it when scaling Scafell Pike in the Lakes, reached the top, and turned to look back the way I'd come. I'd understood then that I would never see the world this way again, never again quite like this, rich with sunlight and stitched together by the shadow of ravens' wings. I couldn't work out the connection. He was just a man in his mid-twenties, a nicely cut profile against bright light, lips pursed in concentration.

He was also just a job. I pushed my reaction aside. I glanced at the long bench beside him, from which he was now rapidly selecting delicate brushes and tools. At his other elbow was a huge ceramic palette, daubed in every colour imaginable. I couldn't make out the subject on the canvas in front of him, but as I watched, he drew one tiny brush-head half an inch across it, and a wound I hadn't realised was there healed itself, a broken line reconnected. I tried not to be impressed. That had to be finicky work. Better than safe-cracking or picking pockets, but not much use in the grand scheme of things. Men like him annoyed me on principle. Fully grown, but locked away in ivory towers doing jobs better suited to graduate students. Hiding away from the world. No matter how talented he was, I doubted the work paid much, and I filled in his background with some neat brushwork of my own—wealthy, indulgent parents, paying for his training and probably still supporting him now. Few worries, and still fewer principles, if he wasn't prepared to come forward as witness to one of the city's most savage killings in decades. An effete dilettante, too dreamy to notice a bloody great policeman walking up behind him...

No. After that one stroke of the brush, he had gone still. His expression didn't change. All I could see of him was that beautiful profile, limned in light, but he was watching me. All right. Game over. I stopped a few yards short of him. “Rowan Clyde?”

He exploded into movement. The easel and his palette went flying. In five years of chasing villains round the city streets I'd never seen anyone shift so fast—he was on the far side of the room before I could draw breath, shouldering open a fire exit. The door slammed behind him and he was gone.

I raised my eyes to the ceiling. "Oh, for fuck's sake," I whispered. This must be a nice peaceful place to work. I could hear pigeons and doves prooking about in the roofspace. There were rain-smeared skylights, seagulls wheeling above them. I could let this go—pull out the stool from under the bench and sit down. My back was killing me already, and I didn't stand a chance—Clyde would know every corridor and broom closet.

But I was here on a last-chance assignment from my boss. Bill hadn't put it to me that way, but I knew. If I screwed up a simple witness interview, how long could I expect to keep my fragile foothold at Mansion Street? As for alternatives—my arse. I was a one-trick pony, a round peg hammered so tight into my nice round hole that I'd never fit properly anywhere else again. And last time I'd looked, I'd still been a copper.

So I ran. I tossed aside my physio's warnings about caution and starting from cold, and I just took off the way I had used to, full throttle. I shoved the fire door open and pelted down the corridor beyond it. No doors, no turnings. My quarry had to be here somewhere, and he hadn't got that much of a head start. I dashed down twenty yards or so of lino-covered floor, and for all but one of them I managed to outrun my damage and pain. On the twentieth, I had to slow to make a corner, and there it all caught up with me. I crashed to a halt, clutching at the wall, fingers scrabbling. Christ, it was like being stabbed—no, worse; I'd taken a knife during a pub fight and not been as royally fucked up as this. I doubled over, bracing one hand on my knee. It had been for nothing, too. I'd run into a storage unit, a bloody dead end. Clyde must have peeled off through a door I hadn't seen. I'd lost him.

Well, at least I was alone. That was a blessing—alone, I could unleash the pain and frustration in a brief explosive roar. "Ah, fuck it! Fuck!"

"Who the hell are you?"

I jolted upright. My balance was screwed and I fell back against the wall in my effort to spin round. My hand flailed for a weapon I hadn't carried in six months. "Police officer," I managed. "You—Rowan Clyde—stay right where you are." That wouldn't work, though—I couldn't see the bastard. "On second thoughts, step out and show yourself. Slowly."

A set of tall cabinets had cast a deep shadow. After a moment, a random patchwork of light and shade stirred and became a human shape. Clyde emerged, as slowly as I could have wished. He was sheet white, and one side of his face—the profile I hadn't seen—was a mass of bruising. Not quite the pussy I'd taken him for—plainly he was terrified, but his spine was straight, the set of his shoulders defiant. "You're from the police?"

"Yeah. Who did you think?"

"Another of Goran Maric's men. You look the part. I want to see your ID."

Swallowing hard, trying to get hold of my breath, I pulled out my badge. I held it at arm's length for him. Maybe I needed to clean up my act a bit. A plain-clothes brief didn't extend to resembling a crack baron's thugs. Maybe I needed a more reassuring, employable face to show to the public. "All right," I said. "I'm sorry I scared you. Are you okay?"

Clyde took a good look at my badge, then a better one at me. After a moment he nodded. "Yes. I'm all right."

"Well, I am too. So can we go back to your workroom and start over?"

I let him lead the way. That gave me the whole length of the corridor to grimace and limp and wipe the cold sweat off my brow. By the time we reached the gallery I had everything more or less under control again. I could even envy Clyde the easy grace with which he hitched himself onto the draughtsman's stool. He was too thin, but nicely built, more on the lines of a dancer than an academic. He gestured at another stool nearby, but that was a chance I couldn't take. Instead I assumed what I hoped was an official-looking posture, propping myself discreetly against the wall. “So,” I began. “One of Maric's lads did that to you?”

“Two of.” A faint smile flickered, poignant against the bruising. “Give me a little credit.”

“Have you had it seen to?”

“No. They told me the fewer people I talked to, the less likely I was to end up in the Tyne with a concrete block tied round my neck.”

Made in the USA
Lexington, KY
26 January 2013